CW00825526

The Malvern Mystery

The Malvern Mystery

Helen Susan Swift

Prelude

'Hurry now, Ruth; we have to get there by dawn.' The frantic rustle of her skirt emphasised the urgency of Sarah's words.

Gasping as they pitted their strength against the slope, they moved upwards through the wind-cropped grass with the hill always rising before them and the chill of the night brushing against their skin.

'There's the sun coming through now.' Sarah pointed eastward across the broad Worcestershire plain. An infinitesimal gleam of light showed on the far horizon. 'Come on Ruth; it's not far. Think of Harry.'

Ruth nodded and lengthened her stride so that every step snapped the material of her skirt against her legs.

'Is that somebody over there?' Ruth stopped and took hold of Sarah's arm. 'I'm not doing anything if there is anybody else here. I'm sure I saw some men.'

'There's nobody there; it's only your imagination; come on,' Sarah pushed Ruth upwards. They stumbled over a steep ridge and down into one of the deep ditches that corrugated the side of the hill.

'I'm not sure I want to do this,' Ruth said.

'Harry will be pleased,' Sarah encouraged. 'Come on and don't hesitate.'

'Here we are.' They stopped before a slight depression in the ground. A sad mountain ash leaned over them, its branches winter- bare. 'Take a deep breath now. The sun has still not properly risen.' A breeze ruffled the dark surface of a pool of water, pushing tiny whispering waves against a bank of rough grass.

'Are you sure this is the right place?' Ruth looked around, narrowing her eyes against the bite of the pre-dawn wind. 'It's very dark.'

'This is Alfreck Well,' Sarah assured her. 'I've been here before,' she hesitated for a moment. 'I had to come here too, Ruth, and it worked. Three times it worked.'

The two women exchanged glances. Ruth gave a nervous smile. 'What do I do now?'

'Strip naked,' Sarah said. 'Quickly now, before the sun rises.'

'What if those men come?' Ruth tried to peer into the dark.

'There are no men foolish enough to come up here,' Sarah said and sighed. 'I'll keep watch just in case. Come on now!' She poked Ruth in the arm. 'Hurry!'

'It's cold!' Ruth said but slipped off her short cloak and then, fingers trembling, unfastened her skirt and top. She placed her clothes in a neat pile and stood, arms-folded and shivering in her shift.

'Stark! You must be completely stark!' Sarah said.

Ruth gave one last pleading glance at Sarah before divesting herself of the last of her clothes, to stand smoothly naked and white beside the black pool of water.

'In you get,' Sarah eyed her briefly and smiled. 'Harry's a lucky man.' She picked up the bundle of clothes and tucked them under her arm. 'You have to be completely immersed as the sun rises or it won't work.'

'It's cold,' Ruth said again. She put a single foot into the water, made a small exclamation of shock, and stepped in further. Sarah watched as the water rose above Ruth's knees, and then lapped at her thighs.

'Get right in!' Sarah said. 'Go on! You won't die! Think of Harry when you give him the good news.'

Ruth whimpered with the shock as the water reached her waist, but set her mouth and stepped on until she was breast deep. 'I thought it would be thick mud underfoot,' she said, 'but it's not.'

'Here it comes,' Sarah ignored Ruth's words.

The sun slid above the eastern plain, a sliver of silver-gold that slowly set the sky aglow. Red and orange streaks radiated from the central orb to fade into the darkness beyond, but even as Sarah watched, the light strengthened to illuminate the land. She saw small islands of trees amid the dark, then villages emerged as beams of sunlight glinted on windows and the tan and gold of thatched roofs. Worcestershire smiled upward to greet another day.

'Now!' Sarah shouted, 'take a deep breath and get right under the water! Now!'

With one last appealing look, Ruth ducked under the surface. For a second Sarah saw her blonde hair floating on top, and then she vanished completely in the still dark water. Sarah stretched across and pushed her head down, struggling to hold her under the surface as she fought frantically to escape.

'No you don't, my girl,' Sarah said. 'You have to be completely under.'

The sun eased higher, sending soft beams of light over the countryside, picking out trees and copses, casting long shadows toward the west, reflecting from windows and glinting from the serpentine Severn as it wound its lazy passage across the awakening landscape. Sarah watched its progress, glanced down to where Ruth crouched submerged in the dark pool and counted the seconds.

'Stay still' she ordered as she felt Ruth's frantic movements within the water. 'You can't come up yet.'

At last the slow beams of the sun crept across the rough grass and touched the pool. The transformation was immediate; the water gleamed silver, with the tiny wavelets glimmering in the light as if alive.

'Up you get,' Sarah said and lifted her hand from Ruth's head.

'Let me out!' The words exploded from Ruth's mouth along with a spurt of water, 'there's something in here with me. For God's sake let me out!'

'There's nothing...' Sarah began until Ruth clutched at her with frantic hands.

'Please Sarah! Get me out of here! Please!'

Sarah grabbed Ruth's arms and hauled her from the water without any regard for her dignity or the flesh she scraped from the rough grass. Both women stared into the disturbing depths.

'There's something down there, I tell you,' Ruth was nearly sobbing, careless of her nakedness. 'Something soft and terrible.' She screamed again, 'Oh God help us; it's coming up!'

They backed away, holding each other, as something burst feet-first out of the water and floated on top.

'It's a man!' Sarah shouted, high pitched. She took hold of Ruth in a close embrace, 'a naked man!'

'And he's dead,' Ruth screamed.

Forgetting about her clothes, Ruth began to run with Sarah frantic at her back. Behind them, floating on the surface of the well, the naked man bobbed unheeded, with his wrists and ankles tied with green cord.

Chapter One

Raindrops raced each other down the outside of the window as the coach clattered around the tight curve on the Great Malvern road. The outside passengers held on and yelled in excitement or fright while those fortunate enough to be inside merely tumbled together in a press of bodies.

'Does this driver know what he's doing?' A large, florid- faced man asked for the fourth time since they had left Worcester. 'I said: does this driver know what he is doing?'

'I hope so.' The elderly woman who occupied the seat opposite him kept one hand on her hat while the other gripped the side of the seat. 'He'll have us over, else.'

Wedged between the florid man and the window, Lorna took a deep breath and wriggled in the leather seat to try and regain some space. She inhaled air laced with the aroma of damp wool and humanity and thanked her good fortune she was not outside in the rain.

'And what do you think, young lady?' The elderly woman asked. 'I say we should complain about his reckless driving as soon as we arrive in Great Malvern.'

'If we arrive safely,' Lorna said, 'we will have nothing about which to complain. If we don't arrive safely, then we will have other things to worry about rather than complaining about a man who may have already broken his neck.' She stared out the window, rather enjoying watching the countryside speed past, with the steam rising from the horses and the driver cracking his whip. There was something quite exhilarating in suddenly rising up the brow of a hill, every village through which they passed provided a quota of excited children who lined the street and waved excitedly at them. It was an interesting method of learning the characteristics of this cool, damp country.

The sudden blare of the guard's horn warned the passengers and everybody else that they were approaching their destination. Lorna rubbed away a clear space in the condensation on the window to give herself a better view of the outside world.

'Thank the Lord,' the florid man thundered. 'We're arriving.'

The horses came to a halt and stood to shiver and steam in the rain, oblivious of the guard blowing his horn once more and roaring out 'Bellevue Inn, Great Malvern! Ten minutes!' He opened the door and peered into the coach. 'Ten minutes to change the horses and have a quick refreshment ladies and gentleman. Great Malvern is your destination, Madam.' The last statement was to Lorna, who was already easing her cramped limbs as she gingerly placed her foot on the small iron step between the body of the coach and the ground below.

Burly and cheerful, as most of his kind were, the guard loaned Lorna his arm and guided her down. 'There we are Miss, all safe and sound.' He looked around, indifferent to the rain that hammered onto his cape and formed large puddles on the ground. 'If you get yourself into the inn I'll get your luggage from the boot. One portmanteau wasn't it?'

'It was, guard,' Lorna pulled her cloak tighter. After the stuffy confines of the mail coach, it was good to get into the fresh air, although the rain that immediately dripped down the back of her neck was not so pleasant. 'I'm not staying at the inn, though.'

'Are you not, Miss?' The guard affected surprised interest. 'Staying with friends are you?'

'No,' Lorna accepted her portmanteau with a smile of thanks. 'I am the new teacher at St Ann's College.'

'Well, good for you, Ma'am,' the guard said. 'You'll need a hand with that bag then. Shall I call a porter from the inn for you?'

'I'll manage,' Lorna retained her smile. 'However, I would be obliged if you could point me in the right direction for the school.'

'If you're sure, Ma'am,' the guard looked doubtful that a woman could carry a case on her own. He indicated a hill behind the inn. 'There is a path up there, Ma'am, known as the Red Lion Bank. The college is about halfway up. It's in a walled garden with the name above the gate.'

'Thank you.' Lorna looked around. The Belle Vue Inn stood in Belle Vue terrace which was parallel to the run of the long ridge of the Malvern Hills. Some of the houses in the terrace looked old, with gables that faced the street, others were Georgian, with shops on the lower levels pushing out to the pedestrians that walked by. The juxtaposition of old and Georgian gave the terrace a unique charm that Lorna quite admired, while the hotels and health spas revealed one reason for the popularity of this town.

At right angles to the terrace, the six lodging houses of Paradise Row marked the top of Church Street that stretched to the walled garden around the Vicarage. Ignoring the rain, Lorna nodded at the Royal Library near the top of Church Street. With its bow front and bustling appearance, this building was the social centre of the town while the spiritual heart, the massive Priory, dominated the surrounding walled churchyard with its holm oaks and ancient yew trees. That was life and death standing side by side, Lorna thought and neither of them of any concern to her.

In front of the Priory, the Abbey Gateway was ornate and prominent, with yellow candlelight glowing behind many of the windows. Lorna took everything in with one long sweep, turned away and looked toward the Red Lion Bank.

'Ready Jem?' The driver took his place on the front of the mail coach; the guard joined him precisely as the whip cracked. The coach pulled quickly away, its wheels buzzing on the wet ground and half a dozen small boys whooping and chasing in its wake.

Lorna shook off her sudden sensation of loneliness. This was a new life in a new country she had always thought of as home; straightening her back, she lifted her portmanteau and stepped on.

The rain was heavier as Lorna passed the Red Lion public house. She ascended what turned out to be a steep, narrow path that curved upward between different levels of buildings and then underneath the overhanging branches of stark winter trees. Rainwater pooled at the side of the road and formed a small gushing channel in the centre.

After ten minutes, Lorna stopped at the sign.

St Ann's College for Young Ladies

It was plain and unpretentious, a simple brass plaque screwed into the centre of a black wrought-iron gate set in a high stone wall. Lorna tried the gate, frowning when she found it firmly closed. She rattled it, hoping for a reply and then walked around the wall, searching for an alternative entrance. The wall entirely encircled two acres of garden ground, hiding all view of the building within. Lorna was back at the brass plate and the entrance gate within twenty minutes, wet, bedraggled and frustrated.

'Halloa!' Lorna raised her voice in a shout. 'Is there anybody there?' There was no answer except the patter of rain on the trees and the call of a lonely blackbird. She tried again: 'Halloa! Is there anybody there?'

This time she heard the ruffle of feet on a gravel path and a stocky man in late middle-age appeared on the opposite side of the gate. 'Who the devil are you?' He looked her up and down and pulled at his grey side-whiskers. 'You're too young to be a parent and too old to be a pupil. What do you want, hollering and shouting fit to wake the dead like that?'

'I am Lorna Buchanan,' Lorna tried to ignore the rain that had reduced her hat to a soggy mess and which dripped from her nose and chin. 'I am to report to Mrs Appleton this morning. She is expecting me.'

'Oh,' the man made no effort to unlock the gate. 'She is, is she?' He eyed Lorna through the black iron bars. 'And what would *Miss* Appleton want with somebody like you?'

'I am to be a teacher here,' Lorna explained. 'So let me in, if you please.'

The man grunted, fiddled in the pocket of his baggy velveteen jacket and produced a small bunch of keys. After a moment's jingling, he unlocked the gate and pulled it open. 'You'd best come in then.' The second Lorna entered, the man closed the door with a clang, turned the key and rattled it thoroughly to check it was locked. 'Miss Appleton doesn't like the gate open. It keeps the girls in and Mad Jack out.'

'Mad Jack?' Lorna queried.

The man did not reply.

'The school is up there; I take it?' Lorna indicated the gravel path that wound gracefully through dripping rhododendron bushes.

'I'll show you.' The man limped forward, round-shouldered. 'So you're to be the new teacher are you?'

'That's the idea,' Lorna said.

The man grunted. 'I give you a month,' he said. 'New teachers never last much longer than that.'

'Oh?' Lorna looked around. The path wound upward, past the rhododendrons and across a stretch of sloping lawn to a large Georgian style house complete with colonnades and a pitched slate roof. Two storeys of tall, multi-paned windows glared down at her with an Italianate tower dominating the north-west wing and rising another two storeys. 'It looks a remarkably satisfying building.'

The man grunted again as they reached the stone steps that led to the closed front door. 'If you wait here, Miss Buchanan, I will see if Miss Appleton will receive you.' He glared at Lorna. 'Don't wander off.'

The lone blackbird continued to sing as Lorna waited in the rain. She heard the sound of chanting as a class of girls learned their lesson and the sharply raised voice of a teacher followed by a moment's silence and then more chanting. Lorna nodded; that sounded exactly like school as she believed it to be.

'Miss Buchanan?' The man had returned. 'Miss Appleton will see you now. This way please.' He held the door open for her with slightly more respect than he had shown a few moments before.

The door opened into an echoing hallway with half a dozen doors opening off, a staircase that rose to the landing above and a wall lined with portraits. Lorna glanced around, thinking that the interior exactly echoed the exterior. The building held a faint aroma of chalk while a young maid knelt on the third step up, furiously polishing the bannister.

'Up the stairs,' the man gave brief instructions, 'follow the corridor to the right and up the stairs again. Miss Appleton is in the topmost room.'

'Thank you,' Lorna wondered if the man would offer to take her bag, but instead, he stomped outside and closed the door. The maid continued to polish, taking no notice of Lorna.

Taking a deep breath, Lorna mounted the stairs. She could hear that rhythmic chanting again, coming from two separate classrooms.

Rather than stop to listen, she continued until she arrived at a plain oak door adorned with a brass plate that announced baldly:

Miss Appleton

'Well, here we go,' Lorna said and knocked.

'Come in.' The sharp-voiced reply came immediately.

Lorna stepped inside, to see an immaculately dressed woman sitting behind a pristine desk. Uniform ranks of leather-bound books covered two walls of the room. Lorna scanned the titles: volumes on manners, decorum, and behaviour filled one bookcase, with another contained books on mythology, folklore and classical and local history. The wind blew rain through the open Venetian windows, while a long cane hung ominously behind Miss Appleton's chair. A grandmother clock ticked serenely in the corner furthest from the desk.

Miss Appleton looked up from behind her desk, her eyes granite-grey in a hard-edged face. 'You're very tall.'

'I know,' Lorna was used to people commenting on her height.

'You must be nearly six feet.'

'I am five foot nine,' Lorna said.

'The girls may not like that,' Miss Appleton perched on her ornate seat like an eagle in its nest. Her smile was surprisingly friendly. 'That might help you keep order. Have you taught before?'

'No, Miss Appleton.'

Miss Appleton nodded and lifted the letter that Lorna had sent. 'You admit that in your little note. Are you sure you wish to embark on this adventure?'

'I'm sure,' Lorna said.

Miss Appleton re-read Lorna's letter. 'You say that you are able to teach History, English Literature and Geography.'

'That is correct, Miss Appleton.'

'You will be aware of the line of the royal succession I take it?' Miss Appleton asked.

'I am, Miss Appleton, from Egbert to our present Queen Victoria, although the Saxon kingdom Egbert founded was temporary and genuine English unification had to wait until the rule of Athelstan.'

'You will know the Romantic poets and the author of the *Lady of the Lake*?' The steel was evident in Miss Appleton's eyes.

'Sir Walter Scott is one of my favourite authors,' Lorna said. 'And Wordsworth and Coleridge are old friends.'

'I am glad to hear it,' Miss Appleton said dryly. 'I hear you have travelled quite extensively. That will help your geography.' She fixed Lorna with that stare again. 'Was your father not regularly employed?'

'My father is in the Army, Miss Appleton. We moved from posting to posting, spending most of our time in India. My mother died in the late Mutiny and father thought it best that I returned home.'

'What rank does he have, Miss Buchanan?' The stare did not waver.

'He is a Major, Miss Appleton.' Lorna stiffened her back.

'Oh,' Miss Appleton gave a little frown. 'Some of my girls have fathers who hold a higher rank. I hope your background does not hamper your teaching.'

'I am sure I will manage, Miss Appleton.'

'I teach manners and deportment to all three classes, and I have and a class of specifically Chosen Girls.' Miss Appleton stood up. 'Your room is beside that of Miss Henshaw. Your first class is at nine tomorrow morning: British history. I will have a timetable sent up to you.'

'Thank you, Miss Appleton.' That had been easier than she had expected.

'That will be all, Miss Buchanan.' Miss Appleton dismissed her curtly.

Chapter Two

'Are you Miss Buchanan? I am Jane Henshaw.' The speaker was bubbly, with blonde hair that was not quite under control, and a wide smile under her snub nose. She peered around the open door. 'May I come in?'

'Lorna Buchanan,' Lorna gave a little curtsey. 'Of course, you can come in.'

Jane's trim grey dress touched the top of her black boots and stopped just short of her neck. She smelled of soap and chalk: the scent of the school.

Lorna looked around the room that was to be her home for the foreseeable future. It was small, with iron bars across a window that gave a view of the stone wall of the basement and nothing much else. The interior was dull and neat, with a single brass candlestick holding a tallow candle that pooled much-needed yellow light. There was a narrow single bed with one cover and a pillow on top of a thin straw mattress. A chest of drawers and a hard-backed chair completed the furnishings.

'This is nice and snug,' Lorna said.

Jane wrinkled her nose. 'They're not bad, but they can get a bit stuffy in summer and in winter you have to break the ice on the water,' she pointed to a blue-and-white ewer and pitcher that stood on top of the drawers.

Lorna smiled. 'I've lived in a lot worse,' she said.

'I'm right next door,' Jane said. 'My room is exactly the same except I have put pictures on the wall to brighten things up.'

Lorna smiled. 'That's a good idea.'

'Have you met Miss Appleton? Of course, you have,' Jane answered her own question. 'She can be a bit stiff, a bit la-de-dah, you know?' She pursed her mouth and drew her eyebrows closer together. 'If you can ignore her ferocious dignity she's all right really as long as you do as she tells you.'

'I'll do as she tells me,' Lorna said.

'You'd better,' Jane said. 'And don't mention her little foibles for goodness sake. There'll be a camality else.' She narrowed her eyes and pursed her lips. 'Her bad side is really bad.'

'A camality? Oh, a calamity! Of course. What foibles should I watch for?' Lorna felt her curiosity rise.

'Oh, you'd better not ask,' Jane said. 'If you see anything unusual, turn away and shut your eyes.'

About to ask more, Lorna thought it better not to push too hard so soon. 'I'll do that,' she promised. 'Have you been here long?' She sat on the bed. It was hard; so was the pillow.

'Fourteen months,' Jane said.

Lorna felt the blanket; it was stiff, clean and sharp- edged. 'That's a long time. You'll know your way around by now.'

'I don't get lost anymore,' Jane reached out and fingered Lorna's cloak. 'You're very wet. You'd better put some dry clothes on before you catch your death.' She dragged a towel from the chest of drawers. 'Here; dry your hair as well; you're dripping water everywhere. You'll quite ruin the floorboards.'

Lorna opened her bag. It did not take her long to choose from the meagre contents.

'Come on,' Jane waited impatiently for Lorna to change. 'I'll give you a tour of the place and get you all settled in.'

'Thank you.' Feeling slightly dishevelled beside the neat Jane, Lorna followed into the corridor outside. She shivered in the dank chill. India had been nothing like this.

'That's the girls' dormitories,' Jane pointed to three doors side by side on the right. 'Lights out is at eight for the juniors and nine for the seniors. We have one week a month on dormitory duty. It's easy enough; just settle the girls in and make sure they stay in bed.' She gave Lorna a sideways look. 'It's important they stay in bed all night. Leaving the school means big trouble, Lorna. Don't forget that.'

'I won't,' Lorna said. 'The man who let me in – the porter I take it? He said that teachers don't last here. Is that correct?'

'Yes, it's correct,' Jane said. 'Ben should not have told you that on your first day. It may be discouraging.'

'I am not discouraged,' Lorna said, 'Only in-trigued. Why don't teachers stay?'

'Teaching is not for everybody,' Jane said lightly. 'Especially in this school.' She smiled briefly. 'Now over here we have the classrooms where you'll be teaching. The middle one is yours.' She opened the door to a spacious room with two tall windows set too high for any pupil to stare outside and day-dream. The teacher's desk faced four rows of desks, while maps of Britain, Europe and the World decorated the walls.

'That looks like a splendid classroom,' Lorna said. 'There is plenty of space.' She walked in to examine the bookcase with its display of slightly tattered volumes of history, grammar, geogra-phy, and religion; each desk had its inkwell and a slate attached by a small cord. She moved the teacher's desk slightly, not because it was in the wrong place, but only to make her mark in the room as soon as possible. 'What was her name?'

'Whose name?' Jane asked.

'My predecessor. She was less tall than me.' Lorna said. 'The desk was too far back to see the whole of the class properly.'

'Oh, *her* name.' Jane screwed up her face. 'Miss Plumbett as far as I can recall. She was not here long enough to make much of an impression. I'm sure that you will be much happier here.'

'I'm sure I shall,' Lorna said.

'It's not that bad if you follow the rules and as I said, ignore the head's strange fixations.' Jane's look was full of meaning.

The sound of a door opening and closing and the clatter of hard-soled boots on the wooden floorboards announced the arrival of a file of girls in the corridor. They were of all ages from minuscule eleven-year- olds with pinched white faces to tall young women who were nearing twenty, and they walked in dignified silence with their hands clasped in front of them and their eyes demurely downcast.

'That's classes finished for the day,' Jane said. 'The girls are going to get washed, have their tea and then two hours homework.'

Lorna nodded. 'That's a long day for them.'

'Keep them busy,' Jane said, 'and they won't get into any trouble. The devil finds work for idle hands.'

'I'm sure he does,' Lorna agreed as the girls passed her. Most still kept their heads down, but as the increased the distance from the class-room, two or three glanced in her direction. One blonde-haired teenager with bold eyes looked Lorna up and down before adopting the same pose as her peers.

'Keep your head down, Margaret,' Jane snapped. 'You know the rules!' She lowered her voice. 'That's your class, Lorna.'

'I'll be watching you, Margaret my girl,' Lorna thought. 'I know your type very well.'

The girls passed them without a word be-fore heading downstairs in a column of two. Only when they were out of sight did somebody speak.

'You stole my pen, Alice!'

'I did not! I only borrowed it.

'Oh, you're such a liar, Alice! You're always borrowing things and not returning them.'

'That's Margaret Smith complaining,' Jane said. 'You'll get to know her.'

'I thought they behaved very well,' Lorna said.

'Oh they have their moments,' Jane gave a small smile. 'They have to be kept in line if you know what I mean.'

'I think I do,' Lorna said.

Jane laughed. 'We've all been through that. Now, this is where we can relax a little.' She brought Lorna into a small room with a central round table and half a dozen straight-backed chairs. Bookcases filled with shabby text-books lined the walls. 'This is the staff common-room, where we gather to mark work and discuss the horrible pupils.' She pulled out a seat. 'The only thing we can't do here is talk about Miss Appleton.' She lowered her voice. 'You don't know who may carry tales to her.'

'I see; thank you, for the warning,' Lorna said. 'Do you intend working here for long?'

'Oh no.' When Jane shook her head her curls bounced from under her cap. 'I am only here to learn what to do. I want my own school where I am in charge, and I make the rules.'

Lorna smiled. 'You are a woman of ambition then!'

'Always,' Jane lowered her voice. 'Be careful of Miss Appleton, Lorna. She and her Chosen Girls get up to some queer things. I don't know what they are doing, sometimes.'

'Oh?' Lorna closed the door. 'I do love a little gossip. What do you mean?'

Jane's voice dropped to a whisper. 'There are peculiar happenings, Lorna. Sometimes it's best not to ask too much or see too much. I just wanted to warn you to be careful, and if you do see or hear anything, it is best not to notice it.'

'You have mentioned that,' Lorna said.

'Good.' Jane pulled a face. 'You have been warned! Now let's talk about something else.'

Quelling her curiosity, Lorna nodded and allowed Jane to complete her tour of the school. It seemed that she had stepped from the fire of mutiny in India to the frying pan of mystery in the heart of rural England.

Chapter Three

Lorna was not sure what woke her. She lay in the unfamiliar bed, trying to make out shapes in the strange room. She could hear the slight whine of the wind through the ill-fitting window and the faint call of an owl outside. These were natural sounds that she would sleep through, so it must have been something else. There it was again; a definite shuffle, as if somebody was trying to walk with her ankles tied together or trying to creep along without making a sound.

Lorna closed her eyes and tried to sleep. She was nervous about her first day at this school. Any novel experience could be nerve-racking but standing in front of a group of hyper-critical teenagers all of whom knew she was brand new and most of whom were expecting and hoping that she made a fool of herself multiplied the apprehension by a factor of ten. That was sufficient to occupy anybody's mind without thinking about unknown sounds in the middle of the night.

Lorna turned over, ignoring the hardness of the mattress beneath her hip. Perhaps her predecessor had been chased away by an unruly class? Maybe she had been unable to keep them in line if they were having, as Jane put it, 'one of their moments'? She turned back, fretful.

'Oh, this is silly!' She told herself. 'A couple of years ago I was in constant danger of being murdered in my sleep or attacked at any time of the day; what does it matter what a handful of teenage girls think of me?

There was that sound again, interrupting her train of thought. Sighing, Lorna gave up her struggle to sleep and dragged herself out of bed. She drew on her dressing-gown and a shawl and quietly opened the door. The corridor outside was black as a December midnight, without even a glimmer of light. There was nothing to see there, so she took hold of the candle, scraped a spark from the old-fashioned tinder-box and carefully cupped the wick until a flame grew to maturity. Only then did she step into the corridor, closing the door behind her. The click of the latch seemed unnaturally loud.

The yellow candle-light cast weird shadows across the panelled walls as Lorna walked cautiously along the corridor. She could hear the sound in the mysterious dark ahead and moved quicker.

The hand on her arm startled her. 'Best not, Lorna.'

'What?' Lorna started; momentarily back in the humidity of Oudh. 'Oh, Jane! What are you doing here?'

'I'm making sure you don't get in trouble,' Jane hissed. 'And keep your voice down.' She pulled at Lorna's arm. 'You'd better get back to your room.'

'Why? What is it?'

'Come on!' Jane pulled harder. 'It's not our concern.'

Lorna gently freed her arm. 'Listen,' she said. 'It's a shuffling sound.'

'I can't hear anything,' Jane said.

She was right. The sound had stopped. Chill silence pressed down upon them.

'Get back to your room, Lorna,' Jane repeated. 'There's nothing out here.'

Lorna nodded. 'Not any longer.'

The candle threw its light around the room when Jane closed the door behind them. 'What's happening here, Jane? What's all the mystery?'

Jane pushed her gently onto the bed. 'Do you remember asking about Miss Plumbett?'

'Of course,' Lorna said.

'Well, she asked too many questions, and they got rid of her.' Jane leaned closer to Lorna. 'This is a good place if you don't ask questions.'

'I see,' Lorna said. 'It's best to be like the three wise monkeys, then.'

'Exactly like them.' Jane said. 'Hear no evil, see no evil and for heaven's sake don't talk about any evil. Now get to sleep, Lorna and don't even think about evil – or anything else.'

'It's not that bad, surely,' Lorna said.

'It's not bad at all. There's nothing about it to be bad. Now get to sleep; you've a big day to-morrow.' Jane smiled, 'I won't tuck you up! I'm on dormitory patrol this week, so I have enough to do ensuring these young misses don't get up to any mischief. Good night, Lorna.'

'Good night.' Lorna lay back down. It was probably all her imagination anyway. Jane blew out the candle as she left. The door closed with a slight click and Lorna was alone with her thoughts and her memories.

Clammy and hot, the Indian night resounded with the sound of insects and night birds. She could hear the soft footsteps of the Pandies creeping around. She shifted slightly until her father's hard hand clamped on to her back. The sounds increased; a twig snapped close by, there was the whiff of body odour, a guttural voice, the gleam of moonlight on a white cross-belt. Lorna felt the hammer of her heart as a predatory brown face flitted from behind a tree. She closed her eyes, stifling her sobs as she heard her father slide the revolver from its holster.

* * *

The girls watched her; fifteen expressionless faces; fifteen pairs of inquisitive eyes; fifteen minds all wondering what she would be like as a teacher; fifteen girls who could make her life impossible, or who could turn out to be the most pleasant and rewarding young friends for which she could wish.

'Good morning,' Lorna said quietly.

The girls stood up immediately. 'Good morning, Miss' they chorused in unison and sat down again in a display of choreographed discipline that would have put the Brigade of Guards to shame.

'My name is Miss Buchanan,' Lorna said, 'and I am here to teach you history.'

The girls looked at her, still expressionless. Lorna allowed her eyes to roam across them. 'Now before we begin, I wish you to stand up one by one and give me your name. Start at the left, please.'

She knew she would not remember half of them, but this was a quick way to break the ice and learn something about their personality.

They stood one by one, gave their names: 'Jessica Headley, Miss', 'Emily Jack, Miss,' 'Alice Weatherby, Miss,' then there was a pause.

'Don't you have a name?' Lorna had known the blonde girl would have been the first to test her. What was her name again? *Margaret Smith*: that was it.

'Yes, Miss Buchanan. You said to start on the left, and I am on the right.'

Lorna raised her eyebrows. 'So you are. Now we know that you can tell your left from your right, you can stand and give me your name.' She paused and hardened her tone. 'Now, please.'

The blonde rolled her eyes and made a huge job of pushing herself upright from her desk. 'I am Margaret Smith.' She did not flinch at Lorna's deliberately stern gaze.

'Sit down, Margaret,' Lorna said quietly, knowing that this girl would be even bigger trouble than she had thought. She could address that later. At present... 'I believe that Miss Plumbett introduced you to the Norman Conquest. Can anybody tell me what happened next?'

'Miss Plumbett didn't get that far,' Margaret Smith said boldly.

Some of the other girls tittered, to immediately quieten when Lorna looked at them. So Margaret Smith was the ringleader, spokeswoman and chief troublemaker with a following in the class. Welcome to teaching at St Ann's College.

'How far *did* she get, Margaret?' Lorna kept her voice deceptively soft.

'Not far at all, Miss,' innocent Margaret said.

'You can remind us all,' Lorna said. 'Step out here and tell the class. I have the notes Miss Plumbett left so I can make sure you leave nothing out. Come on now.'

Margaret's eyes narrowed momentarily as she inwardly debated whether or not she could push Lorna further. Lorna held her gaze all the way to the front of the class. 'Now off you go, Margaret.' She lowered her voice so only Margaret could hear. 'It's better for you to behave.'

Standing in front of the class, Margaret looked a lot less bold than she had only a few moments before. Her voice shook, and her accent broadened until it was as rich Herefordshire as any of the local farmers.

Some of the class mocked as Margaret stumbled over her words; others pulled faces or stuck out their tongues when they thought Lorna could not see. Lorna suddenly understood: Margaret was not a born troublemaker. She was acting a part to gain acceptance. For some reason, she did not belong here.

'Thank you, Margaret,' Lorna had no desire to prolong the girl's humiliation. 'You did well; better than those in the class who sought to distract you.' She allowed her gaze to rest on the culprits, who had the grace to look away guiltily. 'You may sit down now.'

The class shifted uneasily; they had hoped for more drama from Margaret and the new teacher, with one or the other looking foolish. Now the situation was diffused they were not sure what to do. Well, Lorna had ideas for that.

'History now; let's see how much you can tell me,' she smiled to them, making it evident she had drawn a line, and the teaching started fresh. She had survived the first test and learned something about the dynamics of the class. Now it was all about history.

Lorna sighed: Miss Appleton had put her on dormitory duty. She had not expected that to come after only one week at the school. She gave a rueful smile: newcomers to any job were given the unwanted tasks. There was no reason that it should be different for her.

There were two methods of checking the girls in a dormitory. She could either creep along to catch them unawares at whatever they were not supposed to be doing, or make a noise, so they had sufficient warning of her approach to pretend innocence. Lorna chose the latter route; holding her candle in his brass holder, she planted her feet crisply onto the floorboards and made enough noise for the girls in the dormitory to hear her. Lorna smiled as the murmuring within the room ceased, pushed open the door, waited for a moment, stepped in and looked around.

Two rows of beds each complete with its occupant. Two rows of faces either with eyes closed feigning sleep or blinking at her in assumed surprise.

'Good night girls,' Lorna said brightly. 'It's lights out now.'

'Good night Miss Buchanan,' most chorused as Lorna doused the candles.

'Now get to sleep,' Lorna held up her candleholder and spoke into the gloom. 'I don't want to hear any noise in here until morning.' She closed the door quietly, stamped her feet on the floorboards as if she was walking away and waited. After a few moments there was some subdued whispering and then a small giggle. She waited another two minutes as the whispering increased, opened the door and stepped inside.

'Oh!' One of the three girls who were out of bed stared at her while the other two dived back under the reassuring cover of their thin blanket. Lorna raised her candle and looked around.

'You three report to my room tomorrow morning,' she said in assumed sternness.

One of the beds was still empty, and the window was open. Lorna knew without checking who was missing.

'Where is Margaret Smith?'

The silence told her all she needed to know.

'Where is she going?'

The silence continued. Nobody met her eye.

'Why has she left the dormitory?'

Hopefully, it was something simple, such as a trip to the lavatory. Although each girl had a chamber-pot under the bed, some would be too shy to use such sanitary items in public. Nobody even put forward that simple excuse. Anyway, Lorna told herself, a visit to the lavatory would not necessitate an open window.

'There will be trouble tomorrow,' Lorna strode forward and slammed shut the window. She did not lock it. The message of a closed window was sufficient warning. 'If anything happens to that girl tonight you are all equally to blame for not preventing her being stupid. Now get to sleep!'

Shaking her head and trying to repress her smile, Lorna left the dormitory to search for Margaret.

'What's the matter?' Jane's door was open. She looked up as Lorna stepped along the corridor with her outdoor boots and cloak on.

'Margaret Smith has slipped outside,' Lorna said briefly. 'I'm going to bring her back.'

'Best tell Miss Appleton,' Jane said at once.

'Better not, at least not yet,' Lorna said. 'If I can keep this between us it will be better for Margaret. She has been in hot water too often for her own good that one.'

The front door was locked and bolted, with the key hanging on a hook at the side. Lorna spent a few moments fighting the lock before she rushed outside. Luckily it was a dry night, with a full moon sending gentle light onto the grounds. She ran toward the wing where the girls' dormitories were situated, hoping that Margaret had not gone far. That was a vain hope. There was no trace of her save for a few scuff marks on the gravel that Ben raked smooth every day and a patch of flattened grass where Margaret must have slipped. The direction of the crushed grass blades indicated where she had gone.

Lifting her cloak and skirt from the damp grass, Lorna followed the trail, slipped slightly, recovered and continued. She reached the outside wall and looked around. There was a raised seed-bed on this side of the wall, with a cold frame against the wall, a perfect step to cross. Holding the wall for balance, Lorna climbed to the top, looked around to ensure nobody was watching and dropped down to the other side. It was hardly ladylike, but it was effective; she remained still for a second as she gathered her wits and got her bearings. Now, where on earth would a young woman go at this time of night? Lorna could think only of two possibilities, neither particularly palatable; either she had enough of school and had decided to return home, or she was meeting some sweetheart.

Lorna glanced along the narrow lane; had Margaret gone upwards toward the Malvern Hills, or had she gone down to the town? Logic suggested downhill, but Lorna saw a stone loose on the road, sitting beside a slight cavity on the ground. It had evidently been kicked there by somebody walking uphill, and the trickle of dirt beside the stone was still crumbling, so the stone had been moved very recently.

'Uphill then,' Lorna said to herself. 'Right, my girl, I'm after you.' Lengthening her stride, Lorna moved upwards, feeling her skirt snap against her shins with every step and thinking, as she had done so often in her life, how much more practical men's trousers were than women's constricting skirts. She stopped as a faint sound came from above. There was somebody there. Lorna hurried, nearly breaking into a run as she saw a vague shape in the moon-lit gloom above.

The figure was undoubtedly a woman in a long skirt, striding along the path. Even in the half-light, Lorna recognised her as Margaret.

'Halloa!' Lorna shouted, hurrying forward. 'Stop there, Margaret!'

Margaret gave a visible start, looked over her shoulder and broke into a run.

'Don't be silly!' Lorna said and followed. Taller, with longer legs and angry at having to chase down a fugitive school girl, she soon caught up and grabbed Margaret by the shoulder. 'That's enough now.'

'Let me go,' Margaret tried to wriggle free. Her eyes were desperate.

'Calm down.' Lorna held tighter until Margaret stopped trying to escape. 'Now where are you off to, young lady?'

'I was going to watch,' Margaret said.

'You were going to watch what?'

Margaret looked sideways at her. 'You *know* what.'

'Remind me,' Lorna said.

'The full moon ceremony. You *knew* that.' Margaret's tone accused Lorna of deception.

'There is no such thing as a full moon ceremony!' Lorna said sharply.

'You know there is! It's their little secret,' Margaret said, 'and I just wanted to see what it was all about.'

'You're meant to stay safely in bed,' Lorna said, 'not to be running around the countryside in the dead of night. There are all sorts of men going around, and you have no idea what may happen to you, why...'

'Look, Miss. Here they are now.' Margaret pointed down the hill where a short column of white-clad figures was walking toward them.

'Good heavens.' The words were out before Lorna could restrain herself. 'What on earth…?' She glanced around, remembering that Jane had warned her about queer things at the school. 'Well, we'd best not be seen if it's such a secret.' Keeping hold of Margaret's arm, Lorna pushed her to the woodland that hugged both sides of this section of the path. 'Now get behind that tree and keep quiet!'

The figures in white were walking in slow procession toward them. There were nine of them all in long white cloaks that brushed the ground and all with a pointed hood that covered their bowed heads.

Lorna placed a hand over Margaret's mouth, ensuring silence as the nine figures ghosted past. She could not make out any faces.

'That was Miss Appleton and her class; her Chosen Girls,' Margaret said the second that Lorna removed her hand. 'I know it was.'

'You know no such thing,' Lorna watched the white figures vanish between the trees. She desperately wanted to follow them to find out what was happening, yet her duty was to look after her pupils, including this young troublemaker.

'You know it was,' Margaret said. 'What are they doing? Can I go and see?'

'You absolutely cannot go and see!' Lorna said. 'I never heard the like! You are in enough trouble as it is.' Even as she rebuked Margaret, Lorna felt an uncomfortable twist of curiosity. She desperately wished to find out what that file of white-clad people was doing, and even more, she longed to see if it was indeed Miss Appleton leading them.

'If I'm in trouble already,' Margaret said logically. 'I can't get into much more. Anyway, if I don't find out now, I'll come back next full moon, and the one after that until I do. I want to *watch*!'

The white-clad people were already invisible as a cloud shrouded the moon and darkness eased back across the whispering trees. 'Well, Margaret, the only thing you're going to *watch* is your behaviour and your pillow, until you fall asleep.' Lorna pulled her back down the hill. 'Come on my girl. And this is something else we will discuss when you visit me in my room to-morrow.'

Keeping hold of Margaret's arm, Lorna guided her back over the wall and to the dormitory. The room was a-buzz with talk as she entered. 'Get back to bed,' she said. 'All of you!' She dragged a chair over to the door, sat on it and waited until the room was quiet. 'I will sit here until you are all asleep.'

There was an instant rustle of covers and a few moments' silence until a lone voice whispered.

'Miss?' That was Margaret, with a different tone of voice.

'Yes, Margaret.'

'You won't tell Miss Appleton will you?'

'There is no need for that,' Lorna said. 'Once I have finished with you tomorrow you'll wish that Miss Appleton was there to save you.'

'Yes Miss,' Margaret said meekly. A few moments later she added, 'thank you, Miss.'

'Get to sleep,' Lorna kept an edge to her voice even as she wondered what was happening in this school.

Chapter Four

'Did you hear the news?' Jane asked. 'It's all over the school; you must have heard.'

'What news?' Lorna looked at the semi-cooked mess that they called lunch and wondered if she should torture her stomach by eating more.

'They've found a body at the Alfreck Well.' Jane slid down on the bench at Lorna's side. She lowered her voice to a breathless whisper. 'It's poor Mr Findhorn.'

'Oh poor Mr Findhorn,' Lorna said, enjoying the scandal even as the news of a death saddened her. 'I don't know Mr Findhorn or the Alfreck Well. Could you slow down and start at the beginning, please?'

Jane smiled, happy to be the bearer of startling news. 'There were two women at the Alfreck Well this morning. You know why they went there, don't you?'

'No, I don't,' Lorna said. 'Tell me about the body.'

'It was poor Mr Findhorn,' Jane said again.

'I still do not know who poor Mr Findhorn might be.'

'Oh,' Jane paused to explain. 'You must be aware that the Worcester and Herefordshire Railway Company is tunnelling through the Malvern Hills to link the two towns?'

'I did not know that.' Since Lorna had arrived in England, she had been surprised at the mania for railway building that gripped the country.

'Well they are, and Mr Findhorn is the railway contractor. They say that he must have crossed the navvies and they murdered him.' Jane spoke in a soft whisper.

'They murdered him?' Lorna was genuinely shocked. She had not expected a murder in this quiet rural place. She thought she had left that sort of nonsense behind in India.

'I heard that the women found him tied up,' Jane said softly. She lowered her eyes.

'Dear God in heaven,' Lorna said. 'The poor man.'

'Did you hear the news?' Miss Flamborough joined them at the table. Grey-haired and unmarried, she looked as typical a school teacher as one could imagine, yet the girls seemed to like her.

'Jane has just informed me that somebody murdered poor Mr Findhorn at the Alfreck Well.' Lorna said.

'Did you hear the rest?' Miss Flamborough's eyes were wide and green behind her spectacles.

'He was tied up,' Jane said.

'It was worse than that,' Miss Flamborough dropped her voice in case anybody other than the three of them would hear it. 'They had taken all his clothes off. All of them.'

'Dear God,' Lorna said again. Somehow she thought that Miss Flamborough considered it worse that Mr Findhorn should be naked than somebody had killed him. 'Has anybody informed the police?'

'I would imagine so,' Miss Flamborough inched even closer and dropped her voice further. 'The navvies are truly vile and wicked people you know. That is one reason that Miss Appleton has the gate locked and the girls all confined to the dormitories night after night. They say that the navigators would take them away and do terrible things to them.' Her eyes widened with a mixture of horror and fascination.

'I have never seen a railway navigator,' Lorna said. 'So I really cannot tell.'

'He was undressed,' Miss Flamborough repeated in a shocked, fascinated whisper. 'Completely!' She looked at Lorna, hoping for somebody to mirror her interest. 'They are brute beasts, perfect fiends.' Miss Flamborough was pleased to share her knowledge of the railway navigators. 'Some say they are savages that beat their wives, or the women they *call* their wives and spend all their money on strong drink.'

'I see.' Lorna said. 'Best to avoid them then.'

Jane pursed her lips, obviously unhappy that Miss Flamborough had taken over her role of gossip-spreading. 'Have you ever heard the like?' Jane said. 'A murder in Malvern!'

'It is not what I expected,' Lorna agreed. 'And I hope to hear no more about it, although, in a school of some eighty flighty and talkative girls, I doubt that is possible.'

Only when they left for class did Jane slip closer to Lorna. 'They all say it was the navigators,' she whispered. 'I'm not sure it was.'

'Oh?' Lorna said. 'Who do you think it was?'

Rather than reply directly, Jane merely raised her eyebrows. 'That's all I am saying.'

'All right then,' Lorna said. She had been in this school less than a fortnight, and already she had her fill with gossip mongers and half-concealed hints. She was not in the best of humour when she walked to her class.

As she expected, the girls were unsettled at the news that morning, and she had to quieten them down before settling down to teaching. She had barely got them to open their textbooks when the door opened, and Miss Appleton entered, with a stout, be-whiskered man in the blue uniform of the police at her side.

'May I have a word, Miss Buchanan?' Miss Appleton phrased her order as a request.

'Of course, Miss Appleton,' Lorna said and turned to the class. 'You girls read chapter three, and I want no talking from you today.'

'I am Sergeant Caswell of the Worcestershire Constabulary, Miss Buchanan.' The police officer introduced himself in a loud voice that every girl in the suddenly hushed classroom could hear.

'How do you do,' Lorna said.

'You may have heard of the death of Mr Findhorn, the contractor for the Worcester and Herefordshire Railway that is presently engaged in tunnelling through the Malvern Hills.' Sergeant Caswell spoke formally.

'I was informed about that this morning, Sergeant Caswell.'

Taking a small black notebook from the top pocket of his uniform jacket, the sergeant opened it and read one page. 'I believe that you and one pupil from this school left the school grounds last night and were absent for some time.'

Lorna could feel the anger in Miss Appleton's eyes. 'That is correct,' she said.

'Could you tell me why, Miss Buchanan?'

'One of my girls slipped out of the school. I brought her back,' Lorna said. 'It was a simple situation, and I dealt with it.'

'I need the girl's name,' Caswell was writing laboriously in his notebook.

'I do not believe that is necessary,' Lorna said. 'She did not have anything to do with the death of the railway contractor.'

'She broke one of the most rigid of the school rules,' Miss Appleton said. 'Who was she?'

'I assure you, Miss Appleton, and Sergeant Caswell, that the girl was barely out of my sight and had no time to be involved in anything.'

Miss Appleton and the sergeant frowned in unison. 'This is a police enquiry,' the sergeant said.

Miss Appleton stiffened. 'Unless you inform me of the girl's name, Miss Buchanan, I will be forced to take action that could see you removed from your position without a reference.'

'I gave my word to the pupil involved,' Lorna said.

'It was me, Miss Appleton,' Margaret Smith stood up.

'I might have guessed,' Miss Appleton said.

'If both you ladies would accompany me,' Sergeant Caswell said stiffly. 'I have some questions for you.'

Miss Appleton's study was as clinical as before and much more unwelcoming as Lorna and Margaret filed in.

Miss Appleton sat on her chair behind her desk, with the sergeant standing at her side, opposite Lorna and Margaret. The grandmother clock ticked softly in the background.

'I am not accusing either of you of murder.' Caswell said. 'I am only ascertaining the facts. At present, you are both possible witnesses rather than suspects.'

'Yes, Sergeant,' Lorna said.

'First of all, tell me what time you were both out of the school premises.'

'That is a significant breach of school rules,' Miss Appleton interrupted, 'and it will be dealt with, and dealt with most severely, I assure you.'

'I am not interested in school rules,' Sergeant Caswell said. 'I am only interested in finding the facts of Mr Findhorn's demise.'

'It was shortly after bed-time,' Lorna said. 'About twenty minutes after nine o'clock. We would have been back about fifteen minutes short of ten.' She heard Miss Appleton take a quick intake of breath.

'During this half hour outside the grounds,' the sergeant said, 'did you venture anywhere near the Alfreck Well?'

'We did not,' Lorna said.

'Where did you go, if I may ask?' The sergeant was writing in a laborious script.

'We walked a short distance up the path and back.' Lorna said.

'Did you see anybody when you were there?' The sergeant asked the question as if he expected a routine negative.

Margaret replied before Lorna could open her mouth. 'No,' she said.

Lorna sensed Miss Appleton's relief. Now she was in a quandary: if she told the truth, Margaret would appear a liar, but she did not intend to lie. Perhaps the sergeant would not ask her anything?

'And you Miss Buchanan? Did you see anybody out at night?'

'I did,' Lorna said. She felt the tension in the study immediately rise.

'Did you recognise him, Miss Buchanan?'

'I did not,' Lorna said. 'It was too dark to make out any details, and I was far more concerned with returning Margaret here to her dormitory.'

'Of course. Could you give any description? Did he look like a navigator?'

Lorna screwed up her face. 'I could not see much at all, Sergeant. A few people were walking up the path, but I did not see their faces. I have never seen a navigator, so I cannot say what one would look like.' Hopefully, that was vague enough.

'Thank you, Miss Buchanan.' Sergeant Caswell closed his notebook. 'I don't think I need bother you anymore.' He nodded. 'Thank you, Miss Appleton.' Replacing his tall hat, he stepped out of the room and down the corridor.

Miss Appleton closed the door. 'You did not report this incident to me, Miss Buchanan.'

'I did not think it worth mentioning, Miss Appleton. I dealt with it at the time; nobody was hurt, Margaret was barely out of my sight, and I am sure it will not happen again.' Lorna held Miss Appleton's grim gaze.

'This college does not accept that kind of behaviour from its pupils, and still less from its teachers. Please pack up your belongings and leave, Miss Buchanan. Margaret, I should expel you for such a flagrant breach of the rules.'

'She did no harm.' Lorna tried to defend her ex-pupil. 'It was an act of folly, not an act of vindictiveness or malice. She did nothing to warrant expulsion.'

'I told you to leave.' Miss Appleton's voice was cold. 'Unless you go immediately I shall call the porter to carry you out.'

'As I am no longer in your employ,' Lorna said coolly, 'then I do not need to treat you with any respect. The actions of this young lady do not warrant such severe retribution. If you expel her, you will be shown as a brute bully.'

Lorna heard Margaret's sharp intake of breath. She sensed the girl was looking at her.

'Expelling Miss Smith will not be good for your reputation, or for that of the school.' Lorna continued softly.

'I did not say I was going to expel her. I said she *should* be expelled,' Miss Appleton sounded slightly defensive.

'That is also wrong,' Lorna said. 'I would like to hear your assurance that Margaret will not be expelled. Otherwise, *I* shall ensure that your name and reputation is blackened throughout the educational world.' Lorna had no idea how she would do that.

'Margaret, leave the room! Wait outside until I call for you!' Miss Appleton snapped.

Only when Margaret had left did Miss Appleton continue. 'I will not expel that child. Now leave this establishment or I will have the porter remove you bodily.'

Lorna had a brief vision of the middle- aged porter lifting her up as she struggled, legs kicking in undignified protest. 'I will leave gladly knowing that Margaret's place here is not in danger.' Lorna turned her back and left the room, closing the door firmly behind her.

'Miss…' Margaret looked up, her face white and anxious.

'Wait until Miss Appleton calls you in,' Lorna said, 'and then do as she tells you. She is not going to expel you.' She walked on without looking back as Miss Appleton bark at Margaret to enter the room.

Chapter Five

'Well, Jane was right. New teachers don't last. I must be the least successful of the lot.' As Lorna had not completely emptied her case from arrival, it did not take her long to pack up. Having a last look around the room that she had occupied for barely ten days, she shrugged and closed the door. The sound of chanting school girls seemed to mock her as she descended the stairs for the last time.

Where to now?

Ben joined her at the bottom of the stairs, looked at her and grunted. The second Lorna stepped outside the school gates, Ben slammed them shut and locked them with a twist of his wrist. Without saying a word he turned away and crunched back up the gravel path. Lorna had no notion where she would go next. The future was as black as her recent past.

With the next coach to Worcester not until the following day, Lorna found a room for the night in one of the cheapest inns in Great Malvern. A group of hirsute Welsh drovers clustered in the reception area, which stank of cheap beer and damp sawdust. Lorna wrinkled her nose and shrugged; this was not the Britain she had dreamed of all these long years in India. Reality seldom lived up to one's expectations.

'Think of home, Lorna; think of calm green fields and neat villages,' Lorna's father whispered in her ear. They lay in the lee of sun-cracked rocks with vultures circling overhead and a host of insects tormenting them.

Sucking at a pebble to assuage her thirst, Lorna felt the perspiration roll down her back and soak through her matted hair.

'Think of home,' her father repeated. 'We'll get out of this and get you home, eh?'

Lorna forced a smile. She thought of her mother lying in a mess of her own blood back in the bungalow as the Pandies ran amuck, killing and screaming and butchering women and children without mercy or hesitation.

'Home sounds good,' she said, with the pebble clattering against her teeth.

'Are you travelling alone Miss?' The clerk at the desk was less than respectful.

'I am indeed,' Lorna said.

'I see. Room Three,' the clerk said brusquely.

'Thank you,' Lorna rewarded him with her sweetest smile as she took her key. 'I'll carry my bag.' There had been no offer of assistance.

Room Three was one floor up with a view through dusty windows to the street and the back of another building. It was barely large enough to hold the narrow bed and single chair that comprised the entire furniture, and a cleaning woman had possibly visited a week or two ago. Lorna dumped her bag onto the straw mattress, sank onto the chair and sighed. 'What on earth do I do now?'

She reviewed the steps that had brought her here. She could have reported Margaret's absence to Miss Appleton and got the girl into trouble, but she had not. That had been her mistake. Lorna sighed; now she had no means of income and limited capital. Who would employ her without references? Nobody in this little town, that was certain. She would probably have to return to London and search for a suitable situation there.

Standing up, Lorna stared out the window. At that moment she wished she could go back a couple of days and start all over again. She had protected Margaret at the expense of herself. Why?

It was because Margaret reminded her of herself at that age. The girl was wilful, stubborn and independent-minded and even more important, she was out of place, as Lorna had always been.

There was no knock at the door. The woman walked in as if she had every right.

'You are Lorna Buchanan.' She was nearly as tall as Lorna, with the dress and bearing of a lady of leisure and eyes as sharp as a scimitar.

'I am,' Lorna agreed calmly. 'I am afraid I don't know your name.'

'Lady Stanhope,' the woman confirmed Lorna's initial prognosis. 'I hear you have recently lost your situation in St Ann's College.'

'That is correct,' Lorna said.

'Do you have a position to go to?' Lady Stanhope was very direct.

'I do not,' Lorna was equally blunt.

'Then you can work for me. I have a job for you.' Lady Stanhope spoke as if there was no argument.

'That would depend on the job,' Lorna said.

Lady Stanhope glanced out of the window and frowned. 'I've been keeping an eye on you ever since you arrived in my town,' she said. 'You are different from any other teacher I have known.'

Unsure how to take that, Lorna chose not to reply.

'You tracked Margaret Smith in the dark, did you not?' Lady Stanhope said sharply.

'I did,' Lorna wondered how Lady Stanhope knew that.

'And you defended her against that fool of a headteacher.' Lady Stanhope's eyes were very blue.

'I did what I think was right,' Lorna said.

'At the cost of your situation,' Lady Stanhope said.

'My job was already lost,' Lorna said.

'It would not have been if you had reported Margaret Smith to Miss Appleton.'

Lorna nodded. 'That may be true.'

'I do not know any other teacher who would do that for a pupil they hardly knew.' Lady Stanhope spoke with a tone of finality. 'It was that combination of integrity and your tracking ability that convinced me you were the best person for the position you will fill.'

'What on earth do you wish me to do?' Lorna could not restrain her curiosity.

'I want you to find out who murdered Mr Findhorn on my land,' Lady Stanhope said.

'What?' Lorna stared at her. 'I'm a teacher of history, not a policeman.'

'You *were* a teacher of history,' Lady Stanhope reminded. 'At present, you are a woman without a position and with a bad reference from your previous employer.'

'I am no policeman,' Lorna replied.

'I did not say that you were,' Lady Stanhope said. 'You intrigue me.' She leaned against the wall and studied Lorna. 'Where on earth did you learn to track somebody in the dark?'

'India,' Lorna replied. 'My father was stationed there for years. I had a fine *shikari* who took me out hunting.'

'In that case, you can shoot as well.' Lady Stanhope raised her eyebrows.

'Yes,' Lorna said. 'Father insisted I shot; my brothers also learned to handle a rifle in case there was trouble.' She shrugged. 'Which there was, of course.'

'Oh?' Lady Stanhope nodded sagely. 'Your father is obviously a man of sense. Many fathers would not allow their daughters near anything resembling a rifle.'

Lorna smiled at the memories. 'We were often out for days at a time. I did not enjoy the kill. I did like testing myself against the quarry.'

'More and more interesting,' Lady Stanhope said. 'I will arrange for a room for you,' she looked around and pulled her skirt up from the unswept floor. 'Somewhere better than this.'

'I have not agreed yet, your Ladyship,' Lorna said. 'And I cannot afford a better room.'

'Oh, the money,' Lady Stanhope nodded. 'I have no idea what the going rate is for being a police officer. How does payment of two sovereigns a week sound, with board and meals added.'

Lorna started. 'It sounds very well, your Lady-ship,' she said without thinking.

'Then that's settled then,' Lady Stanhope turned away from the window. 'We can discuss the details when I get you into better accommodation. Come on Lorna!' She nearly smiled. 'I detest all the formality of Mr this and Miss that when people know one another. I will call you Lorna.'

'And what shall I call you?' Lorna asked.

'You will call me Your Ladyship,' Lady Stanhope said. 'Now come along.'

Lorna did not immediately move. 'You do realise that I have no idea what I am doing?'

'Naturally!' Lady Stanhope's sudden grin made her look ten years younger. 'I believe you have met Sergeant Caswell? He has no idea either. I have as much faith in him solving this case as I have in Little Jack Horner. Come on!' She strode to the door, with Lorna following her, case in hand. 'Oh leave the case, Lorna. I'll have it taken to your new room.'

'It's all right,' Lorna said. 'I'm used to fending for myself. Father never let the servants run after us.'

'I'll have to meet your famous father some-time,' Lady Stanhope said. 'Major James Buchanan isn't it?' Making no allowances for Lorna's burden, she strode out of the inn without a glance at the desk clerk and to a much larger and grander establishment a hundred yards down the road. The name Pinnacle Hotel was displayed proudly above the door, and a uniformed attendant hurried to open the door for her.

'Thank you, Walter,' Lady Stanhope said. Stepping inside, she gestured to a servant who rushed to take Lorna's bag.

'Take care of this lady,' Lady Stanhope ordered. 'Gibson!' She spoke more loudly. 'Where is that man? Gibson! Come here!'

The clerk at the desk started. 'Mr Gibson is downstairs, your Ladyship.'

'Then bid him come upstairs!' Lady Stanhope snapped. 'We don't have all day.'

Gibson was a middle- aged, smooth- faced man whose smug expression altered to complete servility the second he saw Lady Stanhope. 'Your Ladyship,' he said, bowing. 'It is an honour and a privilege.'

'It's nothing of the sort,' Lady Stanhope said. 'I want the best room for Miss Buchanan. There will be no charge, and the hotel will provide meals. The best meals, Gibson; do you hear me?'

'Yes, your Ladyship,' Gibson bowed again. 'If you would care to come this way, Madam?' He altered the direction of his bow to include Lorna and walked backwards to a sweeping staircase whose polished bannister stretched elegantly toward the upper floors. A thick carpet nearly swallowed Lorna's feet as she climbed upward, while oil-paintings of the Malvern Hills brightened the walls.

'In here, Madam if you will?' Gibson opened a panelled door.

'I can't allow you to pay for this,' Lorna looked around at the hanging crystal chandelier and sumptuous furnishings.

'I'm not paying for anything,' Lady Stanhope said. 'I own this hotel.'

The room was eight times the size of Lorna's previous room, with a four-poster bed in one corner and tall windows that overlooked the Malvern Hills.

'Now,' Lady Stanhope settled into one of the three leather arm-chairs. 'You have work to do. I hear that you and Margaret Smith saw some people walking up the path.'

'Yes we did,' Lorna said. 'Nine people in long white cloaks and white hoods.'

'Hmm,' Lady Stanhope pursed her lips. 'Dressed like that they are not here for the Water Cure.'

'The Water Cure?' Lorna asked. 'I am afraid I don't know the term.'

Lady Stanhope frowned. 'Never mind that at present. I'm sure you'll find out. Now, I would think of these people in white; that would be a good place to start,' Lady Stanhope said. 'After you have spoken to Ruth Finch.'

'Who is Ruth Finch?'

Lady Stanhope tapped her arm. 'Ruth Finch and Sarah Swan were the unfortunate women who discovered Mr Findhorn's body. Ruth Finch lives in a small cottage beside the Common at West Malvern.'

Lorna nodded. 'I will speak to her,' she said as ideas raced through her head, tumbling one after the other in a confused mass that she had to put into order before she began anything. Unconsciously she began pacing the length of the room. 'Nobody here knows me or anything about me. May I use your name as a passport?'

'You are in my employ,' Lady Stanhope said. 'If you have any problems, by all means mention my name. That should help in this area.'

'Who has Mr Findhorn's body?' Lorna asked. 'I wish to see it before it is buried.'

For the first time, Lady Stanhope looked slightly surprised. 'It will not be a pretty sight. Have you seen a dead body before?'

'I have,' Lorna did not go into details. She remembered the carnage at Cawnpore when the rebellious sepoys had slaughtered the women and children, and she remembered the terrible aftermath when the British soldiers had wrought their revenge on anybody they even thought may have been involved. The sight of dozens of men hanging from trees and others blown from guns remained with Lorna with nearly as much force as the memory of her mother's dead body.

'Mr Findhorn's remains are in the Abbey Gateway,' Lady Stanhope had been watching her closely.

'Then that's where I'll go first,' Lorna decided, 'and then I'll speak to Ruth Finch and Sarah Swan.'

Chapter Six

Lorna noticed the figure standing in the doorway opposite the Pinnacle Hotel but thought nothing of it. There were always people waiting for somebody or something or just with nothing better to do than idle their lives away. Lorna thought of the well-prepared meal she had enjoyed in the hotel, smiled and cleared her mind. She had an investigation to perform; something she had never done before and that made it all the more fascinating. Life was bright with promise and filled with challenge.

She was acting the policeman. It was evident that Lady Stanhope had some ulterior motive for wishing to find the murderer, but that was not her concern. She was earning money, and this job was as good as any other until she could find another teaching position.

The Priory Gateway had stood for centuries at the entrance to the grounds of Great Malvern Priory. Two storeys high under a pitched roof, the building dominated a short street that led into the abbey grounds, with the actual gateway wide and high enough for a coach to pass through, or two ladies in crinolines, as Lorna observed when she approached. With a level sun picking out details of the stonework it was an impressive introduction to the abbey, but Lorna did not spare much time to admire the architecture as she mounted the steps inside.

A uniformed police constable stopped her on the stairs. 'This area is restricted to the police.' He must have been all of twenty-one years old and obviously proud of his wispy side-whiskers and incipient moustache.

'Lady Stanhope sent me,' Lorna used the name shamelessly. 'I am working on her behalf.'

'Lady Stanhope has no authority here,' the constable was sure of the power his uniform gave him.

Lorna sniffed audibly. 'You've been drinking,' she said, truthfully. 'Does Sergeant Caswell know about your predilection for alcohol?'

The constable flushed, and Lorna pushed quickly past. The room was larger than she had expected, with a cool breeze coming through the open window. Findhorn lay face up on a plank table with a cloth across his middle and his ankles still tied together. The man who stood at his side was moustached and slender, with a blood-stained leather apron over slightly battered looking clothes. He looked up sharply when Lorna entered.

'Who the devil are you? Are you a relative?'

'I am Lorna Buchanan, here on behalf of Lady Stanhope; and you are?'

'I am Dr Bertram; are you sure you wish to be here? The gentleman is unclothed.' Bertram's tone had moderated at the mention of Lady Stanhope's name.

'Quite sure.' Lorna said cheerfully. 'Was this how Mr Findhorn was found?'

'He was inside Alfreck Well,' Bertram said. 'Two local women found him early on Tuesday morning.'

'Inside the well?' Lorna looked up. 'Had he fallen or was he pushed?'

'That I cannot tell you.' Dr Bertram said. 'May I enquire why Lady Stanhope sent you here?'

'Did she not say?' Lorna acted surprised. 'I am investigating the death.' Her smile was genuine. 'I am a sort of civilian police officer.'

'Good God!' Dr Bertram looked shocked. 'You are a woman! It is not right that a woman should do that sort of work.'

'Would you care to tell Lady Stanhope that?' Lorna asked. Without waiting for an answer, she stepped past the doctor and looked at the body. 'He's been cudgelled on the back of the head.' She pointed to a depression in Findhorn's skull. 'Was that what killed him?'

'He drowned,' Dr Bertram said. 'His lungs were full of water when I opened him up.' He indicated the neatly stitched scars across Findhorn's chest.

'So he was banged on the head and fell or was thrown into the well,' Lorna looked around the room, not quite sure what to do next but unwilling to allow her hesitation to show. She had learned long ago in India that confidence and bluff often replaced knowledge and experience. In India young men of twenty looked after areas the size of Herefordshire with a population of tens of thousands. If she acted like an expert, Dr Bertram might treat her like one.

'Show me his possessions, please; his clothes and the contents of his pockets.'

Dr Bertram shook his head. 'He had nothing,' he indicated Findhorn's body, 'he was like that; naked as a new-born baby.' He looked away as if she would be shocked by his using the word 'naked'.

'Let me see,' Lorna flicked away the scanty covering so Findhorn was completely exposed.

'Miss Buchanan!' Dr Bertram stared at her. 'For God's sake have some propriety!'

Lorna looked at Findhorn. She felt neither interest nor shock; he was only a dead body, a new problem to solve. 'I've seen dead men before,' she said quietly. 'Mr Findhorn was a well-built man. It would take some force to knock him down.'

'He was a railway contractor,' Dr Bertram flicked the cover back across his middle. 'That can be quite a physical occupation.'

Lorna looked again at the wound. 'He was hit on the back of the head. Perhaps somebody crept up behind him, but why tie his hands and feet if he was already unconscious?'

'The navigators apparently took a dislike to him,' Bertram said.

'Perhaps,' Lorna examined Findhorn's ankles. 'Green cord; green silk cord, and tied with quite an intricate knot; that's interesting.'

Dr Bertram stepped closer to the body. 'They must have tied him before they killed him.'

'Is that what navigators do?' Lorna examined Findhorn's wrists. 'I heard that his wrists were also tied.'

'They were,' Dr Bertram agreed.

'Was the same sort of cord used?' Lorna asked.

'Exactly the same,' Dr Bertram said.

Lorna nodded. 'I see; do navigators habitually carry green silk cord with them? And strip a man naked? I had thought they were more straight-forward than that.'

'I cannot comment on the minds of naviga-tors,' Dr Bertie said.

Lorna looked carefully at the cord. 'When I was in India, some of the natives used a green or red thread for symbolic reasons. I think the green was religious while a red thread around the wrist proved a man to be a *ghazi*, a hero; I believe they called it the red thread of honour.'

Dr Bertram hesitated. 'I don't think there are many Indian natives around these parts.'

'Probably not,' Lorna agreed. 'But maybe the green cord means something symbolic to somebody.'

'Nothing that I know about.' Dr Bertram dismissed the theory. 'Mr Findhorn was a cruel man. He drove the navigators hard, and they did not like him at all.'

Lorna examined the cords. 'I doubt that many navigators like their contractors much. Did you see these marks on his knuckles?' She looked up. 'He's been in a fight recently. If the navigators killed him, the murderer might have a bruised face.'

Bertram grunted. 'They're navvies; they'll all be bruised and battered.'

Lorna nodded. She had never knowingly seen a navigator so could not disagree. She gave Findhorn a last look over, decided she could learn nothing more from the body and pondered her next move.

'Thank you, Doctor,' she said. 'You have been most helpful.'

What had she learned? She had learned that somebody had thumped Mr Findhorn on the head either before or after they stripped him stark naked and tied his wrists and ankles with green cord. Then they had drowned him. It was not much, but it was a start.

Chapter Seven

There was undoubtedly somebody following her. Lorna looked over her shoulder in time to see the flicker of movement as someone slid into a doorway. She took a deep breath and stepped into John Farrell's stables to hire a chaise.

'I'm not in the habit of hiring to women.' Farrell was tall and thin, with axle grease on both hands and a lugubrious expression on his face.

'I shall tell Lady Stanhope how you feel,' Lorna said easily. 'I am sure she will find another stable for her people to patronise.'

Farrell wiped the grease from his arms. 'What has Lady Stanhope to do with this?'

'I am working for her,' Lorna said.

'I see,' Farrell grunted. 'I do have a little chaise here. It's not luxurious, and the offside wheel has a slight wobble.'

'That does not matter,' Lorna said. 'Show me, if you please.'

The chaise was dark blue with yellow wheels that creaked and a worn leather seat. Within half an hour Lorna was at the reins, cracking her whip and watching the piebald horse trotting in front of her.

'His name's Harold,' the stable manager called. 'And he pulls to the left a little.'

Lifting her whip in acknowledgement Lorna steered the chaise southward and eastward of the town. A glance behind her revealed that the road was empty save for a lone horseman and a tall woman in a dark cloak. Ignoring both, she settled down to get to know Harold and the chaise.

The cottages were only a few yards apart on Malvern Common, both old and dilapidated, and both occupied. Leaving the chaise by the roadside with Harold nibbling at the grass, Lorna knocked on the door of the nearer.

'Yes?' The woman was in her late twenties, with a long face and red eyes where she had been crying.

'Good evening Madam. I am Lorna Buchanan, and I work for Lady Stanhope. Are you Ruth Finch?'

'Yes,' Ruth stared at her in something like fear.

'It's all right,' Lorna said. 'I just want to ask you a couple of questions.'

Ruth sniffed. 'I'm sorry,' she said. 'I think I've caught a cold or something. Is it about the body in the well?'

'It is,' Lorna said.

'Come in,' Ruth stepped aside.

The cottage smelled of dampness, with a tiny fire spreading very little heat over an earthen floor. A second woman huddled on a three-legged stool with a dark green cloak pulled tightly around her.

'Who are you?' The second woman asked nervously.

'This lady works for Lady Stanhope,' Ruth said. 'This is Sarah Swan; she was with me when we found…'

'When we found Mr Findhorn,' Sarah said. 'And yes he was tied up, and yes he was naked.'

'Thank you, for confirming that,' Lorna said cheerfully. 'Did you see anybody else when you were there?'

'I thought I did,' Ruth said.

'Could you give me a description?'

'I didn't see much in the dark,' Ruth said. 'He wore a white cloak I think.'

'A white cloak; thank you. Are you sure it was a man?' Lorna remembered Jane's doubts about Miss Appleton and the group of nine cloaked figures she had seen that same night.

'I thought so,' Ruth sounded so doubtful that Lorna realised she had no idea who, or what she had seen. 'It might have been a woman.'

'I see,' Lorna said. 'I have one more question, please. Why on earth were you out there at that terrible time of morning?'

'I can't give my man a son,' Ruth sounded ashamed. 'If you go to the Alfreck Well at dawn or full moon you can get fertile again.'

'Oh,' Lorna said. 'I had not realised that.'

'Everybody knows that you go to the Alfreck Well to get a baby,' Ruth said. 'It's to do with the power of the moon or the sunrise on the water. People have been using the well forever.'

Momentarily taken aback, Lorna was not sure what to ask. 'Is it some sort of fertility well?'

'It is the best place to go,' Sarah said. 'I went there three times, and each time I fell with child before the next full moon.'

Lorna tried to hide her surprise. 'Would that be why Mr Findhorn was there, do you think?'

'It don't work for men,' Sarah spoke as if rebuking a slow-witted child. 'Men can't fall pregnant.'

'So there was no reason for Mr Findhorn to be there in his state of undress?'

'His what?' Sarah gave a hard laugh. 'His state of undress? He was stark naked, Miss Buchanan. Stark. All of him.' Rising from her stool, she stepped closer. 'The navigators done for him.'

'That might be true,' Lorna said. 'Thank you, ladies. You've both been very helpful.'

Lorna left the cottage surprised at what she had discovered. Rural England was not the home she had dreamed of all her life. She had not expected to find such superstition in England, with people roaming around in white cloaks and others leaping into fertility wells to become pregnant. It was 1859 for goodness sake, the middle of the nineteenth century. This nineteenth century was the age of industry and progress, of steam railways and steamships, of spreading Christianity and agricultural improvements. There was no room left for silly superstitions and centuries-old beliefs. Lorna sighed. She was very little further forward except for that information about the fertility well and the possibility of somebody else on the hill at the same time that the women found Findhorn's body.

Chapter Eight

A band of grey light acted as the harbinger of dawn as Lorna left the Pinnacle Hotel and breathed in the sharp air of morning. She shivered and pulled her cloak tighter around her. 'It's cold.' After many years in India, she could never get used to what was considered a warm day in Britain, let alone the raw chill of March. As always in Great Malvern, the street was busy with portly and dignified gentlemen who had come here for the exercise, the fresh spring water, and the mysterious Water Cure that Lorna resolved to investigate.

Glancing upward, she followed the line of the hill ridge and moved on. If she had thought, she could have asked the stable lad to get the chaise ready, but it was too late now, and she would have to walk. She shrugged; oh well, the exercise would not do any harm, and she would have more time to think.

The boy slipped out of the shadowed doorway and limped toward her, his bare feet making no sound on the ground. 'Mistress,' his voice was a piteous whine as he proffered cupped hands toward Lorna. 'Have pity on a poor boy, mistress. I have not eaten all day.'

Although Lorna was well used to beggars in India, she had not expected any in this prosperous area of England; that was another surprise in this country. She was reaching for her purse when a group of three passers-by stopped. The stoutest of the men spoke.

'Neither have I eaten all day,' the stout man told the boy. 'It's too blasted early for breakfast. Be off with you!'

'Please, Sir; spare a penny for a poor beggar boy,' the boy's fair hair flopped across his huge eyes. 'Only one penny Sir; you have a generous face.'

'And a hard hand,' the stout man said. 'Be off with you, you little blaggard!'

The boy's duck was instinctive, 'no, Sir, please, Sir; only a single queen's head to feed me.'

'Here,' Lorna fished a silver threepence from her purse and flipped it toward the boy. 'There you are. What's your name?'

The boy started and caught the coin with his left hand. 'Thank you, Mistress! I am Peter.'

'Well Peter, you would be better finding some useful employment rather than begging from strangers.'

Peter stepped back. 'Yes, Mistress.' When he looked up his smile revealed yellow teeth in a face whose features were almost concealed by layers of dirt.

'And wash your face as well,' the stout man added sourly. 'God knows there are plenty of wells around here.'

Lorna smiled. 'Best take the gentleman's advice. The police like to arrest dirty-faced boys.' She watched Peter's expression alter to one of fright. He turned around and ran across the road with his bare feet splashing through muddy puddles.

'That made him leave,' the stout man said, laughing. 'You'd think the devil was prodding a pitchfork into his tail the speed the little scoundrel can run.'

Lorna raised her eyebrows as the stout man joined the others and they strode together toward the hills. They were of all ages from early twenties to mid- fifties and exchanged banter as they lifted their hats in greeting to any passing woman. Other men hurried in the same direction.

'A good morning to you, Madam,' one red-faced man said. 'Off to the Worcestershire Beacon now for our health!'

'Will you join us, Madam?' his younger companion asked politely. 'There's nothing like company on the hills.'

'Not today I'm afraid,' Lorna replied as the red-faced man expressed his disappointment. 'I'm heading for the British Camp this morning!' She indicated the Herefordshire Beacon in case there was any doubt as to her destination.

'Have a good walk!' The red-faced man said and increased his pace to head for the path to St Ann's Well. 'But be careful in case these blasted navigators are around.'

'Thank you; I'll be careful,' Lorna said and frowned as something caught the periphery of her vision. She turned in time to see the figure slip into an alleyway beside the hotel. That was three times she had seen something like that. There was no doubt someone was following her; that was a little unsettling.

'They're still behind us, Father,' Lorna glanced over her shoulder.

'I know.' Major Buchanan checked the cartridges in his revolver. 'Keep moving, Lorna. 'Don't look back.'

'Yes, Father.' Lorna stumbled and would have fallen had her father's hand not held her up.

'There are loyal sepoys ahead, and British soldiers.'

'Yes, Father.' The vultures circled above. They would not have much difficulty in finding food in this bloody summer of 1857.

'If you look, they'll think you're scared,' Major Buchanan said. 'And you're not scared are you?'

'Of course not, Father.'

'Good girl! You're the daughter of a British officer and as brave as anybody in the world. Keep your head up now girl and face the world.'

Keep your head up now girl, and face the world, Lorna told herself. She was in the rural heart of England, not the burning plains of India.

Stepping aside to allow a train of donkeys past, Lorna thought it best to act casual, and caught the eye of the elderly woman who led them. 'I've never seen such a fine collection of donkeys all together before,' she said. 'Is there use for them here?'

The donkey woman stopped for a second. 'They take the less energetic up the hills to get their morning exercise.'

'That is nonsense,' Lorna said.

The woman smiled. 'They get their fresh air, and I make my living,' she said, 'so everybody is happy.'

Lorna nodded. 'Do you ever go as far as the Alfreck Well?'

The woman's face immediately closed into a frown. 'I go to the Worcestershire Beacon and round about' she said. 'I never go near the Alfreck. I got six children, and I certainly don't want any more.'

'Six is sufficient to keep anybody busy,' Lorna decided to act as if she had not heard of Alfreck's Well's reputation for enhancing fertility. 'Although I don't see why it should keep you from the Alfreck Well. Or is it too far away?'

'Too far away? Lord save us; it's only a couple of miles.' Hooting with mocking laughter, the woman slapped the nearest donkey on the rump and led them away, muttering to herself. 'Too far away she asks. Too far away.'

Lorna watched as the donkey woman halted abruptly when a tall man spurred his black horse past her. The donkey woman waved her fist as the horseman galloped away, his mane of white hair blowing in the wind and his old-fashioned swallow-tailed coat flapping over the rump of his horse.

'This is indeed a busy town,' Lorna said and walked on.

Alfreck Well was near the western summit of the Herefordshire Beacon, a hill made conspicuous by the massive earthworks of an ancient British fort that circled the upper half. A thin mist drifted across the fort, settling in the grassy ditches of the millennia-old defensive works and distorting every sound and shape.

As she strode up the path, Lorna was again aware of somebody dogging her, yet every time she turned around in seeming casual appreciation of the views, the person vanished behind a tree or slipped into the cover of the uneven ground. Lorna looked at the sketch map she had obtained from the hotel clerk and pushed on.

'Here we are,' Lorna stopped beside the lone mountain ash on the western slope of the hill and looked at the well where the women had found Mr Findhorn. She could not prevent her shiver as the mist clung to the surface of the dark water, grey and chill. 'I hope this is the correct place,' she tapped the bole of the tree, speaking to herself. 'The clerk said that it's the only well to have a guardian tree although I don't know how a mountain ash can guard against anything. It's got no thorns.'

That figure was there again, hovering fifty yards away, hazy through the mist.

'Challenge him,' Lorna said quietly. 'Take the initiative.' 'Halloa!' She raised her voice. 'You can come out now; I'm not going any further today!'

There was no response. A slant of wind thickened the mist, so the dark waters appeared even more mysterious. Sighing, Lorna draped her travelling cloak over a branch beside the well and slid into the thickest of the mist. From a distance, her cloak would be indistinct and may even appear to be her.

'*Deception is as good as a battalion of men,*' her father said. '*Baffle the enemy, confuse them, and hit them hardest at their weakest point.*'

Circling one of the yawning grassy ditches, Lorna judged where her follower was and peered outward. The figure was crouching behind a bush, her long dark dress contrasting with the blonde hair that escaped from her tight round hat.

'Margaret Smith! What on earth are you doing here?'

Margaret whirled around and stared at her. 'How did you see me? I hid well.'

'I asked you what you were doing here? You should be at school!'

Margaret looked away. 'Not any longer,' she said.

Lorna frowned. 'What do you mean? Did Miss Appleton expel you after all?'

'No…'

'Then you should be at school.'

'There were other things.' Margaret said. 'I thought you might need help.' She stood up. 'You spoke up for me,' she said. 'Nobody ever done that before.'

'No one ever *did* that before,' Lorna corrected automatically and then frowned. 'Margaret, I only said what was right. You'll get into worse trouble now. Get you back to school. Go on!' She shoved her ex-pupil downhill.

Margaret brushed a hand across her face. Her eyes were moist. 'I was trying to help like you tried to help me.'

'You'll help me best by helping yourself,' Lorna said.

'It guards against witches and the like,' Margaret said suddenly.

'What does?' Lorna asked.

'The mountain ash does.' Margaret said. 'I heard you say that the mountain ash can't guard against anything. It does. It guards against witches and fairies and things.'

'What?' For a second Lorna was bemused. 'How can it do that?'

Margaret shrugged. 'Everybody knows that mountain ash protects against evil. That's the elf tree.'

'Why is it called that?'

'This is the Alfreck Well; the well of the Elf Kingdom.' Margaret looked puzzled. 'Don't you know anything, Miss?'

'Nothing about that sort of thing,' Lorna said. 'Are you going back to school or not?'

'Not never again,' Margaret said. 'Not after what she done to me.'

'Not *ever* again and not after what she *did* to me,' Lorna corrected. 'What happened?' She remembered the long cane that hung on Miss Appleton's wall and the inherent strength of the head mistress's stringy body. 'No, don't tell me. I can guess. You'll live. You need an education you know. Even if Miss Appleton is a bit strict.'

'She's an evil bitch,' Margaret said charmingly. 'And a witch.'

'Your mother will send you back to school,' Lorna warned.

'My mother's dead,' Margaret said.

'Your father then,' Lorna felt as if she was losing this argument.

Margaret shrugged. 'I've never met him. He was either an Irish harvester or a swaddie. My ma didn't know which one it was. Or maybe he was somebody else.'

'I see.' Lorna said. 'Who cares for you then?'

Margaret shrugged again. 'Nobody cares for me. I'm not a child.'

'In that case, who pays your school fees?'

'I don't know. Some man came along and told me I had to go to school. There were free food and a bed, and it was winter.' Margaret shrugged again. 'It sounded better than the Union. They never said there was a witch in charge, though. They never said that at all.'

'We'll talk about this later,' Lorna fought her frustration. 'If you're not going back then you may as well help me. That way at least I'll know where you are.'

'That's what I said!' Margaret nearly shouted. 'Lady Stanhope got you to find the murderer, and you don't even know a mountain ash keeps away evil.'

'You can teach me that sort of thing until I decide what to do with you,' Lorna said. 'In the meantime... I don't know. Here come the police so behave yourself.'

The mist seemed to alter Sergeant Caswell's shape, so he looked immensely tall, with his top hat strangely elongated and his arms apparently detached from his body. As he approached, Lorna could see that he was frowning.

'What are you doing here Miss Buchanan?'

'The same as you,' Lorna said. 'Lady Stanhope asked me to make some investigations into Mr Findhorn's death.'

'You're a woman!' Caswell said.

'I know,' Lorna said sweetly. 'And you're a man.'

'Women don't know anything about this sort of thing,'

'And men are born with all the investigatory skills, I suppose,' Lorna was still upset at Margaret not being at school and Caswell's attitude was not helping.

'This type of work is not suited to women,' Caswell did not attempt politeness.

'He's rather out of humour this morning,' Margaret murmured.

Lorna thought she had better change the direction of the conversation. She pointed to the pool. 'Is this where Mr Findhorn's body was found?'

'It is,' Caswell confirmed reluctantly.

'Could you describe the scene to me please?'

Caswell's frown deepened, so his face looked longer above his luxuriant whiskers. 'I have no intention of doing such a thing!'

'I would be grateful,' Lorna continued. 'And so would Her Ladyship.'

'I don't answer to Lady Stanhope,' Caswell sounded smug rather than annoyed.

'Mrs Caswell won't like to hear that,' Margaret interrupted. 'Not with Her Ladyship sending a doctor to her last time she was with child.'

Caswell's previous glower could have melted glass, but his expression softened at the mention of his wife. He pulled the collar of his coat higher and adjusted his scarf. 'Mr Findhorn was in the water,' he said. 'Tied up by his hands and feet.'

'It was two local women who found the body, I believe?' Lorna nodded her thanks to Margaret. She thought there was no need for the sergeant to know that she had already interviewed Ruth and Sarah.

'Ruth Finch and Sarah Swan,' Caswell confirmed.

'Indeed,' Lorna passed over a small notebook and a pencil. 'Here Margaret; make yourself useful and take notes. Your writing is not the best, but it will do.'

Margaret's smile showed surprisingly white teeth. 'Thank you, Miss.'

Lorna nodded. 'Was there anything else found here, Sergeant? Findhorn's clothes perhaps, or his belongings?' Lorna peered at the ground. 'I suppose you did check for footprints and the like?'

'Of course, we did,' Caswell said irritably, 'but this is a well- used place. There was nothing else found here, no clothes, no pocketbook, and no boots: nothing.'

'So either he came here naked, he was taken here naked, or the killer carried away his clothes,' Lorna was thinking on her feet. 'Either way, if we find his clothes we have a chance of finding the killer.'

'My men looked all over the hill,' Caswell said. 'We thought of that.'

'Did you find out what he generally wore?' Lorna asked and nodded when Caswell shook his head. 'All right, I'll ask around. Did you ask about his movements or any enemies or quarrels? He had scarred knuckles.'

'He was a railway contractor working with navvies,' Caswell said, 'everybody would dislike him. There would be too many enemies to list.'

'Do you have any theories, Sergeant?' Lorna wondered what else she could ask.

Caswell shrugged. 'I believe it was one or more of the navvies. I know Findhorn paid some off a week or so ago so they would harbour resentment against him.'

'That could be significant,' Lorna ensured that Margaret noted everything down. 'Do you have the names of these men?'

'No. The navies at the camp told us that the men who were paid off were long gone.'

'I'll see what I can do,' Lorna said.

Caswell shook his head. 'The best thing you can do is leave it to us. We are quite capable of solving a simple murder, Miss Buchanan. If Lady Stanhope did not employ you, I would have you run out of the county.'

'Lady Stanhope certain has some power around here.' Lorna said, more to herself than to anybody else.

Both Margaret and Caswell looked shocked. 'Lady Stanhope,' Caswell said quietly, 'owns the land you are standing on and all the land you can see or could see if this damned mist ever lifted.'

'I see,' Lorna nodded. 'But what does she have to do with the police and this murder?'

'Lady Stanhope has something to do with everything,' Caswell's voice was quieter than ever.

'I see.' Lorna decided to find out more about Lady Stanhope. 'Thank you, for your help, Sergeant. I intend to find Findhorn's clothes and possessions. If I do, I will tell you.'

That peace offering worked as Caswell gave a small nod of appreciation.

'I'll also talk to the navigators and see if they are more forthcoming with me than they were with you.' Lorna added.

'You'll what?' Caswell looked visibly alarmed. 'You cannot go into that place with these people!'

'I shall,' Lorna said.

'No,' Caswell shook his head. 'It's not safe.'

'Safe or not,' Lorna said, 'I'm going. Her Ladyship would expect no more.'

Caswell opened his mouth, closed it again and looked away. 'I can send a man to escort you.'

'That will only stir the hornet's nest,' Lorna said. 'I'm safer alone. I'm used to rough men; probably more rough than your navigators.'

When Caswell answered, his Herefordshire had broadened, proving both that he was genuinely concerned and that he had done some research work of his own. 'I heard that you grew up in the Army, Miss Buchanan.'

'That is correct,' Lorna said.

'It is uncommon for young ladies to remain in India with their parents,' Caswell said.

'My parents did not wish their daughter to grow up not knowing them,' Lorna said.

'They preferred to expose you to the diseases and cruelties of India?' Caswell sounded aghast.

'In all my time there,' Lorna said, 'I never came across a naked man murdered in a well.' She thought it better not to admit that she had seen a lot worse.

Caswell's smile was slow and welcome. 'I am glad to hear that, Miss Buchanan. Once is enough for anybody.'

'It's not only a well,' Margaret stepped back a little from Sergeant Caswell. 'It's a sacred well.'

'So I have been informed,' Lorna said.

Margaret nodded. 'That's right, Miss Buchanan. It's known as a sacred well.'

Lorna raised his eyebrows. 'Does it work? Do women actually become with child after visiting the well?' She tried to discard her scepticism. Her father had always told her never to discount local beliefs in India. Perhaps it was the same in Britain.

'Women have used it for centuries,' Caswell did not give a direct reply.

'Was Findhorn childless as well?' Lorna asked. 'Was he here to become a father?'

'It doesn't work with men,' Margaret sounded scathing.

Caswell consulted his notebook, 'Mr Findhorn had eight children,' he said.

Lorna nodded. 'So he did not come here to seek fertility; indeed he was quite the opposite of a woman seeking fertility. He was a very vigorous man.' She looked up, 'Thank you, sergeant. You have been most helpful.'

Sergeant Caswell nodded. 'Sir John Garston informed me that there were two people at the murder site.' He touched a hand to the brim of his hat. 'I had hoped to catch the murderer revisiting the scene, not two women playing at amateur detectives.' He stamped his feet, splashing mud up the leg of his trousers. 'That was an abominable waste of my time.'

'But not of ours,' Lorna said softly as Caswell slid into the mist. 'I have no idea who this Sir John Garston might be, but I must thank him sometime. Come along Margaret; if you have not yet had enough, we have a hill to examine.'

'I know this hill already,' Margaret said.

'Good; what else is there except for the well and the British hill fort?' Lorna waved a hand in front of her face in a vain attempt to clear some of the mist. 'Is there anywhere that the murderer could have hidden Mr Findhorn's clothes?'

Margaret edged a little closer. 'Do you honestly want my help?'

'I honestly want your help for this one thing,' Lorna said. 'And then you go back to school.'

'There's Clutter's Cave.' Margaret said at once. 'It's not far at all, and that's where I would go.'

'We'll finish here first,' Lorna decided, 'and then you can take me there.'

A westerly wind was shredding the mist so one moment the surface of the hill was shrouded, the next there were patches of rough grass visible together with sections of the defending ditches. The improving weather encouraged a number of the hardier of the early spring visitors to venture onto the hill, so donkey women in their long baggy skirts and cheeky-faced donkey boys led their health-seeking passengers to the highest summit to join the energetic if portly walkers.

'No use searching for footprints now,' Lorna indicated a woman who led a pair of donkeys past the Alfreck Well. An overweight man sat astride each donkey. 'Look at that: all these health-seeking people will have obliterated any traces.' She looked around. 'Let's walk, Margaret.'

Remembering how her father had searched for tigers back in India, Lorna began a slow circuit of the Alfreck Well, increasing the radius every time she passed the guardian mountain ash. 'Look at the ground, Margaret. Don't bother about footprints but look for drag marks. There may be some; there may not.'

'Do you think the murderer dragged Mr Findhorn here?'

'I can't rightly say,' Lorna knelt to examine the grass, 'but he may have been hit on the head and hauled to the well, or maybe he met his killer here.'

'What do drag marks look like?' Margaret asked.

'Flattened grass with all the stalks close to the ground and facing the same direction.' Lorna crouched at a tuft of rough grass, shook her head and moved on.

Margaret joined her. 'No, miss, I can't see any.' She looked at Lorna curiously. 'How do you know these things?'

Lorna smiled as they stood up together. 'I learned as a child,' she said.

'You had a queer childhood,' Margaret said. 'What do you think happened, Miss?'

'If Findhorn was not dragged here, then he either came here on his own accord, or he was carried or led,' Lorna crouched beside a curious stone. 'And that leads to two questions: why would he want to come here, or who carried or led him?'

Margaret scratched her nose. 'We know he was not looking for fertility, Miss, and I can think of no other reason for anybody to come here, except one of these health seekers.'

'Agreed,' Lorna said. 'That leaves the second possibility: somebody brought him here. Do you agree?'

Margaret again looked pleased to be asked. 'I do agree,' she said.

'In that case, we want to know who brought him and why the green cords around wrist and ankle.'

'Green cords?' Margaret said. 'I never knew about them, Miss.'

'Do you have any ideas?' Lorna saw that the cords meant something to Margaret.

'I knew the murders tied up Mr Findhorn, Miss but I didn't know they used green rope. That's the fairy colour.'

'Fairy colour?' Lorna asked. She felt a little lost. She had expected to hear about brutal navigators or savage thieves, and here she was being told about elf trees and fairy colours.

'Green is the fairy colour,' Margaret explained seriously. 'It is sacred, like this well.'

'Who told you all this sort of thing?' Lorna asked.

Margaret shrugged. 'Everybody knows it,' she said. 'Everybody around here knows anyway.'

Lorna nodded. She took that to be a rebuke for not being local. 'I'll try to learn. Now, Margaret, if you could show me this Clutter's Cave, please?'

Margaret's smile could hardly have been broader. 'This way, Miss.' She nearly ran to the southeast, turning around every few steps to ensure that Lorna was still with her. After ten minutes, she stopped by a sheer rock face, with a short, gradual climb to a dark entrance around which the mist eased.

'Here it is, Miss.' Margaret was obviously pleased that she could help. 'It's known as the Giant's Cave as well, or the Hermit's Cave or Waum's Cave.'

Lorna viewed it. She could walk into the cave quite easily without stooping, and although the interior was dark, it was not oppressive. There were no clothes inside; there was nothing but bare rock and a thin covering of soil.

'Do you want to see the Sacrifice Stone as well?' Margaret asked. 'It's where the druids of King Caractacus sacrificed people.' She was so eager to help that Lorna did not have the heart to say no.

'See?' After another short walk, Margaret showed Lorna a recumbent, moss-furred stone lying in a small clearing surrounded by scrubby trees.

'It's very unusual,' Lorna looked under the stone in case the murderer had hidden Mr Findhorn's clothes there. Again there was nothing. She looked around; there were a thousand hiding places among the budding trees and bushes. 'This could take some time,' she said. 'Come on Margaret; let's look for Mr Findhorn's clothes.'

It was some hours later before Lorna was satisfied that Findhorn's clothes were not in the immediate vicinity. By that time an early spring sun had dispersed the mist, and the hillside was crisp and clean- lined. Tired, hungry, dirty and slightly disappointed, she led Margaret back down the path which was now busy with visitors seeking fitness. Some strode up individually; others came in convivially chatting groups, and the less dedicated rode astride the patient donkeys.

'This place has not seen so many people since Caractacus fought the Romans,' Lorna grumbled as a small gathering of portly men stepped aside, lifting their hats politely as she passed. 'It seems that a murder does not deter people from visiting the hills.'

'No, Miss,' Margaret accepted the salutations of the men as if it was her right.

Lorna did not see the thin, round-shouldered man until they rounded a sharp bend banged into each other. 'Oh, I do beg your pardon!' The man looked up from his study of the ground and stared at her through thick spectacles.

'No harm done,' Lorna said.

'I am dreadfully sorry,' the man adjusted his spectacles. 'I was concentrating so much on the ground that I quite forgot to look where I was going.'

Lorna stood still as the man bowed politely and stepped aside as a donkey-woman tried to pass him. The donkey's hooves clumped dangerously close to his feet.

'He must have been a big man to kill Mr Findhorn. He was tall and sturdy enough.' Margaret said suddenly.

'More than one man I would say,' Lorna instinctively put out a hand as the thin man tried to walk, stumbled on a loose stone and nearly fell. 'Careful there, Sir.'

The man started at Lorna's touch. 'Oh; thank you!' He gave her a near-vacant smile and walked on. Lorna watched him go, shaking her head. 'Now there is a man whose mind is elsewhere.'

'Never mind him,' Margaret said. 'We get all manner of queer folk coming here to take the waters. They come from London and all sorts of foreign parts. You were talking about Mr Findhorn being a big man.'

'He was all of six feet tall.' Lorna spoke more to herself than to Margaret.

'Mr Findhorn was a big man, too' Margaret said. 'It would take a very powerful man to overcome him, unless he sneaked up from behind.' Margaret swung her arm as if wielding a club. 'Whacko! Whack on the head! Dead!'

'Did you know Mr Findhorn?' Lorna asked.

'I saw him around,' Margaret said. 'I used to watch the navvies working.' She gave a secretive little smile. 'There's some handsome lads there.'

'You're too young for such things!' Lorna reverted to her school-teacher role.

'I am nearly nineteen, I think,' Margaret replied.

'You *think*?' Lorna frowned. 'Don't you know?'

'Not for sure,' Margaret sounded guilty as if the circumstances of her birth were somehow her fault. She looked away.

'Railway navigators are very brawny.' With Margaret unwilling to say more, Lorna changed the subject. 'And if they were paid off, they would be wild as well.' She looked around as a group of health-seekers sunk to the ground. One fanned his flushed face with a newspaper while another drew a bottle from inside his jacket and took a surreptitious sip.

'They're the hardest workers in the world,' Margaret was smiling at some secret thought.

'You should not be thinking of them,' Lorna said.

'It entertains me,' Margaret was still smiling.

'I can take you back to school this afternoon,' Lorna said sharply. 'That should keep you entertained.'

Margaret shook her head so violently that her hair flicked around her face like a blonde cloud. 'No.'

Lorna looked sideways at her. 'You appear determined not to go back to school today. Very well, you know the probable penalty.'

'The witch is not going to touch me again,' Margaret's face twisted in genuine anger. 'I'll kill her first.'

'That's not a good thing to say when we're dealing with a murder.' Lorna said. 'All right then. Maybe you can help some more. These clothes of Findhorn; I still want to try and find them.'

'They could be anywhere,' Margaret said immediately. 'We looked all over the hillside and found nothing.'

Lorna stopped, faced Margaret and took hold of her arms. 'If you were to hide a man's clothes, Margaret, and you knew the police would be searching for them, where would you put them?'

Margaret screwed up her face. 'If it was me,' she said slowly. 'And I had murdered the witch; I would not stuff her clothes in any cave or hole up the hills. There are too many people up here; all the health seekers wandering about with their queer accents. No, I would get some money for them and still put them somewhere safe.'

'Where would that be?'

'In a pawn shop,' Margaret said at once. 'There's none in Malvern, but Worcester or Hereford have plenty. Once they are there, any Tom, Dick or Harry could buy them and then they're gone forever.'

Lorna nodded. 'That was a smart thought.' Her smile was genuine. 'I'll go there tomorrow, Margaret.'

'I'll come too.'

'You'll be back at school tomorrow,' Lorna said firmly.

'Where are we going now?' Margaret did not pursue that conversation.

'I'm going to see Mrs Findhorn.' Lorna sighed. 'I suppose you can come along as well. You've missed today's schooling already. You make sure you behave yourself and remember that Mrs Findhorn has just lost her husband.'

'Yes, Miss,' Margaret said meekly.

Chapter Nine

They heard the noise of children as soon as they opened the garden gate. Lorna stopped for a second, wondered how Mrs Findhorn must feel left alone with a family to bring up, shook her head and walked on.

'Are you all right, Miss Buchanan?' Lorna thought she detected concern in Margaret's voice. 'You looked a bit queer for a moment.'

'No, I'm well enough,' Lorna tried to push the thoughts away. 'It's a lovely house.'

The Findhorns had leased a cottage in the village of Mathon on the western slopes of the Malvern Hills. Two stories high and set beside a small stream, it was of traditional cruck construction with black timbers set against white-washed clay walls. Two children played outside the front door with another, older girl gathering fruit from a well-tended garden at the side.

Other youngsters shouted from inside the house. It could have been an idyllic scene except for the woman who leaned against the inside of the door, crying.

Lorna swallowed hard, wondering what to say. 'Mrs Findhorn?' She tried to keep the emotion from her voice. 'I am Lorna Buchanan, and this is Margaret Smith. Lady Stanhope sent us to find out what happened to your husband. I know this is a terrible time but may I ask you some questions about Mr Findhorn?'

Mrs Findhorn's eyes were red-rimmed. 'Yes, of course, if it helps.' Her smile was vacant. 'It's unusual for a woman to do this sort of job.'

'I know,' Lorna agreed. 'It is unusual.' She moved her foot aside as another child rampaged past, yelling. 'Could you tell me about Mr Findhorn, please?'

Mrs Findhorn nodded. Her eyes were moist and her voice dull. 'He was a good man, Miss Buchanan and the best of husbands, whatever they say about him.'

'What do they say about him, Mrs Findhorn?' Lorna asked.

'They say he was cruel,' Mrs Findhorn stooped to pick up a crawling baby that tried to escape from the house. 'But it was not true. He was a good man.' She held the child close, as if for comfort.

Lorna nodded. 'You were in the best position to judge that, Mrs Findhorn. Nobody knew him better.' She winced as two more children thundered past, with one crashing onto her left foot. 'May we come inside?'

Mrs Findhorn shook her head. 'Please no: the place is a mess, and if I am here I can keep an eye on the children. We have eight, you know.'

'You are a busy woman,' Lorna reconciled herself to the fact that her feet may be under siege during this interview. 'I am going to ask you some difficult questions Mrs Findhorn, but please believe me when I say the answers may help us find your husband's killer.'

Mrs Findhorn took a deep breath. 'Carry on,' she said. Her voice shook.

'We noticed that Mr Findhorn had some marks on his knuckles. Do you know if he fought with anybody in the days before he was killed?'

'I know he had to get rid of some of the navvies,' Mrs Findhorn said. 'They threw stones at the house later, and Findhorn chased them away.'

Lorna glanced at Margaret, who wrote the details down.

'Do you know their names?' Lorna asked.

'No; they were just navvies,' Mrs Findhorn handed her charge to a tousle-haired girl with advice to change and wash it. She raised her voice to tell the girls outside to hurry with the fruit. 'Findhorn might have recorded their names somewhere.'

'Do you know where that may be?' Lorna stepped aside as the two girls from the garden rushed past, wielding baskets of fruit like battering rams.

'In his office somewhere. Findhorn had his office at the navvies' camp near the workings.'

'Thank you. We will look there.'

'You'll need the key,' Mrs Findhorn slipped inside and reappeared with a large iron key. 'He never left it unlocked in case the navvies wrecked it or stole everything. They are the most filthy beasts you know. Do you think the men he paid off were the ones to…?

'I don't know yet,' Lorna said, 'at present, we are looking at every possibility.' She studied Mrs Findhorn, wondering how strong she was. 'Did you hear details of how Mr Findhorn was discovered?'

'He was unclothed and tied up,' Mrs Findhorn held his gaze with eyes suddenly direct. 'Nobody has seen Findhorn in that condition except me, Miss Buchanan. He was not a man to parade himself in that state.'

Lorna nodded. 'I am sure he was not, Mrs Findhorn.'

'There was not another woman involved Miss Buchanan, whatever people say. He was not that kind of man.' Her voice hardened although her tears were not far away.

'That is something that bothers me,' Lorna lowered his voice. 'Would navvies go to all that trouble, stripping him and tying him up? I have no experience of such men.'

Mrs Findhorn shook her head. 'I don't know Miss Buchanan. How would I know that? But I do know that he was not dancing naked up the hill with some woman. These navvies are the devil incarnate. They are capable of anything if the drink is in them.'

'Mr Findhorn's clothes were not at the scene,' Lorna said. 'If we can locate them they may give us a clue about the murderer. Could you tell us what Mr Findhorn was wearing that last day?'

'What he always wore; moleskin trousers that I washed only that morning,' Mrs Findhorn shook her head, 'he was always tearing the knees of them; I can't count the number of times I darned these trousers.'

'Moleskin trousers and what else?' Lorna prompted.

'A sharp shirt, like the men, bright yellow it was, with mother-of-pearl buttons, and a buff waistcoat.' Mrs Findhorn absently lifted another child and wiped its nose with a square of linen she took from her sleeve. 'We bought that waistcoat at the market in Ledbury. One and nine pence it cost and cheap at half the price. There was a button missing from the shirt; the third one down I recall. I was going to replace it when my Findhorn got back. He looked grand in his waistcoat, Miss Buchanan, so grand, and now he's gone, murdered naked and stuffed down a well like the pussy in the nursery rhyme.'

'Would Mr Findhorn have anything in his pockets, Mrs Findhorn?' Lorna glanced at Margaret, who continued to take notes, 'maybe some money to tempt somebody to rob him, or a gold watch?'

'He had a watch,' Mrs Findhorn said. 'Of course, he had a watch. A silver coloured one with a silver chain it was. We bought that in London three summers ago when Findhorn was working there.'

'Was his name on it, Mrs Findhorn?' Lorna asked, 'or an inscription that we might identify it by?'

'No,' Mrs Findhorn shook her head. 'It was just a watch. Findhorn used it at his work, and it was all battered and scratched. It was not real silver of course, but it was Findhorn's watch.'

'Was the watch sufficiently valuable to tempt anybody to steal it?' Margaret made her first contribution.

Mrs Findhorn shook her head. 'Hardly that. It cost us a shilling three years ago, and Findhorn's used it well since then. I doubt you would get a farthing for it now.'

'Would Mr Findhorn have any money, a pocketbook or anything else of value?' Lorna asked, but Mrs Findhorn shook her head again.

'No, Miss Buchanan. With eight children to support, Findhorn did not have money to throw away. He was a good man, a good man and all his money came to me.'

Lorna nodded. 'Two last questions, Mrs Findhorn, and then we will leave you in peace: did Mr Findhorn have any enemies and was he in the habit of going out alone at night?'

'He was a railway contractor,' Mrs Findhorn said. 'The navvies disliked him because he made them work. The landowners disliked him because he drove railways over their land and the engineers disliked him because he altered what they wanted to do. The local people disliked him because he brought the navvies to plague them, and then there was that strange woman who watched him at work the last few days.'

'What strange woman?' Margaret paused her scribbling.

'I don't know who she was!' Mrs Findhorn's voice rose an octave. 'How should I know who she was? Findhorn mentioned her a few times. He said there was a woman in white who stood watching the workings and sometimes pointed at him. He said it gave him goose-bumps.'

Lorna exchanged glances with Margaret. 'Did anybody else see this woman?'

Mrs Findhorn frowned. 'How should I know? I never asked anybody else! Why should I ask anybody else?'

'Of course not: I am sorry to ask that,' Lorna tried to soothe the situation. She waited until Mrs Findhorn calmed herself. 'Just one last question,' she continued, 'was Mr Findhorn in the habit of walking alone at night?'

Mrs Findhorn nodded. 'Yes of course. He checked the workings at all hours of the night and sometimes had to make sure the navvies were not having a randy.'

'Thank you,' Lorna said. 'We will do our best to find your husband's murderer, Mrs Findhorn.'

As they walked away, Lorna heard the sobbing. He did not look back; there was nothing she could do to help.

'That poor woman,' Margaret said. 'It must be terrible to be left like that with all these children!'

Lorna nodded. 'The only thing we can do to help is to try and find her husband's killer. I know it won't ease her pain, but it might give her some release.'

'How do we do that?' Margaret asked.

Lorna glanced at her. 'Well, if you insist on not attending school today...'

'Or ever again,' Margaret interrupted.

'If you insist on not attending school today you can help me some more. Or I can personally take you back to Miss Appleton.'

'Yes, Miss.' Margaret tucked her notebook away. She glanced over her shoulder to the neat black and white house. 'What will happen to her?'

Lorna was quiet for a moment, more interested in this new caring side of Margaret than in the question. 'Unless she has a very understanding family she faces a lifetime of heartache and poverty, with her only hope the workhouse. If she can't afford to keep her children, the parish authorities will place them elsewhere, and they will end up working as servants or factory hands if they are lucky.' Lorna took a deep breath. 'Life is not easy, Margaret. That is one reason that an education gives some advantages.'

'There is not just one victim in this murder, is there?'

For the first time, Lorna felt a glimmer of genuine affection for Margaret. There was more to this girl that wilful stubbornness. 'No. I think that a murder leaves parents, children or spouses bereft all their lives, while a theft can push poor people to destitution and starvation.' She pushed her hat firmly on her head. 'Come along Margaret. If we can clean up some of these sordid parasites that cause so much misery we have achieved something.' He stopped at her chaise. She had intended to visit the navigator's camp next, but if they were even half as rough as their reputation, she had no intention of exposing Margaret to their language and behaviour. 'I'm going to follow through on your suggestion of pawn shops.' She wondered if she was allowing Margaret too much latitude and shook her head. She would have to move quickly or else the clothes would be bought and lost forever.

Margaret looked at her. 'Are you really, Miss?'

'It was a good idea.' Lorna gave grudging praise. 'No; it was more than that. It was an *excellent* idea.' She saw Margaret's eyes widen and guessed that she was not used to praise. 'Come along then, Margaret. You know Worcester far better than I do. Jump in!'

'Are we going to Worcester?' Margaret looked slightly shocked.

'I was going tomorrow, but I think we should go now. Right at this minute!' Lorna said. She climbed into the chaise. 'In you come!'

Cracking the reins, Lorna set off for Worcester. It was late afternoon now with dusk not far away, and she did not know the road or the town, but if Findhorn's clothes were in a pawn shop, every wasted hour increased the chances of them being bought and disappearing forever.

'Are you sure you wish to come?' She asked Margaret. 'It's late now.'

'Where else do I have to go?' Margaret said.

Although she was acutely aware of the tragedy of this case, Lorna admitted to herself that she rather enjoyed this new freedom she had to wander around the countryside, probing into the mystery. The feel of the crisp air on her

face and the sound of the horse's hooves clopping on the road were exhilarating; far better
than sitting in a classroom trying to interest a
score of young women in the lives of long- dead
kings, queens, and commoners.

'I don't know Worcester all that well,' Margaret admitted.

'You know it better than I do,' Lorna said. 'I've
only been there once when I caught the mail to
Malvern.'

'Yes, Miss,' Margaret fidgeted uncomfortably
in her seat.

Lorna frowned, remembered Miss Appleton's
cane and tightened her mouth. 'When were you
there last?'

There was a long silence as Lorna eased the
chaise onto the main Worcester road and worked
Harold into a reasonably fast walk.

'I've never been there at all, Miss,' Margaret
sounded guilty as she admitted the fact.

'Oh.' Lorna digested this piece of information.
Worcester was around ten miles from Malvern
and was the nearest large town.

'Oh well, you will still be able to help,' Lorna said. 'You may know Hereford better if we have to go there.'

'I've never been there either,' Margaret admitted. 'I've never been anywhere really, except the Malverns.'

'I see.' Lorna said. She had heard that country people did not travel much, but as her life had consisted of various military postings with her father she had not paid much attention. 'It will be a new experience for you,' she said cheerfully. 'It will broaden your education!'

'Yes, Miss,' Margaret shifted in the seat. 'This is good, Miss, doing things and talking to you like this.'

Lorna glanced at her and smiled. 'You are a big help,' she said.

Worcester was busy when they arrived. It was a town full of ancient buildings, some of them of the traditional black-and-white painted design, with the River Severn broad and serene flowing past. Carriages, coaches, and carts rumbled over the streets and crowds jostled together on the pavements. Lorna felt Margaret wriggle on her hard seat.

'Are you all right, Margaret? Do you want me to stop so you can walk for a while?'

'I'm fine Miss, thank you. I never seen so many people before.'

'I *have* never seen so many people before,' Lorna corrected automatically. 'Right; let's find somewhere safe for the chariot, and we'll get to work finding these pawnshops.'

'Yes, Miss,' Margaret edged closer to her.

'It's busy isn't it?' Lorna had not expected the apprehension in Margaret's eyes. 'We should stay together I think.'

'Yes, Miss,' Margaret sounded relieved.

Easing the chaise into a quiet lane, Lorna pulled on the reins and hopped out, followed by Margaret. A group of small boys immediately crowded round.

'If you give them two-pence they'll watch the chariot,' Margaret advised. 'And if they don't' she raised her voice, 'I'll boot their arses for them.'

'Quite,' Lorna said. 'You boys. I'll give you a penny to watch the chaise and another two-pence if it's here and undamaged when we get back.'

'Here!' Margaret grabbed the tallest and scruffiest of the bunch. 'No queer business, right?'

'It'll be all right,' the boy wriggled in Margaret's grip.

'It better be!' Margaret said. 'Now, where's the best pawnshops in this town. If I was a-wanting to dump some shady stuff, where would I go?'

'Are you a thief?' the boy sounded impressed.

'Never you mind what I am and what I'm not,' Margaret gave the boy a cuff on the head and shook him vigorously. 'You just answer my question, or I'll smack your head so hard your brains will come out your ears if there was any inside, to begin with.'

Lorna turned away to stroke Harold. Margaret's methods left a lot to be desired, but she knew how the local people worked.

'There's Ma Flannigan's,' the boy said at once, 'and Joe the Jew's place by the Cross, or Miffy Sadler's; that's where I would be going if I had anything worth more than threepence.' He reeled off half a dozen names, with Margaret paying close attention and scribbling them down in her notebook.

'You'd better not be pulling the longbow,' Margaret said, 'I'll hammer you if you are, you little ding boy.'

'I'm not throwing the hatchet, Miss, true as my mother's life.'

'Right then,' Margaret released the boy. 'And that chariot better have all its wheels and paintwork when we get back.'

Lorna turned back from her inspection of the horse. 'That was good work,' she approved.

'You got to be firm with that type,' Margaret said. 'They'll steal the clothes off your back, else.'

'You stick close by me,' Lorna remembered how nervous Margaret had looked at the crowded streets. 'Don't you go wandering off on your own.'

Ma Flannigan's was in Angel Street, a short walk from the Cross. Lorna hesitated at the doorway until Margaret, who had been pressing close to her since they left the chaise, pushed ahead. 'I heard that you got to look bold as brass in these places,' she gave her nineteen-year- old wisdom. 'Otherwise, they'll take you for all you've got and charge you for the pleasure.'

The interior smelled of damp cloth and sour cooking, with a plain wooden counter prominent in a shop lined with shelves packed with clothing and cheap household goods. Behind the counter was a glass case with half a dozen metal watches and a few items of jewellery.

The plump woman behind the counter summed them up in a single glance. 'Good afternoon ladies,' she said politely to Lorna. 'What can I do for you?'

'I'm looking for something,' Lorna said. She took the list that Margaret had written down. 'Some items of clothing and a watch.'

'Plenty clothing in here,' Ma Flannigan's smile was as insincere as a cat at a mouse-hole.

'I'm looking for some things in particular,' Lorna said.

'What kind of things?' The smile faltered as Ma Flannigan looked at them. 'Who are you?'

Lorna read out the list.

'I never saw them,' Ma Flannigan was immediately suspicious. 'What are you wanting these for, a well set up gentlewoman like you? I'll call George, mind!' She lifted a stout stick from underneath the counter. 'I run a clean shop; none of your shady stuff here!'

'I did not think there was anything shady...' Lorna began.

'George!' Ma Flannigan thumped her stick on the counter. 'George! There's two foreigners here causing trouble!'

'Time to leave, Miss,' Margaret took hold of Lorna's arm. 'Come on; it's time to leave!'

'George!' Ma Flannigan screamed. 'They're still here! Throw them out George and don't worry about breaking bones!'

George proved to be a lumbering giant with a bald head and forearms as thick as most men's legs. Lorna did not wait for him to arrive before she allowed Margaret to haul her outside.

'And stay out!' Ma Flannigan's bellow followed them down the street. 'Accusing honest folk of theft and robbery!'

'That was unpleasant,' Lorna said after they retreated a good hundred yards down the street.

'If you don't mind, Miss, I'll ask in Joe the Jew's shop.' Margaret hesitated. 'You sound a bit too respectable for these places. They think you're a peeler or something.'

'You try and see,' Lorna agreed.

Joe the Jew's was a smaller shop with shutters across the lower half of the window and a gas-lamp burning low inside. Joe himself greeted them with a smile and a bobbing bow. His kippah was inconspicuous at the back of his head.

'Hello Joe,' Margaret smiled in return. 'My da lost his clothes in a card game, and we want to replace them.'

'You've come to the right place,' Joe was about forty with quiet eyes in a featureless face.

'He wants a yellow shirt with mother of pearl buttons and a buff waistcoat,' Margaret said. 'He's very particular about what he wants.'

'Is he now?' Joe looked at her shrewdly. 'I have not anything like that just now but if you give me your name I can send the boy to you when something comes in.'

'Thank you, Joe,' Margaret said. 'We'll come back when you have more stock.' She ushered Lorna out of the shop.

'That was short and sweet,' Lorna said.

'Never give your name to nobody,' Margaret said. 'And if anybody asks for where you live … run!'

'He's only a pawnbroker,' Lorna said. 'I don't think he's any threat to us.'

'Joe may be only a pawnbroker,' Margaret said, 'but we don't know who his friends are. They may be even bigger and uglier than George.'

Lorna nodded slowly. 'You are not as silly as you pretend,' she said. 'Miffy Saddler's next, in St Switching's Street.'

They did not have to look far in Miffy Saddler's. As soon as they stepped in the door, Margaret snorted in a most unladylike fashion and fingered a yellow shirt with mother-of-pearl buttons that hung on a rack by the counter.

'That looks like it will fit him.' Lorna passed her gaze over the shirt. The third button down was missing, as Mrs Findhorn had said.

'Are you interested in that shirt?' Miffy was a smooth- faced woman in her thirties, with a score of rings disguising her fingers and earrings that jingled every time she moved. 'It came in recently from a most respectable source.'

'Most respectable?' Lorna fingered the material and remembered the phrase Margaret had used. 'I hope so. I don't want my man to have a shirt that any old Tom, Dick or Harry has worn.'

'Only three shillings,' Miffy clattered her hands onto the counter.

'Three shillings!' Margaret hooted when Lorna reached for her purse. 'You'll get one shilling and like it!'

Miffy's earrings jangled in anger as she turned to Margaret. 'You best keep your opinions to yourself!' she snapped.

'Three shillings does seem an inordinate amount for a second- hand shirt,' Lorna followed Margaret's lead. 'Now if you could find a waist-coat to match…'

Miffy's anger faded as the prospect of another sale loomed. 'We have a huge selection of vests. We have green, blue or many coloured, just like Joseph's coat…'

'Buff I think,' Lorna held up the shirt as if wondering about a match. 'My man would suit buff.'

'I have the very one!' Miffy said. 'From the same respectable source.' A few seconds rummaging found her lifting up a buff waistcoat.

'It's stained,' Margaret pointed out. 'That's dirt.' She bent closer to the waistcoat. 'It may be blood.'

'It will wash,' Miffy said.

'It will do,' Margaret fitted into her role. 'My da won't mind a little bit of dirt. He's a navigator you know,' she said, facing Miffy across the counter.

'You don't have a pair of moleskin trousers too, do you?' Lorna asked. 'He's a big man…'

'Alas, no. I had a pair, but they went only this morning,' Miffy said.

'These will do fine,' Lorna said. 'Now if you only a had a watch as well…'

'We've a handsome silver Hunter,' Miffy was eager for a sale. 'Only half a sovereign.' She glowered as Margaret forced out laughter.

'A silver Hunter for a navvy. That won't last ten minutes in the workings!'

'I can't run to half a sov.' Lorna said. She saw Margaret slip behind the counter and quickly distracted Miffy's attention. 'How much for both shirt and vest?'

'Shall we say six shillings the pair?' Miffy was too ready with the figure.

'How about three shillings for both?' Lorna countered.

'Three shillings! I'd be cutting my throat if I let them go at that price! Why they cost as much to buy!' Miffy's earrings jingled again as she shook her head. 'Five and sixpence and that's my last offer.'

Lorna pretended to consider. 'Could you tell me who brought them in? This respectable gentleman who brought them. Who was he?'

'Oh it was no man; it was a lovely respectable girl. Quite charming she was,' Miffy said.

Margaret returned from her trip on the other side of the counter and nodded to Lorna, who took a step closer to the door.

'Five shillings the pair; how's that?' Miffy asked.

'Four shillings and that's my final offer.'

'Done,' Miffy spat on the palm of her hand and extended it. Lorna took it gingerly, parted with the money and guided Margaret out of the shop.

'You *were* done,' Margaret said.

'I don't care,' Lorna responded. 'What on earth were you up to behind the counter? I hope you were not stealing anything.'

'What do you take me for? I'm not a thief!' Margaret sounded so indignant that Lorna nodded.

'Of course not. Now let's find an inn and get something to eat. You can tell me there.' Lorna fingered her purchase. If it was the right shirt and waistcoat, her trip to Worcester had been worth four shillings.

The Talbot Inn nestled close to Worcester Cathedral. There was a carriage pulled up outside and a small group of loafers pulling on pipes; they stepped aside when Lorna and Margaret asked them nicely, and one opened the door as he touched the brim of his hat.

'I never been in an inn before,' Margaret looked around her.

'Stay close to me,' Lorna guided her to a table and ordered the fish pie, bread and cheese and tea for two; she parted with three shillings and checked her purse, hoping her money would last. Her reward was the look of utter gratitude on Margaret's face as she saw the plate of food.

'I never seen so much on one plate,' Margaret said.

'I *have* never seen so much,' Lorna said. 'I thought you looked hungry.' She watched as Margaret tasted gingerly and then ate with a fine appetite. 'Now, what have we discovered?

We have these items of clothing, and we know that a girl handed them in.'

'We know more than that,' Margaret spoke through a mouthful of fish. 'I got her name as well.'

'How did you manage that?'

'What do you think I was doing when Miffy was cheating you over the prices? I got her tally book and ripped out the pages. Here...' she handed over three ragged sheets of paper to Lorna. 'They got a bit torn.'

'So they have. That's breaking the law, you know.'

'So is charging four shillings for dirty old working clothes, so it serves her right; her with her dangly ear- rings and flashy fingers. I bet she got them all from her customers and cheated them for the price too.'

Lorna smiled. Margaret had unique concepts of right and wrong and acted accordingly. 'You're quite a girl aren't you?'

'Don't forget that some people never give their real names, though,' Margaret ate quickly, as if afraid that somebody might come and snatch the plate away from her.

Lorna ran her gaze and forefinger down the pages. 'Here we are,' she said. 'One buff vest; one shirt with mother of pearl buttons; one pair mole-skin trousers; one cheap watch; one and nine pence halfpenny the lot.'

Margaret nodded vigorously. 'I told you Miffy cheated you. Did I not tell you she was a cheat?'

'You did,' Lorna agreed. 'Please keep your mouth shut when you're eating. Here's the name too: Sam Bellamy.' She looked up. 'Sam: that's a man's name. Miffy told me it was a girl that handed them in.'

Margaret stared at her and said nothing, still chewing.

Lorna thought out loud. 'Maybe it was one of the navigator's wives. I'll ask when I visit the camp. Maybe it is a young wife, or even a daughter using her father's name. Unless Sam is not short for Samuel.'

Margaret screwed up her face. 'I was wondering if I knew a Sam Bellamy, but I don't, and I've lived in the area all my life.'

'Could be a navigator then, or the daughter of one, as we thought.' Lorna gave a small smile. 'I can't see a young girl knocking down a great hulking man like Mr Findhorn, tying him up and stealing his clothes. There is more to this than that.'

'Green thread and the sacred well,' Margaret blurted out. 'That's what this is all about.'

'You might be correct,' Lorna said. 'I haven't forgotten that. All the same we – I – had better search for this Sam Bellamy in case the name is real. Now eat up, and we'll get you home.'

'I haven't got a home,' Margaret lifted her head and faced Lorna. 'I was in the workhouse when the man took me to the school, and I amn't going back there again neither.'

'This man who took you to the school,' Lorna said. 'Who was he?'

Margaret shrugged. 'I don't know. It was just a man. I never seen him before and I don't want to see him again.'

'All right,' Lorna came to a hard decision. 'I'll take you back to the school and see if Miss Appleton will take in again. If I use Lady Stanhope's name, she should go easy on you.'

Margaret said nothing. Lorna noticed that she cleared her plate and also lifted any left- overs on her way to the door.

'I see you are not arguing,' Lorna said.

Margaret shrugged. 'There's no point is there? You're going to do it whether I want to or not.'

'I'm doing what is best for you,' Lorna said. 'It is far better that you are warm and housed and fed at St Ann's College than hungry and sleeping under a hedge in the rain – or worse. It's either that or the Union workhouse.'

'I'm not going back to that place,' Margaret said.

'That's settled then,' Lorna hardened her heart. She could imagine what sort of reception Miss Appleton would give Margaret. However, the alternative was worse. 'Come on Margaret.'

'Yes, Miss.' Margaret said sullenly.

The chaise was where they had left it, with the group of small boys sitting inside. Lorna gave them the promised two-pence, added another penny and boarded the chaise in silence. Although she felt guilty at taking Margaret back to a place she hated, she knew there was no choice. Glancing sideways at Margaret's deliberately expressionless face, she cracked the reins and set off.

The ten miles or so to Great Malvern was one of the most uncomfortable journeys that Lorna had undertaken since she arrived in England.

'Father,' Lorna said. 'What if the Pandies have killed all the British?'

'Don't even think that,' her father said. 'It will be all right; you'll see.'

They stood outside the burning bungalow. The corpse of Mrs Hewson was outside, spread-eagled on the ground, naked and torn. The bayonet protruded obscenely from her.

'Don't look.' Father guided her away.

'Are we not going to bury her, Father?'

'No, Princess. We don't have the time, and it will let the rebels know we have been there.'

'All right, Father.' Lorna did not mention the corpse of Dougal. She had been playing with that little tousle-haired dog only last week, and now it was dead, hacked to pieces by Pandy swords and bayonets.

'Come on, Lorna.' Taking her by the hand, Father led her into the terrible darkness. Behind them, the burning thatch of the roof collapsed into the bungalow. Close by, a pi-dog howled.

A vixen called off to the left, breaking the silence of the first few miles. Lorna glanced sideways at Margaret's white, set face and spoke again.

'Would you like me to come to the school with you?'

'No.' One word.

'It might make it better.' Lorna said. 'I can explain that you were helping Lady Stanhope and me.'

Silence. Margaret shifted, easing the pressure on the hard wooden seat.

'It might help if I was there.'

Still silence.

Lorna felt anger overtaking her guilt and sympathy. 'All right then, Margaret. I'll take you to the front door and leave you there.'

The silence was even denser as they drove on with the faint light from their lamps bouncing along the road in front of them and the occasional coach or farmer's cart rumbling past. In the dark, the long ridge of the Malvern Hills was stern and strangely oppressive, as if sheltering sinister secrets.

'Here we are,' Lorna turned into the steep road that led to St Ann's College. 'Now keep calm, Margaret. Tell Miss Appleton that you have been helping Lady Stanhope and me... Margaret!'

'I'm not going!' Margaret shouted, and before Lorna could reach across she had jumped out of the chaise and vanished among the trees.

Lorna hauled back on the reins and climbed out. There was no sign of Margaret. 'Oh you odious little minx!' She took half a dozen steps in pursuit and stopped at the edge of the trees. 'Margaret!'

Did she genuinely want to hunt Margaret down and hand her over to Miss Appleton's less-than-tender care? Lorna pondered waking up the school and organising a search, and then shook her head. No; the thought of half a dozen teachers blundering around in the dark after one reluctant young woman was not inviting. Sometimes it was better to let things run their course without interfering. Margaret was nearly nineteen by her own reckoning. She was hardly a child and probably knew more about surviving in this part of the world than most.

Sighing, Lorna returned to the chaise. 'Come on Harold,' she said. 'Let's go home. It's been a long day.'

Chapter Ten

The Navigators' camp was arranged in two long rows of huts set on the western slopes of the Malvern Hills and a hundred yards from the noise, dust, and labour of the railway workings.

Perseverance Hill loomed above, a great green sentinel over the grafting men. Lorna hauled on the reins of the chaise and looked around, getting her bearings and assessing the situation before she began work. The navigators were hacking a tunnel through the hills as they pushed the line from Hereford to Worcester. Within a few hundred yards of where Lorna stood, scores of brawny men were toiling through some of the hardest rock in England, sweating and swearing as they laboured with pickaxe, gunpowder, and shovel.

Smoke from a score of fires took the place of the mist that had lately hovered on the peaks of the hills and a dozen hard-faced women emerged from the huts as Lorna hooked the reins up and adjusted her hat.

'Good day to you all,' Lorna dismounted and smiled as the woman stared at this lone stranger who dared to come to their camp. 'My name is Lorna Buchanan, and Lady Stanhope has sent me to find answers to some questions.'

The women gathered around. 'What sort of questions, Mistress?' The accent was Welsh, and the words came from a young face with ancient eyes.

'Questions about the death of Mr Findhorn,' Lorna said.

The women looked at each other. Two drifted away while a third spat a mouthful of tobacco juice on the ground at Lorna's feet.

'He was a black-hearted bastard,' the Welsh spokeswoman gave her opinion. 'He was a cold-blooded, wicked scoundrel of a bugger.'

'That may be so.' Growing up in a military environment, Lorna was unmoved by foul language and rough behaviour. She had seen worse; a lot worse. 'However, I am not asking about his character. I am only asking about the last few days of his life and the manner of his death.'

The Welshwoman stuck a short-stemmed pipe in her mouth. 'The last days of his life were the same as the rest, Mistress Nosey. He used folk and robbed them blind.' She took the pipe from her mouth and jabbed the stem into Lorna's arm. 'Some of the boys went on the randy, and a public house got damaged. Her bloody Ladyship demanded that the peelers toss them in the lock-up, but the local bluebottles were too scared to touch them.'

'That would be Lady Stanhope I presume?' Lorna asked.

'Aye; that's what I said.'

'I thought it was,' Lorna realised that a dozen men had joined the women. Dressed in the navigator's uniform of moleskin trousers, canvas shirt, heavy hobnailed boots and the ubiquitous felt hat with the brim turned up, the men did not look friendly. 'So Mr Findhorn sacked them instead? Is that what happened?'

'Findy did that,' the woman confirmed. 'He owed them a week's pay but kicked them out with nothing. He sez the wages would pay for the damage to the public.'

The crowd was inching closer. 'Move back a little please,' Lorna asked. 'You may unsettle the horse.'

'Or the driver,' a dark-haired woman said. 'What are you asking such a heap of questions for, Mistress Nosey?'

Lorna tried to control her unease. However tall she was, she knew that these immensely tough women and men would overpower her in a moment and she did not expect much mercy if they turned against her. She remembered a maxim of her father's when dealing with recalcitrant natives or unhappy soldiers. If in doubt tell the whole truth.

'Lady Stanhope wants me to ask,' Lorna said. 'I work for her.' Reaching under the driving seat of the chaise, she produced a square bottle. 'I thought this might help.'

'Well, you're a trump! I don't mind if I do,' the nearest woman snatched the bottle the second it appeared. Removing the cork with her teeth, she put the neck to her mouth and took a deep draught. 'Mother's ruin,' she said. 'That's the real stuff.'

'Leave some for me,' the Welsh woman snatched the bottle. 'You still haven't told us why you're asking the questions.'

Lorna watched her bottle disappear into a dozen willing hands. 'You're not children. Why do you think? Mr Findhorn was found murdered a day or so after he paid off three navigators. Naturally, the navigators are the prime suspects.'

'It's always the navvies that get the blame,' a hoarse voice sounded. 'We never done for him.'

Lorna nodded. 'I didn't think you did,' she said truthfully. 'I am here to try and clear your name; not to blame you.'

'The bluebottles think some of us murdered him?' the Welsh woman's laugh was as coarse as anything Lorna had ever heard in barracks. 'Listen Mistress Nosey; he deserved to be killed, but it was no navvy that did it.'

'So who was it then?' Lorna asked, 'if you can vouch for the actions of all the navigators, working or not, I will tell Sergeant Caswell.'

'None of us,' the woman repeated. 'Any decent navvy would have smashed his skull with a shovel or kicked him to pieces, not stripped him stark and drowned him.' The Welsh woman looked up at Lorna, suddenly cunning. 'You inspect their boots, Mistress Nosey; look for blood on them. You won't find a bit cause they never done it, sure as God Almighty is sitting on his throne.'

Lorna nodded; it was the sort of answer she expected from a soldier or a navigator. 'You don't believe a navy murdered Mr Findhorn then?'

'No,' the woman said. 'What's all this stuff and nonsense about him being naked and tied up. Who has time for that sort of nonsense?' She poked her pipe against Lorna's arm again. 'I tell you who would do that: some bloody dollymop that he struck would do that.'

'Was there a dollymop … a prostitute?' Lorna asked. 'I thought he was a family man.'

'Oh he was a family man all right; Findy loved to make families. He took any woman he fancied and helped them into the family way.'

'Did you see him with another woman?'

'We seen the woman,' the Welshwoman said, 'didn't we see her, ladies?'

There was a loud chorus of assent from the gathering. 'We seen her,' the women said, 'she was always watching him.'

'There was more than one of them,' a thin-faced woman shouted, 'I say there was more than one.'

Lorna stepped away from the chaise 'Is there somewhere we can talk in more comfort?' She knew she was taking a chance by entering the den of these navigators. Their reputation for drunken violence was formidable.

The crowd closed in with the women all talking at once, each one apparently determined to shout louder than her neighbour as they gesticulated to catch Lorna's attention.

'Come into my hut,' the Welshwoman said, 'and don't be afraid. We won't eat you.' Her smile revealed discoloured teeth. 'Maybe.'

Leaving the chaise outside, Lorna ducked under the low entrance to the hut the Welsh woman shared with a dozen others. Long and dark, it was stuffy with the smell of cooking and lack of air.

'Over here; I am Bridget; this is Maggie,' the Welshwoman indicated the thin-faced woman, 'and Katie,' a woman who had once been handsome but was now broken with fatigue and hardship, 'and Lizzie.' The last mentioned gave a small smile and looked away. Lorna recognised that look: Lizzie was a woman guilty at having been in trouble. She was unhappy in the company of respectability.

With no furniture except a double row of shake-down beds, Lorna lifted the hem of her skirt and squatted cross-legged on the ground as the women gathered around her. A gaggle of children yelled in the background until Katie chased them away with curses and well-placed blows. 'Now, Bridget, tell me about this woman, please?'

'I say there was more than one woman,' Maggie repeated.

'He must have been a busy man,' Lorna said. 'He had a wife and eight children as well as working on this job. Are you certain he would have time for another woman, let alone more than one?'

'We saw her. We all saw the woman. She stood up the hill watching the workings the day or three before Findy got himself killed.' Bridget gave Maggie a look that would have bored through granite. 'There was just one, whatever Maggie thinks.'

'Calm down!' Lorna spoke as she would to a noisy class before the women became physical. 'Could you give me a description, please?'

'She always wore white, like a bride,' Bridget said.

'More like a bloody ghost than a bride,' Katie stepped closer, so her hip nearly touched the side of Lorna's head. 'A ghost; that's what she was like with that hood pulled over her head.' When Katie smiled, Lorna could see a shadow of her once-good-looks.

'Was she tall? Short? Old or young? Did she speak?'

'She was medium height,' Bridget said forcefully, 'not tall or short, and she never said a word. She just stood and watched with that hood up like a Catholic monk or something.'

'Like Bridge says, the woman never said a word,' Katie emphasised her point by pressing against Lorna's head. 'But she pointed at the men like a ghost claiming her own.'

'Did anybody try to talk to her?' Lorna asked.

'Oh aye,' Maggie said. 'The men shouted out to her and invited her to join them. Some of the comments were…' She stopped then, 'well you know navvies. The comments were a bit…'

'Rude?' Lorna prompted.

'Yes,' Maggie said, 'they were rude enough for sure. The woman never spoke, and when the men tried to get near her, she ran away.'

'She never ran,' Katie said. 'She drifted away like a ghost. Like this,' Katie demonstrated by moving over the earth floor in what Lorna assumed was intended to be a gliding motion. 'Like ghosts do.'

'How many ghosts have you seen?' Bridget asked.

'Just the ones that watch the diggings,' Katie shouted, 'so watch your lip, Bridget; I'm handy with my maulies, see?'

'Let's leave the ghosts for now,' Lorna suggested before the women began tearing each other's hair out by the roots. 'I also wish to know the names of the men who were dismissed.'

'So you can have them hanged for nothing.' There was bitterness in Kate's voice.

'So I can question them and ensure they are not guilty.' Lorna corrected.

'You'll get nothing from me,' Kate moved away.

'Peter Morgan, Michael Jones and Samuel Wilce,' Bridget said at once. 'All good honest men.'

'Did you know them well?' Lorna wondered how honest and good these men had been.

'I knew Peter and Michael well enough,' Bridget said. 'Welshmen from the hills, they were. Samuel Wilce,' she screwed up her face, 'he was a local man, an Englishman from Worcester or somewhere.'

'Was he not so honest then?' Lorna asked.

'You watch your mouth, Bridget Jones!' Maggie pushed in, 'you aren't getting Samuel Wilce hanged for a murder he never had nothing to do with, see?'

'If Mr Wilce had nothing to do with the murder he has nothing to fear from the police let alone from me,' Lorna said quietly. 'I will say that there are some who believe that these three gentlemen were involved in Mr Findhorn's death.

I can only disprove that theory by interviewing your companions and removing any suspicion.'

'Her bloody Ladyship and the bluebottles always blame the navigators for everything,' Maggie said. 'The lads only went on the randy; they never killed anybody!'

'I hope to prove you correct,' Lorna said, 'and if you could advise me where these gentlemen might be now, I will attempt to establish their innocence of this crime.' When the women stared blankly at her, Lorna realised that her words were not understood. 'If you tell me where they are I'll talk to them and inform the police they're not to blame.'

Maggie grabbed hold of Bridget's arm and glared at Lorna. 'We'll tell you nothing,' she said.

'Well thank you, ladies.' Realising that pressing the issue would not be wise; Lorna stood up, brushed the dirt from her coat and skirt and smiled. 'You have been most helpful.'

'Ghosts!' Bridget scoffed, 'what nonsense.'

'Oh: one last thing,' Lorna turned around at the entrance to the hut, 'could you direct me to Mr Findhorn's office? I believe he had one here.'

'Over there,' Bridget flapped her hand toward a small hut that stood slightly apart from the rest. 'He's not in, though.' The women echoed her cackle.

Timber built with a solid roof and a simple brick chimney, Findhorn's hut was by far the best constructed in the whole ramshackle collection. Lorna put in the key Mrs Findhorn had given her and was surprised to find the door already open. She pushed in to see an immaculately tidy interior, with a fire, laid ready on the grate. There was also a sturdy chair behind the plank that acted as a desk and which was almost invisible behind a pile of papers held in place by a single rock paperweight.

Lorna sat on the chair and sifted through the papers: geological reports on the type of rock, costings for the work, reports of the amounts of dirt removed each day, engineer's reports, letters to Lady Stanhope and wages bills. She checked the wages bills and noted that the three names Bridget had mentioned were there. There was also a very brief loose-leaf journal with the heading: *Problems encountered.* The entries were short, sharp and written in elegant copperplate writing.

'Three spades missing today.'

'Twenty pounds of gunpowder found soaked in water.'

'Woman in white followed me home.'

'One of the huts set afire during the night; nobody injured.'

Lorna frowned; the workings seemed to have been plagued with minor acts of theft and destruction, while Findhorn had mentioned the woman in white on three separate occasions. Lorna shook her head; clearly, Mr Findhorn did not know the identity of the mysterious woman and nor had he sought her company.

Lorna lifted the letters and scanned them quickly. Most were about land access and the progress of the works, day to day events and the behaviour of the railway labourers, the navigators. The letters were filed in order, a day-by-day account of the workings. Lorna returned to the journal, aware that something was not right: with a small nod, she noted that two pages were missing: the 3rd and 4th of March.

'Now why is that?' Lorna asked herself. 'Find-horn was a methodical man; why miss out these two days?' She looked on the ground in case the papers had fallen. There was nothing there.

'Why miss two days? That makes no sense. I wonder if anything else is wrong in here?'

Lorna realised that she had taken it for granted that the hut had been untouched be-cause the place was in good order. Now she stepped back and looked again. The hut had been unoccupied since Findhorn had died so there should be a week's film of dust on top of everything. She knelt down to inspect the top of the desk from eye level. There were undoubted clear spaces, some of which she had doubtless made herself. There was also a palm-size dust free circle at the top corner of the desk where she had never been. Something had lain there and had been recently removed.

That meant one of three things: either Mrs Findhorn had taken away some possession of her husband, as she had every right to do, or some-body else had entered the hut and taken some-thing away. Who had that been, what had they removed and why had it been taken?

The sudden explosion of sound took Lorna by surprise. She heard the upraised voices and the thunder of feet as she left the hut to see what had happened.

'Bridget!' She shouted as the woman rushed past, 'what's happening?'

'There's been a rockfall!' Bridget screamed, 'my man is inside.'

'Oh, good Heavens!' Lorna joined in the rush toward the brick-faced entrance to the tunnel. Surrounded by worried men and women, she had no idea what to expect when she pushed into the lantern-lit darkness that led into the bowels of the hills. Once past the high entrance, the roof lowered, with the air becoming staler by the yard and the sides seeming to close in on them.

Lanterns cast bouncing pools of light that afforded brief glimpses of hard, sweating faces and muscular bodies, digging equipment and discarded shovels, wheelbarrows and piles of spoil.

'What's happened? Can I help?' Lorna pushed through the press. 'What can I do to help?'

'Rockfall,' somebody said, 'we've got men under there,' he lifted a shovel and threw it to Lorna.

'If you want to help, get digging. Otherwise get out of the bloody road with your fancy togs.'

Lorna looked around. Most of the wives and other women had already grabbed shovels and were beginning to work alongside the men, grunting and panting with effort as they fought the shifting mountain of earth, stones, and boulders.

Lorna raised her voice. 'Where do you want me?'

'There!' The navvy pointed to a corner of the tunnel, where a huge pile of rocks, had cascaded from the roof, 'get digging,' he looked Lorna up and down, 'who are you anyway?'

'Just a woman trying to help,' the shovel was heavier than Lorna had expected. She joined the half-dozen navvies in the corner. Only one looked around, said nothing and continued hacking at the rocks.

There were no words, just the gasps of struggling men and women and the clatter of steel shovels on rock, the slide of soil and the battering echo from the roof.

'Careful!' a rough hand pulled Lorna back as a rock slid from the pile, bringing a small avalanche with it. 'Take your time, woman; we don't want another fall.'

'How many men are trapped?' Lorna asked.

'Two: David Hughes and Edwin Williams.' The man was about forty, with a clay pipe in his mouth and a trickle of blood from a cut somewhere above his soft cap.

Lorna nodded. 'Let's get them out.'

'Who are you?' the navigator asked as he thrust his shovel hard into the loose soil. 'You're not a navvy's wife. Not in these clothes. Not with that accent.'

'No,' Lorna shook the sweat from her eyes. 'I'm Lorna Buchanan. I work for Lady Stanhope.'

'Oh do you now.' The navigator did not seem impressed. 'I'm Henry Clayton, the ganger here. That's a foreman to you.'

Lorna thrust her shovel into a load of spoil and moved it aside. 'I heard about Findhorn; I heard three navvies might have murdered him.' She shovelled away another small pile of stones and looked upward; the rock-fall extended in a sliding slope from the roof of the tunnel some ten feet above their heads to the ground on which they stood.

'Is that what you heard?' Clayton navigator lifted a pickaxe and levered a rock the side of a child free from the top of the pile. 'Could somebody brace here?' His voice echoed around the tunnel.

'That's what I heard,' Lorna stepped aside as two men brought a length of dressed timber and thrust the end under the roof of the tunnel. They looked upward as a small shower of earth descended on them.

'He was a hard man, was Findhorn, but not unpopular.' Clayton wrapped both arms around his rock and carried it away from the fall. He dropped it with a crash whose vibrations caused loose stones to roll from the pile. The echo seemed to last for minutes, stopped, started again and stopped a second time. In the momentary hush, Lorna heard a tiny sound that was out of place. She frowned, remembering long nights out in the Indian jungles, hunting for game, listening to every sound of nature. If she had missed the snap of a twig or the rustle of a bough there, a tiger could have torn her apart, or a cobra sunk its curved fangs deep into her body. There had been no margin of error.

She held up her hand, 'wait!'

'What? We must get on! There's men's lives at stake.' Clayton rammed his shovel into the pile.

'No!' Lorna grabbed the ganger's arm. It was as solid as the trunk of an oak tree. 'Wait! I think I heard something.'

Clayton stopped. 'Silence!' he roared, 'shut your bloody mouths you lot. This woman has heard something.'

'Who is that woman?'

'Who cares? Shut your teeth and listen!'

There was silence in the tunnel broken only by the irregular drip of water from the roof and the occasional slide of a stone.

'Nothing,' Clayton said. 'Get back to work lads!' He lifted his pick and landed a mighty blow on the surface of the fall. There was a mini avalanche of stones and dirt that Lorna began to shovel away. A younger navigator joined her, swearing with every sweating shovelful.

They moved the fall, inch by inch and shovel by shovel, with the brawny Clayton man-handling the heavier rocks. Lorna coughed as the dust rose, wiped the sweat from her face and carried on. Looking around, she peeled off her jacket and threw it aside.

'About time you did that,' Clayton said. His eyes glowed in a face blackened with dirt, except where a trickle of blood had washed out a small channel from forehead to chin. 'Come on *Miss* Buchanan! There are more rocks to move.' He pointed.

There were always more rocks, and then more after that.

'Brace!' Clayton shouted, and silence fell as two men ran forward with another length of timber. They thrust it in place, and the rescuers had made another few feet of distance.

'There it is again: listen!' Lorna held out a hand to stop the timber carriers. 'Wait!'

There was something in her voice that caused even the turbulent navigators to stop. 'Now listen,' Lorna ordered.

'Who the hell are you to tell us what to do?' A man asked.

'Shut your mouth and listen!' Clayton said.

The sonorous drip-drip-drip of water seemed to dominate the dark, emphasised by the guttering flicker of the bull's eye lanterns.

'I hear something,' somebody said. 'It's a clicking sound.'

'That's bloody Edwin,' Clayton said, 'he's not dead.'

'It might be Davie,' somebody else said.

'It's bloody Edwin; he's too stupid to be killed.' Clayton raised his voice to a shout, 'Eddie: where are you?' His voice echoed around the tunnel. 'Edwin!'

'Try this,' Lorna tapped on a rock with her spade. Within a few seconds, there was an answering tap. She tapped twice, and two taps came back. 'At least we know that somebody is alive.'

'Back to work, boys,' Clayton said, 'get that brace in place!'

With another section of roof shored up, they returned to the digging. The gasping of labouring men and women and the click and rattle of shovels again filled the tunnel.

'Look!' A bearded man pointed ahead. 'We'll never get past that.' He rested on his pickaxe. 'We're done.'

'Bring the lanterns, boys' Clayton said. Two lights danced forward, revealing a rock three times the height of a man and twice as wide.

'That's a bugger,' Clayton's voice was quiet.

'How do you usually clear a thing like that?' Lorna asked.

'We blast it with gunpowder and shovel the rubble.' Clayton said, 'but with Davie and Edwin trapped underneath we can't do that.'

'If they were underneath, they would be dead,' Lorna pointed out. 'They must be behind it.'

One of the other navigators shrugged, 'underneath or behind; it makes little difference; we can't blast it, and we can't hack it down.'

'So we go around,' Lorna said.

'What's it got to do with you?' The bearded man asked.

'Around it?' Clayton asked.

'Why not?' The solution seemed obvious to Lorna. 'We just need enough space for one man to squeeze in or out.'

'Dig around it, boys!' Clayton saw the logic. 'Hack into the wall and let's get Eddie and Davie out.'

Despite the time they had already spent at the workings, there was no sign of fatigue as the navigators returned to work. Clayton led the way with huge swings of his pick and the others followed, crowding around Lorna as they shovelled the rocks, stones and dirt to the rear, where a chain of others eased it out of the tunnel. Lorna had thought the navigators would have taken hours to hack around the massive rock but with the ganger showing the way by swinging his pick like a man demented they created a sizeable gap within twenty minutes.

'Eddie! Davie!' Clayton roared.

There was no response until Lorna again tapped her shovel on the rock and immediately heard an answering click.

'We've cut a little space around here,' Clayton said. 'We need a small man to squeeze through.' He looked around and pointed to the youngest navigator, a wiry man with short red hair. 'Matthew; you'll do. Get through there, see who's there and if we can get them out.'

Lorna was not sure of Matthew's age; somewhere between eighteen and twenty- five she guessed, even although his eyes were as old as time.

Matthew stepped from the crowd and tried to squeeze through the gap. 'It's no good,' he said a few moments later. 'I'm too big.'

'Can we make the gap larger?' Lorna asked.

'Not without bringing the roof down.' Clayton said.

Lorna looked at the gap and shook her head. Most women could have fitted through that space, but she was tall and broad-shouldered for her sex.

'I'll try.' The voice was familiar, feminine and completely unexpected.

Lorna turned around in mingled surprise and anger. 'What in heaven's name are you doing here?' She stared at Margaret. 'It's too danger-ous for you. Don't even think it!'

'Let me try. I'm small enough.' Margaret pleaded. 'Please, Miss!' She hopped from one foot to the other.

'No!' Lorna snapped. 'Get back outside!'

'You're a game one, young 'un.' Clayton said. 'Off you go then.' He watched as Margaret stepped into the gap.

Margaret looked back at Lorna, gave a small, nearly apologetic grin and edged forward. Lorna heard her gasp. 'I'm too big!' she called. 'No… I might do it.'

The rumble of falling stones filled the tunnel.

'Margaret!' Lorna lunged forward to try the gap. 'Margaret!'

'Wait!' Clayton stopped her with a single massive hand on her chest.

'I'm through!' Margaret shouted. 'There are two men in here, but they're hurt. They need help. One is unconscious.'

'Can you help them?' Clayton shouted.

'No,' Margaret's voice echoed through the dark. 'They're half buried.'

'We'll have to make the gap bigger.' Clayton decided, 'and hope the roof stays in place. You – girl - what's your name? Margaret; come out of there.'

'They might need me.'

'Come out of there, Margaret!' Lorna shouted. She could not contain her thrill of something. What was it? Pride? It was certainly an unfamiliar emotion for her.

Dirty, dishevelled and with the skin scraped from the knuckles of her left hand, Margaret appeared a few minutes later.

'I told you not to go,' Lorna said.

'You're not my teacher anymore,' Margaret responded with some of her classroom impudence. 'Anyway, they men needed help.'

'You're a devilish self-willed woman,' Lorna snapped.

'Yes, Miss.'

The navigators began work again, slower and with more care. Twice they halted as the rock above them groaned, and each time Clayton ordered more braces and carried on, leading from the front.

'Right.' Clayton finally gave the order. 'I'm going in first.'

'I'll go,' Margaret said. 'I know the way.'

Clayton put a battered and bleeding hand on Margaret's shoulder. 'No.' His voice was gruff. 'You're a spunky piece and no mistake but you done your bit, Margaret. Leave it to us now.' He pushed her gently toward Lorna. 'Stay with your sister.'

'She's not my sister,' Lorna caught firm hold of Margaret. 'You stay here; I'm going through.'

Four navigators followed Clayton before Lorna could get elbow her way to the far side of the rock-fall. The entire tunnel was blocked by a huge pile of stones, with light filtering in from an air vent cut through from the hillside above and the upper half of two men trapped beneath.

'They're half buried,' Clayton sounded concerned.

Hughes and Williams were face- down under a pile of mixed stones and soil.

'Get them out,' Clayton looked up, 'before the roof collapses again.' He raised his voice. 'Bring braces lads, and take care.'

A dozen navigators eased around the rock and immediately began work with some digging around the two men, others dragging sawn tree-trunks to brace the roof secure.

'David's gone.' Somebody said. 'He's dead as mutton.'

'Leave him then,' Clayton ordered. 'We can do nothing for him. Help Eddie.'

Lorna nearly felt the compassion in the air as the navigators cleared the spillage from around the man named Edwin.

'It's all right Eddie. We've got you now.' They dragged him clear. 'His leg is broken,' Clayton said, 'we'll have to splint it.'

'Leave Edwin to us,' a squat man tapped Lorna on the shoulder with a forefinger as hard as a metal bar. 'He's our mate.'

Lorna nodded and knelt beside David. Something heavy had crushed his head, and his right arm was stretched fully out with his fist tightly closed.

'Now why is your hand clenched? What were you grasping at?' Ignoring the scrambled mess of the man's head, Lorna prised open the fingers. A small silver coin slid out.

'Oh dear God,' Lorna lifted the coin and slipped it into her pocket before helping to drag the dead man through the gap to the main tunnel.

'We'll take him from here,' the bearded navigator said.

'Thank you,' Lorna stood up. Taking her now filthy jacket she grabbed Margaret's arm with an equally dirty hand.

'Come on Margaret. We can't do more here, and I have words to say to you.'

Lorna took a deep breath of air that smelled sweet after the dust-laden confinement of the tunnel. She looked around. More time had elapsed than she had imagined and it was now full dark, with the flicker of torches and probing beams of lanterns casting weary shadows across the camp. It seemed that all the navigators at the diggings had gathered to see Edwin carried to his hut, with those wives who had not been inside the tunnel clustering around to hear what had happened.

'Those two women helped,' Clayton pointed as Lorna stood in the midst of the navigators with Margaret at her side. 'The tall one's called Buchanan and the other's Margaret something. I don't know who they are, but they came to help.'

Faces turned to Lorna; men smeared with mud and sweat and women with expressions of wonder or suspicion.

'That is moonshine,' a familiar voice sounded. 'Do you know who this is?' Katie pointed to Lorna, 'that's her Ladyship's black spy, come to ask questions and get us all hanged. I dunno the young one but she'll be as bad.'

The babble of friendly noise ceased. All the faces turned to Lorna. Some of the men with whom she had worked shoulder to shoulder only half an hour before glowered at her as if she was their deadliest enemy.

'A bloody spy? She's a bloody spy?' The bearded man repeated. Some of the navvies began to move closer, some hefting their spades and picks like weapons.

'Mistress,' Bridget sounded concerned, 'you'd best get away from here. The boys have lost one of their own, and they are angry. They very badly want to hurt somebody.'

'Leave them!' Clayton's voice rose above the hubbub. 'She helped get Edwin free.'

'She's working for Lady bloody Stanhope.' The bearded man shouted. 'She's spying on us!'

'Do you have something to hide that I should spy on you?' Lorna held the bearded man's gaze.

'Don't rouse them for God's sake,' Bridget advised, 'get out before the boys realise you're alone and tear you apart.' She took hold of Lorna's arm, 'come away Mistress, please. Your chariot is still here, safe for you.'

'She's not alone,' Margaret said. 'I'm with her.' She stepped beside Lorna, folded her arms and faced the navigators.

'Go!' Clayton pointed to the entrance to the encampment. 'I'll help you this once but never again.' He raised his voice. 'Go!'

Bridget held the horse steady as Lorna and Margaret mounted the chaise. 'Thank you.' Bridget said softly.

Lorna nodded, flicked the reins, ducked under a slowly spiralling bottle and walked Harold out of the encampment. She paused at the entrance, turned around and raised her whip in a formal farewell. Only Clayton responded, lifting a massive hand and watching until she left the camp. When Lorna glanced back, Clayton was still there, impressively huge and seemingly as enduring as the Malvern Hills.

'You were brave back there, Margaret' she said. 'I won't forget it.'

'Oh,' Margaret sounded surprised. 'I thought you was going to...'

Lorna stopped her with a brief shake of her head. 'Were you following me again?'

'Yes, Miss.'

'My name's Lorna, and you'd better stay with me for now.'

'Miss?' There was incredulity in Margaret's voice.

Smiling, Lorna flicked the reins and increased Harold's speed.

They emerged out of a patch of jungle into the fringes of the British camp. The sentry raised his Enfield rifle and shouted a challenge. 'Halt, or I'll blow your bloody head off!'

'You'd best not, private.' Major Buchanan said, 'unless you wish court- martialled for murdering an officer.'

'Oh, sorry Sir!' The private slammed to atten-tion. 'I did not know.'

'There is no way you could have known,' Major Buchanan said. 'Stand easy man; this is no place for parade-ground soldiering. Who's in charge here?'

'I am Sir; Sergeant O'Hara.' He was stocky and red- faced, with Irish blue eyes.

'Good man sergeant. The young lady is my daughter, Lorna and we've come through the Pandy lines.'

O'Hara slammed to attention and threw a smart salute.

'I said there was no need for that, Sergeant,' Major Buchanan snapped.

'Yes, Sir. That was not for you Sir; it was for the lady. Bravery deserves a reward.'

Lorna drew herself erect and saluted in turn. Despite her rags and the tears that streamed down her cheeks, she felt ten feet tall.

'You deserve it, Margaret,' Lorna said. 'You proved yourself back there. I was proud of you.' She did not look around; she knew Margaret was crying.

Chapter Eleven

The reception area of the hotel was busy with health-seekers and a few local people. The clerk was busy, yet Gibson rushed over as soon as Lorna arrived at the desk. 'Yes, Miss Buchanan?'

'Good morning Mr Gibson,' Lorna was still surprised how much power her relationship with Lady Stanhope afforded her. 'I am looking for somebody named Sam Bellamy. I am not sure if it is a man or a woman, or even a girl.' She gave her most charming smile. 'Her Ladyship did say that you were the best person to ask about any such thing.'

Gibson preened himself at the supposed praise. 'There are a few Bellamies in these parts,' he said. 'I don't know a Sam, though.' He leaned forward across the counter and screwed up his face in thought. 'Let's see; there is Old Peter Bellamy and his wife Mary; there is Jack Bellamy the carter and William the wheelwright with Susan, his daughter, and ...' the innkeeper counted them on the fingers of his left hand.

'It may be a woman,' Lorna reminded. 'Perhaps a Samantha Bellamy?'

'Can't say as I know of any more,' Gibson said.

'We'll keep looking,' Lorna said. 'If you think of any, please let me know.' She hesitated for a moment. 'Mr Gibson,' she said. 'I do have another question for you.'

'I shall help in any way I can,' Gibson said.

'These health seekers,' Lorna's gesture covered all the overweight men in the reception area as well as half the town. She lowered her voice slightly. 'I know they wander up and down the hills and drink gallons of water from the various wells but what is this mysterious Water Cure that they speak of.'

'Ah,' Gibson smiled. 'It is something unique to this area. Our water is the purest in the world you see.'

'Yes, Mr Gibson, I don't doubt that,' Lorna said.

'Have you heard of Dr James Wilson?' Gibson asked. 'No? Dr Wilson reasons that we wash our faces in water so why not wash our stomachs too. The health seekers come to Great Malvern from all over the country. They are mostly …' he hesitated, 'perhaps a *little* on the heavy side through over-indulgence and soft living, so they enter a strict regime of early rising, healthy walks in the hills, a limited diet and plenty of pure Malvern water to cleanse them inside and out.'

'Inside and out?' Margaret pressed closer. 'Could you explain more please?'

Gibson did not give Margaret anything like the respect he showed to Lorna. He glanced at Lorna, who nodded.

Gibson cleared his throat in slight embarrassment. 'The health seekers also undergo various practices with the water,' he said. 'They are bathed and wrapped in wet towels and may opt for a douche of cold water.'

'I see,' Lorna said. 'Thank you, Mr Gibson.' She waited until Gibson hurried away to attend to his other clients. 'You knew all that already, Margaret.'

Margaret smiled. 'Yes Miss, I wanted to see Mr Gibson's face. I wondered if he would tell you that the men are naked when they are douched.'

'Of course, they are!' Lorna snapped. 'You can't have a bath with your clothes on.'

'I know,' Margaret was not in the slightest put out by Lorna's abrupt response. 'I wanted Mr Gibson to say it, that's all.' Her soft giggle reminded Lorna how young she was and what sort of natural feelings would be raging through her body.

'Well, I will tell you instead,' Lorna said. 'Men and women both bathe without their clothes on, and I don't want to hear any more of that sort of talk from you.'

'Yes, Miss.' This time Margaret looked slightly abashed.

Lorna gave her a few moments to ponder what she had said and recover before taking her by the arm. 'Right, Margaret, I've been wondering how much I should take you into my confidence.'

'Yes, Miss,' Margaret sounded brighter already.

'Well, I've decided that you are trustworthy.' Lorna guided her to a table and sat down. 'That means you never repeat anything I tell you until I say you can. Understand?'

Margaret's smile was slow to come. 'I think so, Miss.'

'Good. What do you *think* about this?' Lorna tossed the silver coin she had found in David's fist across the table.

Margaret examined it. 'This is old,' she said. 'I've never seen a coin like this before. It hasn't got the queen's face on it, so it's not a British coin. That means that it's foreign. It may be French.'

'Thank you, Margaret,' Lorna knew that French was about as foreign as Margaret could imagine. 'David, the navigator, had it in his hand when he died; he may even have died because of it.'

Margaret spat on the coin in a most unladylike fashion and rubbed it clean on her sleeve, leaving a black smear on the cloth. 'It looks silver to me,' she said, 'and I'm sure that it's French, Miss.' She passed it back. 'Do you think that is French?'

Lorna shook her head. 'It's not French,' she said. 'I think it's Latin.'

Margaret took the coin back. 'I never heard of a place called Latin, Miss. This penny is different to anything I ever saw before; that's a horse on it; I thought people only ever put the heads of kings and queens on coins.'

'And horses too, it seems.' Lorna said with a smile, 'but I would like to know more about it.'

'Dick Temple's your man,' Gibson had slid up unobserved and gave his unrequested opinion. 'He knows everything about that sort of thing.' He placed two plates piled high with chops and potatoes on the table; a simple and robust luncheon that contrasted sharply with the diet afforded to the health-seekers or the tasteless fare doled out at St Ann's College. 'You find Dick Temple, and he'll know. When he is not teaching, he spends all his life walking around the hills looking for pieces of old rubbish that people threw out years ago.'

'Why does he do that?' Margaret had already started on her breakfast.

'You'd better ask him that, Miss Smith,' Gibson said.

'Where will we find him?' Lorna asked.

'He lives in the schoolhouse beside the old school,' Gibson said. 'You can't miss it.'

'Well then,' Lorna smiled her gratitude. 'That is where we will go right after this formidable breakfast. Thank you, Mr Gibson.'

Gibson bowed and withdrew.

'I know the place,' Margaret said through a mouthful of food. 'I don't know this Dick Temple fellow, though.'

'You probably move in different circles,' Lorna said. 'And don't eat with your mouth full.'

'Yes, Miss,' Margaret said.

'And call me Lorna.'

'Yes, Miss.'

The schoolhouse was small and thatched, with a dejected air that spoke of an occupier whose mind was elsewhere other than maintaining the property. Lorna gently pulled the reins and allowed Harold to graze on the ragged grass outside the fence. 'Now let me do the talking, Margaret, unless you've something important to say.'

'Yes, Miss,' Margaret fondled Harold's muzzle as Lorna rapped on the door.

'Good morning,' Lorna said to a slatternly –looking woman she took to be the housekeeper. 'Is your master in?'

'He's in the study,' the woman stomped away, and Lorna stepped inside, passing a case of stuffed animals and a stand of walking sticks that leaned drunkenly against a damp-smeared wall. A chipped bust stood on a pedestal, with a two-penny wide-awake hat placed on top at a rakish angle.

They entered a cold room that was dominated by a long deal table, cluttered with pieces of what Lorna would have considered rubbish had she not heard of Temple's reputation.

Temple sat with his back to the door, poring over a book. He looked up irritably and turned around as Lorna and Margaret stepped in.

'I don't receive many visitors,' he said at once.

'Then thank you, for seeing us,' Lorna gave a bright smile. 'We won't bother you for long. I hear that you are an expert in all things ancient.'

Temple removed his spectacles, polished them and replaced them. 'I am not quite an expert in all things,' he gave a small cough. 'I do, however, possess a little knowledge on such matters. I am what is known as an antiquarian.'

'Then you are exactly the man I seek,' Lorna said. 'May I ask you to delve into your knowledge for me?'

'You may,' Temple said graciously, and stood up, eager to impress.

'I've seen you before,' Lorna realised. 'You were up on the Herefordshire Beacon the other day.' She recalled the thin man who had bumped into her.

Lorna looked around. Bookcases covered three walls of the room with a multi-paned window in the fourth.

'Yes,' when Temple nodded his thick spectacles slid down his bony nose. 'I walk all the hills.'

'So you are an active man as well as an antiquarian,' Lorna said.

'I certainly do not need to try the water cure.' Temple looked pleased with the compliment. He indicated the stones, pieces of broken pottery and strange metal objects that cluttered the table, 'as you can see I am a collector of curios. I found most of these pieces on the hills or round about.'

Margaret lifted what looked like the handle of a vase. 'This is just a pile of useless rubbish.' She dropped the handle, which landed with a clatter on the table.

Temple extended a hand too late to catch it. 'That's a Roman jug handle!' His benevolence vanished as quickly as the handle had fallen. 'It's priceless!'

Margaret laughed, 'do you mean that people actually pay for this sort of thing? So I can go round the ash pits and find smashed plates and sell them.'

'No, I mean it's nearly two thousand years old…'

Lorna watched as Temple fondled the handle back to its original position on the table. 'Could you identify this coin, Mr Temple?' She handed over the silver coin the dead navigator had held.

Temple held it delicately between forefinger and thumb, and then lifted an ivory-handled magnifying glass and examined the coin for a long three minutes. When he looked up his eyes were wide. 'Where did you get this?'

'In the railway tunnel,' Lorna said truthfully. 'Do you know what it is?'

'Yes of course.' Temple sounded impatient at the question. 'It is a coin of the Trinovantians.' His voice smoothed over the last word as if he was praying to some sacred deity.

'The what?' Lorna was not sure if Temple had made the name up. 'We think the inscription is Latin.'

'The Trinovantians; they were a British tribe. Of course, the inscription is Latin; it's the name of the tribal king. That's why it has the name Rex after it. Where did you say you found this?'

'In the railway tunnel,' Lorna told him.

'That's impossible,' Temple looked up in anger. 'It could not be in there. How could it get in there?'

'Maybe one of the navigators carried it there,' Margaret suggested cheerfully.

Temple shook his head. 'Oh, I hope not. Artefacts like this are wasted on people like that!'

'Is it valuable?' Margaret asked bluntly.

Temple screwed up his face and had a second look through the magnifying glass. 'To an antiquarian such as myself, naturally, it is but intrinsically not really.' He shook his head and explained further. 'The navigators might raise sixpence for it in a pawn shop; enough for the price of a night's drinking at most. Nobody except a collector would give any more than that.'

'Thank you, Mr Temple,' Lorna said.

'Do you wish to sell it?' Temple sounded casual, but his fingers were shaking. 'I could give you a shilling for it; two if you wished.'

'Thank you, but I wish to keep it,' Lorna retrieved the coin before Temple added it to his store of battered treasures. 'Now Mr Temple, you told us that you spend a lot of time walking over the hills.'

'I am an antiquarian,' Temple repeated. He spread his arms to indicate the contents of the table as if that explained everything.

'You must see a lot that happens up there,' Lorna said.

Temple sighed. 'I see all these health seekers trampling over the hills, probably crushing underfoot all the valuable remains from the Romans and British tribesmen. You do know that King Caractacus had his last stand on the Herefordshire Beacon, don't you?'

'I had heard that,' Lorna said. 'Do you remember seeing Mr Findhorn on the Herefordshire Beacon?'

'Mr Findhorn?' Temple looked confused for a moment and then nodded. 'That's a terrible business.' He shook his head and slumped on one of the two chairs. 'What a shocking way to die.' He looked up. 'Why are you asking such things? Did you know the poor chap?'

'Her Ladyship has asked me to find out what I can,' Lorna said. 'Miss Smith here is assisting me.'

'Oh, I see,' Temple gave a faint smile. 'Her Ladyship must be obeyed.' He sat back down and glanced at his book, evidently anxious to lose himself within the pages.

'Quite,' Lorna agreed.

'Have you noticed anything suspicious in your perambulations?' Lorna asked, 'I saw you in the vicinity of the Alfreck Well: did you happen to be there on the night somebody murdered Mr Findhorn?'

Temple gave a half smile. 'I'm sorry; I can't remember which night that was.'

'Wednesday the 9th of March,' Lorna said.

Temple took a visibly deep breath. 'I would be marking the pupil's work that night,' he said. He looked up. 'Do you know what happened?'

Lorna glanced at Margaret. 'That is what we are here to find out,' she said.

Temple lowered his voice and leaned across the table. 'You will have to be very careful here. You are dealing with forces beyond your knowledge.'

Margaret nodded vigorously. 'You're right Mr Temple. I told Miss Buchanan that it was about witches and things. The sacred well...' she stopped when Lorna frowned at her.

'And what sort of forces are we talking about, Mr Temple?' Lorna asked.

Temple looked at her. 'Miss Buchanan; excuse me please.' Rising, he closed the shutters so nobody could see into the room. Lorna moved closer to Margaret in the resulting darkness as Temple busied himself with a box of Lucifers. He lit the single candle that he sat in the middle of the table. The flame was small at first and then rose to cast short shadows and highlight the lines and creases on Temple's not-quite-elderly face. 'I am talking about forces of darkness, Miss

Buchanan; things that should have been con-signed to history thousands of years ago.'

Lorna frowned as Margaret muttered 'they're still there' under her breath. 'Could you elabo-rate, Mr Temple? I am afraid I do not know of any forces of darkness around here.'

Temple looked around the room and dropped his voice so far that Lorna had to strain to hear him. 'You must know what the Alfreck Well means?'

'Tell us,' Lorna encouraged.

'It means Elf Reich, that means *Elf Land*,' Temple sounded smug. He leaned back as if he had made a significant point. The candle flame wavered slightly, shifting the shadows of his strange collections and giving the impression that the ancient artefacts were moving.

'Oh? Everyone knows that. How is that sup-posed to help us find Mr Findhorn's murderer?' Margaret was not easily impressed. 'I thought you were the antiquarian who knew everything.'

'Margaret!' Lorna touched her arm in gentle rebuke.

'Don't you see?' Temple leaned forward again. He lifted a finger as if he was lecturing a reluctant pupil in his class, 'Elf Reich: it was a well devoted to something spiritual but not Christian, something pre-Christian.'

'Oh, indeed?' Margaret tapped long fingers on the table. 'Thank you, for telling us that information we already knew.'

Lorna stepped in tactfully. 'Please forgive my young friend's rudeness. I understand you are trying to make a point Mr Temple; please continue.'

'I am sure you will have heard of the druids,' Temple waited for confirmation.

Margaret stared at him. 'Yes, we have.' She looked at Lorna as if to say 'I told you so.'

'Mr Temple,' Lorna said, 'we are trying to find a murderer. If you have any information that may help us, I'd be obliged if you would tell us. How can these long gone druids have any bearing on the murder of Mr Findhorn?'

Temple opened his mouth, closed it again and swallowed. When he spoke, his erstwhile smugness had vanished entirely. 'Elf Reich Well is a sacred spot for the druids, the religion the old people had before the Romans. They used to have human sacrifices there.'

'Go on,' Lorna encouraged. 'Although I heard that it was a fertility well.'

'That is correct,' Temple agreed. 'The druids, the old Celtic priests, used to sacrifice a chosen victim of proven virility to ensure the water retained its power.'

Lorna started as he remembered that Findhorn was the father of eight children. She exchanged glances with Margaret. 'Mr Temple,' she said slowly, 'are you suggesting that druids sacrificed Mr Findhorn?'

Temple was suddenly silent. 'I did not say that Miss Buchanan, but the druids used to sacrifice their victims by drowning them head first in cauldrons or sacred pools.' He touched one of the fragments of pottery. 'I would be happier if you did not mention that you spoke to me about this matter.' He took another deep breath. 'How was he found?'

'He was in the well.' Lorna said shortly.

'I heard he was upside down as well,' Margaret added helpfully. 'And he was naked as a newborn baby.'

Lorna frowned at her. 'Could you take notes please, Margaret?'

'I am already taking notes,' Margaret said.

'Was he bound?' Temple did not seem surprised at the news. 'The druids bound their sacrifices.'

'He was bound,' Lorna said.

Temple looked up suddenly. 'As long as it was not with green rope.'

'It was with green cords.' Margaret's look at Lorna was of pure triumph.

'Oh, God in heaven,' Temple stared at Lorna across the length of the table. 'That means it was the druids. It was not merely a coincidence. They're back; God help us all; they're back!'

'How can the druids be back?' Lorna was in very unfamiliar territory here. 'I thought the druids died out centuries ago.'

Temple looked away and said nothing.

'I am sorry to ask so many questions.' Lorna gave her most charming smile. 'I am afraid ancient religion is a subject about which I know nothing, so I am drawing on your expertise. Do you know of any druids around here?'

'I don't know,' Temple said. 'I can't say any more.' He seemed close to tears.

'I don't mean to upset you,' Lorna put a friendly hand on Temple's thin but surprisingly wiry arm. 'I thank you, for your time, Mr Temple, and for your advice about the coin.'

'Miss Buchanan,' Temple was shaking. 'It's not safe for you to ask questions if the druids are back.'

Patting his arm, Lorna nodded to Margaret. 'Come along, Margaret,' she said.

Night was falling as they left the schoolhouse, with a pink sky over the sharp ridge of the Malvern Hills.

'Druids!' Lorna shook her head. 'Have you ever heard the like? Druids and sacred wells and human sacrifice; I thought I had left all that superstitious nonsense behind in India.' She looked upwards. The moon was faint and the stars unfamiliar. She knew the Indian sky far better.

'I told you so.' Margaret said. 'Did I not tell you? It's all to do with witches and druids.'

Lorna took a deep breath of the sweet, cool air, so different from the scented night-air of Bengal. 'I have heard of some strange religions,' she mused, 'but not in this country. My father was an army officer, and he drilled into me that we should respect the religion of the country that we were in, even when we found their beliefs strange. I never thought to meet this sort of thing in England.'

Margaret stood close by her. 'The old man Temple was telling the truth.'

'The old man was scared,' Lorna said. 'I don't know what of, but he was scared.' Inwardly she told herself that it was Old Wives Tales. She tried to convince herself that these people were yokels who still lived with scares of hobgoblins and demons. Yet she knew that was not entirely accurate. Temple was an educated man, and Miss Appleton had her bookcase crammed with books of folklore and fable. There was no doubt that Findhorn had been stripped naked, tied up and drowned in a well that supposedly had fertility properties.

'Mr Temple was telling us the truth about druids and human sacrifice,' Margaret said. 'And we saw them, remember?'

Lorna frowned. 'Absolute moonshine,' she said. 'I've never seen a druid in my life. I would not know what a druid looked like.'

'We saw them walking up the path when you stopped me following them.' Margaret reminded. 'The people in white robes, remember?'

'I remember the people in white cloaks,' Lorna said. 'They were just some people playing the fool.' She did not mention the woman in white who had been following Findhorn.

'I know who the druids are.' Margaret spoke hesitantly.

The sky was darker now, with the stars more prominent, pricking bright holes in the velvet night. Lorna looked up; it would be easy for a superstitious person to believe that the moon and stars had some power, out here in these quiet, lonely hills.

'Who?' Lorna asked.

'You know too,' Margaret said.

'Who?' Lorna repeated, hardening her voice.

'It was Miss Appleton and her Chosen Girls.' Margaret said. 'That is why she never let anybody out of school and kept the gates shut. She went up to the holy wells with her Chosen Girls.'

A sudden cold wind made Lorna shiver. 'I don't think so,' she said. 'I can't see Miss Appleton as a druid.'

Margaret shrugged. 'She's a witch,' she said.

Lorna hid her smile. In many ways, Margaret was still very young. 'I know you have reasons to dislike her,' she said. 'I don't think she is a witch, though. I can't see the elegant Miss Appleton flying around the skies on a broomstick.'

Climbing into the chaise, she waited until Margaret jumped in, flicked the reins and began the short journey to their hotel.

'What do you think then, Miss?'

'I think you should call me Lorna,' Lorna said with a smile and made a sudden decision to trust Margaret further. 'When I was with the navigators, the wives told me about a woman in white who watched the men at the digging, and Mrs Findhorn revealed that her husband had seen a woman in white as well.'

'See?' Margaret sounded quite aggressive. 'A woman druid.'

Lorna eased the chaise around a corner. 'What if the navigators were wrong, Margaret and the woman in white was not a woman? What if it was a man?'

'A man dressed as a woman? That's disgusting!' Margaret looked away in distaste. 'What sort of man would do that?'

'That is not quite what I mean,' Lorna said. 'I mean, what if the person watching was not a man dressed as a woman, but a man dressed as a druid.'

'Oh.' Margaret was quiet for a few moments. 'That could be true. I still think it was Miss Appleton. I think she and her Chosen Girls murdered Mr Findhorn.'

'Now why would she do that?' Lorna asked.

'Because of the fertility well.' Margaret sounded impatient. 'Mr Findhorn had lots of children, and Miss Appleton is getting old. She must want a husband and children. You know why she has her Chosen Girls don't you?'

'No,' Lorna pulled the chaise into the courtyard at the back of the hotel. The stable boy ran to greet them and took hold of Harold, quietly talking. 'I thought the Chosen Girls were the most senior class in the school.'

'No,' Margaret shook her head. 'That's not it. That's not why they're at school. Miss Appleton is preparing the Chosen Girls for a husband. She's teaching them how to be perfect wives in every way.' Margaret ensured that Lorna was listening by holding her gaze. 'And all men want children to follow them.' She slid out of the chaise in a flurry of skirts and fondled Harold's muzzle. 'The rest of us: the class you got, we are not good enough to be Chosen.'

'The Chosen Girls are not quite druids then,' Lorna handed the reins to the stable boy and climbed out. Margaret pressed against her. 'Now we have to find out more about druids and how they dress and what they do. We have to learn about human sacrifices as well.'

'Why do we have to find out how the druids dress?' Although Margaret was a full head shorter, she matched Lorna stride for stride as they walked into the hotel.

'I want to know if they really did dress in white,' Lorna explained. 'I'm sure I don't know, but the local clergyman might know. We'll talk to him tomorrow,'

'Would we not be better asking Mr Temple?'

'He's had enough for now. He was shaking like an autumn leaf when we left him. I think he would have said anything to get rid of us,' Lorna decided. 'No; the local clergyman will know best. What's that big church called?'

'Malvern Priory,' Margaret said. 'Everybody knows that.'

'We'll speak to the Malvern prior then,' Lorna said.

'Miss,' Margaret spoke softly, without looking at Lorna. 'Miss; can I ask you a favour, please?'

'A favour? What sort of favour?' Taken by surprise, Lorna was instantly suspicious. 'Go on, then.'

'There's a young man,' Margaret said.

'Oh?' Lorna encouraged.

'I want to meet him.' Margaret was unexpectedly bashful and then spoke in a rush. 'I want to meet him, but I don't know how. His name's William.'

Lorna took a deep breath, surprised at this abrupt turn in the conversation. 'You'll need a chaperone, at least the first time,' she said. 'Are you asking me?'

'Yes, Miss,' Margaret said.

'I would be honoured.' Lorna took Margaret's hand. 'Thank you, for asking.' She had never seen such gratitude as Margaret had in her eyes.

Chapter Twelve

'Come along and let me show you around,' the prior extended a hand in welcome. 'We are quite proud of our priory here, even although the Bible does not recommend Pride.'

'So I believe,' Lorna took an immediate liking to this cheery man as she looked around at the tall Norman pillars of the priory. Sunlight filtered through the stained glass windows, making a multicoloured rainbow across the stone interior. 'You have a fine church here, Sir.'

'It is a fine church in need of much repair,' the prior said, 'but funds are lacking.' He shook his bald head. 'The spirit is willing, but the purse is weak.'

'That is not uncommon,' Lorna did not restrain her smile.

'So, Miss Buchanan; how can I help you? I assume you are not here merely to admire the architecture.' The prior's gentle demeanour did not hide the intelligence in his eyes. 'I have heard that you are making inquiries on behalf of Lady Stanhope. Are you here about that unpleasant business with Mr Findhorn?'

'It is related,' Lorna said, 'now Sir, could you tell me anything about the druids who once lived in this area?'

The prior stopped dead. 'That is a very unusual request. I am not sure that I am the best person to ask. Mr Temple is the local expert on that sort of thing.'

'I am aware of that, Sir,' Lorna said. 'I have spoken to him already. Do you happen to know what the druid priests wore?'

'They wore white robes I believe,' the prior said, 'although I cannot see how that is relevant to your inquiries.'

'Thank you, Sir,' Lorna said. 'It may not be. I hope it is not! Do you know if the druids performed human sacrifice?'

'My word,' The prior sat down on the nearest pew. 'I haven't been asked that before. According to Julius Caesar, they did, and he should know.

They burned people inside huge wicker men I believe.'

'Oh,' Lorna glanced at Margaret. 'And did they drown the victims as well?'

'I have heard so,' the prior said. 'In sacred cauldrons or sacred pools.'

'Thank you, Sir,' Lorna said again. 'And do these druids still exist?'

She had expected the pause that followed his question. The prior looked at her through suddenly narrowed eyes. 'What makes you ask that, Miss Buchanan?'

'Please bear with me, Sir, it is just a fancy of mine. Do you think there may be a vestige of druidism remaining?'

The prior looked suddenly old. 'Sit down, Miss Buchanan; have a pew,' his attempt at a smile did not work. 'This little grey town is an ancient place. The old Forest of Malvern protected us from the worst of the ravages during the Civil War, but isolation can be a curse as well as a blessing.'

'Carry on,' Lorna encouraged.

'For centuries the outlying areas were cut off from the mainstream...' the prior looked up when the front door of the church slammed suddenly open.

'For heaven's sake…' Lorna rose in alarm as a horseman clattered right inside the church.

The prior stood up suddenly and stepped in front of her. 'You stay behind me, Miss Buchanan.'

The horseman rode straight to where they stood and hauled hard on the reins, so his horse reared up, hooves flailing at the air only a yard away from the prior's face. The prior flinched, leaving Lorna staring at the rider as the hooves clattered to the floor of the church.

The rider looked down at him. 'You are Lorna Buchanan?' He was about fifty, Lorna judged, with a mane of white hair on his uncovered head and an aquiline nose that thrust downward arrogantly. The tone of his voice indicated nothing but authority. Lorna remembered seeing him riding through the town.

'I am Lorna Buchanan,' Lorna agreed. She felt Margaret step to her side and pushed her out of harm's way. 'And who are you, Sir, to break the sanctity of the church?'

The man blinked pale blue eyes as if he had expected instant recognition. 'I am Sir John Garston.'

'It's Mad Jack!' Margaret's whisper seemed to echo around the church.

Sir John glared at Margaret. 'Some call me by that name.' He did not act ashamed at the title. 'You must be Miss Smith.'

Lorna could feel the hammering of her heart, yet she determined not to show fear. 'You seem to have sought me out, Sir. I hope there was a good reason for you bursting into a holy place in such a dramatic fashion?'

Mad Jack's right arm twitched as if he wanted to slash Lorna with his riding whip. Instead, he lowered his tone very slightly. 'Don't you think to bandy words with me, Madam!'

Lorna held his gaze, hoping her fear did not show. 'You must know that I am working for Lady Stanhope and investigating the strange death of Mr Findhorn. Have you come here with any information that may further my investigation, Sir John?'

'Why did you not come to see me immediately you arrived here?' Mad Jack's tone had not altered as he glared down at Lorna.

She ignored the implied slight. 'Do you have any information that may further my investigation, Sir?' She lifted her chin as Mad Jack half raised her arm.

'If you had come to see me you would have found out,' Mad Jack was first to retreat from the deadlock. He lowered his arm.

Lorna breathed out in relief. 'Well Sir John, here we both are. If you have something to say I am listening.'

'Are you always so insolent to your superiors?' Mad Jack asked.

'Are you always so rude to a lady?' Lorna countered. She did not consider that Mad Jack was her superior in any way except social position, and that was of little interest to her.

'Good God!' Mad Jack stared at her. 'You do have a mouth on you, don't you?'

'I am not inclined to give respect to a rude and arrogant man,' Lorna said. 'However long his pedigree or high his position.'

'You, madam, are impertinent!'

'And you, Sir, are no gentleman!' Lorna raised her chin slightly higher as Mad Jack raised his crop, but rather than strike her, he tucked it into a small holder at the side of his saddle.

Mad Jack sidestepped his horse around Lorna until he towered over Margaret. 'You are Margaret Smith,' he repeated.

'Yes, Sir.' Margaret did not flinch.

'Mmmph,' Mad Jack looked her up and down. 'What the devil are you doing here?'

'I am helping Miss Buchanan.' There was a trace of nervousness in Margaret's voice.

Mad Jack nodded. 'Are you indeed? Is Miss Smith any help, Miss Buchanan? Or is she merely a hindrance.'

Lorna stepped to Margaret's side. 'She is proving an excellent help, Sir John.'

'And she is picking up your insolence, no doubt.'

'I hope she will learn to be polite when people earn politeness and to return bad manners with what they deserve.' Lorna said.

Mad Jack rapped his reins on the flank of the horse as it fidgeted, 'Quiet, Randolph!' She looked down at Lorna. 'Miss Buchanan, you would be well to look at St Ann's School. Things are not all they seem there. That is all I have to say.' Wheeling his horse, he walked out of the church with the echo of Randolph's hooves remaining long after he banged through the front door.

'Don't show fear!' Major Buchanan said softly.

The natives surrounded them, some naked except for loin cloths, some wearing the battered remains of British uniforms, all armed with swords or knives or British rifles.

They spoke to each other in Urdu, asking each other what they should do with these British intruders. One poked at Major Buchanan with a stained bayonet. Without a word, he took hold of the man's arm, twisted it and grabbed the weapont.

'If we show fear,' Major Buchanan said, 'they will kill us.' He threw the bayonet aside.

Lorna nodded. 'How are you all?' She spoke in their language.

'Have you gentlemen seen the 78th Highlanders¿Major Buchanan asked pleasantly. 'They are meant to meet us here.'

The man who had held the bayonet stepped back as one by one the natives slipped away. Within a few moments, Lorna and the major were alone.

'Good girl,' Major Buchanan said. 'Never show fear; predators take advantage of that.'

'How did Mad Jack know my name?' Margaret whispered.

'I don't know,' Lorna said. 'There is a great deal about this little town on the hills that I do not understand.'

The prior had been a silent spectator. Now he wiped a cloth across his sweat-beaded forehead. 'You are a brave woman, Miss Buchanan. I don't know anybody else who would have stood up to Sir John.'

Lorna did not mention that her knees were trembling so badly she nearly collapsed. 'He is a bully,' she said. 'The only way to deal with a bully is to stand up to him, or her.' She forced a smile. 'You were about to tell me about the druids, I believe?'

'Oh indeed yes,' the prior indicated that they should all sit down. A beam of sunlight through the stained glass windows settled on him, painting him multi-coloured. 'You were asking about the druids. As you know, they were the Celtic priests and wielded great power before Christianity revealed their religion to be as false as the Norse or Roman gods.'

'I know little about them,' Lorna admitted. 'Except what Mr Temple has told us.' She realised she was shaking with reaction from Mad Jack's visit. 'That was a long time ago, surely.'

'Evil can return at any time,' the prior said. 'It only requires good men and women to turn aside for a moment, and evil can slide through the cracks in our society.'

'That is a bit obscure,' Lorna said. 'Do you think that they have returned?'

The prior looked at Margaret and frowned.

'It's all right, you can talk freely in front of Margaret,' Lorna glanced at her and lowered her voice. 'I trust her implicitly.' She saw the pleasure cross Margaret's face.

'She is rather a young woman to hear such unsettling things,' the prior said.

'Admiral Nelson commanded a ship at age 21,' Lorna said. 'I'm sure that Margaret at 19 can hear about druids.'

The prior tapped a long finger on the back of the pew. 'I have heard disturbing things, Miss Buchanan and Miss Smith. I have heard that people in white cloaks and hoods have been seen walking the hills and,' he glanced at Margaret. 'I have heard other things as well; things too unpleasant to talk about.'

'Try us,' Lorna included Margaret. After the brief visit of Mad Jack, hearing about obscure religious rites would be a relief.

'No, Miss Buchanan.' The prior made a decision and stood up. 'Some things are not suitable for female ears. It is my duty to struggle against spiritual evil. Sufficient to say that I do believe there are druids back on our hills. I cannot say whether or not they were involved in the murder of poor Mr Findhorn. I hope not. I hope to God that they were not or we could be entering a very black time. A very black time indeed.' He stood abruptly. 'I advise you both to keep clear of that so-called sacred well and all that is associated with it. Good day to you.' Turning aside, he walked crisply away with his footsteps echoing in the vastness of the priory.

'Well,' Margaret said. 'He wasn't much help!'

Lorna sighed and stood up. 'No; he is even more scared than Mr Temple I think. Are you sure you wish to continue, Margaret?'

'Quite sure,' Margaret said.

Lorna nodded. 'If you don't…'

Margaret stood up. 'Come on Miss. We have a murder to solve.'

Chapter Thirteen

Lorna and Margaret sat in the room they now shared, with a silver sun sinking outside and a bright fire crackling in the grate.

'So what do we have,' Lorna sipped delicately at a cup of tea and looked across to Margaret, who sat, slightly hesitantly, on one of the armchairs. 'Let's put it all together and see where we go from here.'

Margaret produced her notebook and opened it on the table. 'We have a lot of information, Miss, but nothing that makes sense.'

'Remind me what we have,' Lorna said.

Margaret looked pleased to be asked. 'Most of this is just moonshine,' she said. 'We have Findhorn found naked.' Margaret said the word softly, as if afraid to be heard. Only when Lorna nodded encouragement did she continue. 'And he was tied, upside down in a well. The police think the navvies did it, but you don't think so.'

'I don't think so' Lorna agreed. 'I can't see navigators being so subtle and elaborate.' She sighed. 'I still don't know how we can trace the three men who were paid off. What else, Margaret?'

'There are confused reports of a woman, or perhaps a man, dressed in white who has been watching the workings. He or she also followed Mr Findhorn,' Margaret looked up, 'and Mr Temple and the prior both think that there were druids; and so do I. It is Miss Appleton and her Chosen Girls.'

'Anything else?' Lorna did not mention Miss Appleton.

'You found that silver coin in the tunnel,' Margaret reminded, 'and there were Mr Findhorn's clothes in the pawnshop, handed in by some girl who called herself Sam Bellamy.'

'We also have Sir John's suggestion of the school to follow,' Lorna reminded.

'St Ann's School.' Margaret screwed up her face at the memory. 'Mad Jack apparently thinks that Miss Appleton murdered Findhorn. I know she did. She is an evil witch.'

'I don't know what Sir John thinks,' Lorna said, 'but as you said, it was some girl who named herself Sam Bellamy who handed in Mr Findhorn's shirt and waistcoat, and there was nobody of that name at St Ann's.'

Lorna sat back in the chair, allowing the warmth from the fire to relax her. 'There was something else,' she said, 'when I was in Mr Findhorn's hut two pages were missing from his day-to-day journal, and he mentioned minor thefts at the workings, as well as that woman in white.' Lorna sipped at her tea, 'something was missing from his hut as well, something round, a snuff box perhaps- there was a gap in the dust.'

'In a navvies' encampment, I am surprised the whole hut was not looted and burned to the ground.'Margaret said. 'What do you think was stolen?'

Lorna shook her head. 'That, I could not tell you.'

Margaret smiled. 'We have far more questions than answers here, Miss.'

'We have indeed,' Lorna said. 'I think you are enjoying this.'

'Margaret's smile broadened. 'Yes, Miss. It is far better than being at school. It is exciting! When Mad Jack came clattering into the priory, I nearly jumped through the roof, and when we helped the navvies at the tunnel … Well, I never had so much fun in my life.'

Lorna hid her smile. 'You should be at school. However, we have work to do. We have this Bellamy girl to trace, and three navigators, and this woman in white. Lots to do yet and we are no closer to finding poor Mr Findhorn's murderer than we were days ago.'

'I'm not coming with you to the school,' Margaret said quickly. 'I'm not going back near that witch.'

Lorna nodded; she was not surprised. 'All right Margaret. I'll go alone. If you want something to do, you can look for this Bellamy girl.' She was aware of the intense gratitude in Margaret's eyes.

St Ann's School stood as unwelcoming as ever behind its screen of dark rhododendron bushes and tall trees. Surprisingly the gate to the grounds had been open, so Lorna had been able to walk right up to the front door.

Despite the early hour, candlelight flickered behind the multi-panes of the tall windows, and the black-uniformed maid was on her knees scrubbing the front steps as if her life depended on it.

'Good morning,' Lorna remembered the maid although she had never before spoken to her. 'I wish to speak to your mistress. Pray inform her that Lorna Buchanan is here on the business of Lady Stanhope?'

The maid was about fourteen, with a thin face and acne on her chin. She stood up and flicked soap suds from her hands. 'I'm sorry, Miss but Miss Appleton is out with her class at present.'

'At this hour?' Lorna looked up, 'it's scarcely dawn! I thought we would catch Miss Appleton before school started.'

'Oh they won't be long, Ma'am,' the maid said, 'they'll be down off the hills in no time.'

'Is there anywhere I can wait indoors?' Lorna asked. 'I won't steal the silver, I promise.'

The maid gave a small smile. 'I know Miss; I remember you. Miss Appleton might not approve.'

'Lady Stanhope will certainly not approve if you make me wait outside the school,' Lorna said. 'She may withdraw her funding and her goodwill.' She smiled. 'Come on now: my apologies, I have never had the opportunity to learn your name.'

The girl looked momentarily confused, 'I'm not called by my name here. I'm called Mercy.'

'Mercy: that's a fine name,' Lorna said.

Mercy sighed. 'If you say so, Miss. Oh come in then, Miss!'

Mercy led Lorna into a small room on the first floor. 'This is the parent's waiting room. Shall I light the fire for you, Miss?'

'No, no; that's not necessary, thank you.'

'You can look out the window if you like and see Miss Appleton come down from the hills.' Mercy cleared a film of condensation from one of the panes and pointed. 'Indeed, there she is now, Miss Buchanan.'

'Thank you, Mercy,' Lorna stepped to the window.

The girls descended from the hills in a short crocodile walking sedately two by two. Every girl wore an identical long green dress with a matching dark green jacket and a straw bonnet tied on to their head. They walked with their backs straight and their heads erect, not speaking as they negotiated the steep slope.

Lorna counted eight pupils, knowing that she was looking at Miss Appleton's Chosen Girls.

Miss Appleton was last to come. Dressed in an identical manner as the girls, she shouted something and stepped off the path, so they had to file past her, unsmiling as they approached the school. She overtopped each of her pupils by a head.

They look like soldiers on parade Lorna thought. *Where is the fun in that?*

As the pupils walked past Miss Appleton barked the occasional order and twice landed a stinging blow with the flat of her hand.

Lorna studied Miss Appleton as she took her place at the back of the crocodile and marched into the school like a guardsman.

The girls retained their silent march until Miss Appleton left them and then the noise levels rose as they began to talk together. Lorna waited until the headmistress ascended the stairs before she stepped out of the waiting room.

'Good morning Miss Appleton.'

Miss Appleton stopped sharply. 'What are you doing back here? I ordered you out of my school.'

'I am working for Lady Stanhope,' Lorna had expected that reaction. 'And I am here to ask you some questions.'

'Indeed you are not.' Miss Appleton said flatly. 'I will answer none of your questions.'

Lorna smiled. 'In that case, Miss Appleton, I will inform Lady Stanhope that you refuse to co-operate with her private inquiry and Sergeant Caswell and some of his uniformed constables will return instead.' She gave a deliberately un-pleasant smile. 'I am sure that will do wonders for the reputation of your establishment.'

Miss Appleton flinched visibly. 'You had better come into my study, Miss Buchanan, although I cannot for the life of me think how I can be of assistance.'

The room was as immaculate as Lorna had remembered, with nothing altered. Only when Miss Appleton invited her to sit did Lorna realise that the desk stood on a subtly raised platform so that Miss Appleton looked down on her. The grandmother clock gave its slightly sinister tick as a constant backdrop to their conversation.

'Well, Miss Buchanan?' Miss Appleton pressed her palms together and looked steadily at Lorna. 'Be brief. I can't think why Her Ladyship would employ a woman who cannot follow simple rules.'

'I am investigating the murder of Mr Findhorn,' Lorna spoke deliberately slowly. 'And I wondered if you or your girls had seen anything untoward on your excursions through the hills.'

'What exactly do you mean, Miss Buchanan?' Miss Appleton's angular face did not alter expression. 'What sort of untoward thing would you expect us to see?'

'Anything that did not seem right,' Lorna said. 'For example, I have had reports of women wearing white robes near where Mr Findhorn was working, and where his body was discovered.'

Miss Appleton's face was impassive. 'Many people use the hills, Miss Buchanan. I am sure that some wear white clothes. My girls, as you must have noticed, have a uniform of a different hue.'

'I did not accuse your girls, Miss Appleton,' Lorna pointed out. 'I asked if you had *seen* any women wearing white.'

'Not that I recall,' Miss Appleton said.

'Thank you, Miss Appleton.' Lorna said.

'My girls do not have time to dawdle and gape at the other users of the hills,' Miss Appleton said. 'They are walking for a reason, not for the pleasures of the company or the romantic vistas.'

'What reason is that?' Lorna was genuinely interested.

'My young ladies are trained to keep fit and healthy, and are trained in all the arts and skills they will later require. They walk uphill to St Ann's Well and onward every morning, rain and shine.' She nodded grimly. 'My girls always marry.'

'Is that why you have your Chosen Girls?' Lorna asked, 'to prepare for marriage?'

Miss Appleton's gaze was bleak. 'A lady's role in this life is to find a husband. He will be the provider, and she will guide and look after him and bear his children. I prepare my young ladies for all aspects of their life of obedience, guidance and motherhood.'

Lorna nodded. 'I see, Miss Appleton.' She decided to set a verbal cat among the pigeons. 'You said you prepare them for all aspects of their life. You are preparing the upper classes for their role.' She sat back and waited for a reaction.

'We also allow in two local girls as well.' Miss Appleton said. 'We place one in each of the lower forms. Sometimes they do quite well, but often they are not of the required standard and fall by the wayside. You met Margaret Smith; she was one of the local girls we allowed in. That was a major miscalculation as Smith was nothing but trouble until she left.'

Lorna decided not to pursue that subject. 'Do you have a young lady by the name of Sam Bellamy in your school?' She decided that with Miss Appleton a blunt approach was best. 'I believe she is a local girl.'

'I do not divulge the names of my pupils.' Miss Appleton said. 'If that is all, Miss Buchanan, I have work to do.'

Lorna nodded; it was clear she was getting nowhere here. She would have to take a different approach. 'Thank you, for your time, Miss Appleton.' She walked outside, deliberately taking her time.

'Well, that was a complete failure,' she said to Margaret, who had waited a hundred yards from the school. 'I learned nothing.'

'Miss Appleton is a witch,' Margaret gave the expected response. 'And a murderer.'

Rather than respond to the words, Lorna watched as a beggar approached a group of water-cure invalids who had left the hills and were heading for their hotel. 'I was not particularly interested in the school until today. Miss Appleton is undoubtedly hiding something from us.'

'She's a witch,' Margaret insisted. 'She should be burned at the stake.'

'Maybe that's a bit extreme' Lorna said.

'What do we do now, Miss?'

Lorna kept her voice low. 'We will visit the school tonight.'

'It'll be shut,' Margaret was blunt. 'Ben the porter won't let you in.'

Lorna gave a small smile. 'It won't be shut for us, Margaret; we'll get in.'

'I don't want to come,' Margaret said at once.

'I hope that you do come,' Lorna said. 'I might need you.'

'Oh.' Margaret looked astonished. 'Nobody ever needs me.'

Lorna leaned over and touched her arm. 'I do.'

Margaret's breathing roughened. 'I'll come,' she said slowly, 'if *you* need me.'

'Thank you.' Lorna knew how much courage it would take for Margaret to re-enter the school.

An owl hooted mournfully from the trees that surrounded St Ann's, and somewhere in the dark, a dog barked, once, twice and then again, ending in a series of sharp squeals and the ugly snarl of a man.

Lorna looked to her right, where Margaret crouched, white- faced, in the swaying shadow of an elm. 'Are you all right?'

Margaret nodded. 'Yes.' Her voice was small. 'Do we go in now?'

'Not until all the lights are out,' Lorna indicated the yellow flicker from the attic window. 'The maid is still awake.'

'Mercy,' Margaret reminded.

'I wonder how much mercy Miss Appleton allows that poor girl,' Lorna said. She eased deeper into the dark as the maid's wan face appeared momentarily at the window, framed by the flickering glow of a candle. The light vanished. 'Give her ten minutes to settle down,' Lorna said. 'And relax, Margaret. It will be all right.'

Margaret shook her head. 'I'm all right, Miss. I only hope that the peelers aren't watching. I don't want the jail. You can get transported for robbery.'

'If we get caught, Margaret, you tell them that I made you do it.' Lorna was already having second thoughts about this escapade. 'If we're not caught everything is bright.' She checked Margaret with a quick glance. 'I'm glad you have dark clothing; it suits you.'

Margaret gave a brief and very nervous smile.

'Come on then, and be quiet.'

They slipped over the wall and stepped flat footed across the gravel walkway to the back door. 'I saw draw bolts on the front door,' Lorna explained, 'but I hope there are none on the back.'

Without outside lighting and with no moon Lorna took the bull's eye lantern from the small pack she carried. She applied a Lucifer match to the wick and slid the metal shutter across the front until only a thin beam of light shone out.

'The only thing wrong with this type of lantern,' she whispered, 'is that it gets very hot, so mind your fingers.'

'Yes, Miss,' Margaret whispered. 'Here we are.' She tested the door. 'It's locked.'

Lorna eased her aside. 'Mercy will have seen to that, Margaret. Let's see if it is also bolted.' She applied pressure. 'See how the door holds in one place when I push? If it were bolted, it would also hold at the top and bottom.'

Margaret nodded, 'I see, but what about the lock?'

Lorna took a lock-pick from her pocket. 'It just happens that I know how to use this. I need you to keep a lookout for anybody coming. That Mercy is sharp as a pin.'

'Miss!' Margaret looked and sounded shocked. 'I thought you were a teacher!'

'I was a teacher.' Lorna glanced around as a sliver of moon rose above the hills. 'We'll have to do this the hard way.'

She slipped the lock-pick into the keyhole and felt for the mechanism of the lock.

'Hurry, Miss,' Margaret hissed, 'I think somebody is coming.'

Lorna took a deep breath. 'Put that lantern out, please.' She glanced around; the door was flush with the wall; there was no doorway in which to hide. She bent to the lock, listened to the faint clicks from within and finally twisted her pick. The lock gave a distinctive clack as it shot back.

'That's it,' Lorna said, eased the door open and stepped inside. The interior was cold, with stone flags underfoot and bare plaster walls punctured by four panelled wooden doors. At the end of the short corridor, a flight of steps led both upstairs and down. 'We'll check upstairs first.' Lornaspoke quietly, 'and work our way downward. Stay close to me.'

Margaret nodded. She looked pale.

'Are you all right, Margaret?'

'Yes, Miss.' Margaret's voice shook.

'Follow me then,' the first wooden step emitted a soft creak under her boot, 'and be careful.'

The narrow beam of light bounced up the stairs, passing over portraits of grim-faced men and even grimmer- faced women. At the very top was a wooden ladder that led to a plain unpainted door. 'That is the attic where Mercy lives,' Lorna said, 'we'll leave her in peace.' She led the way to the tower where Miss Appleton had her study.

'Here we are.' It took Lorna only a minute to pick the lock. 'Come in.'

Margaret closed the door and stood with her back to it as Lorna stumbled toward the desk.

'Lantern!' Lorna saw the fear on Margaret's face. 'Come on. The sooner we finish, the quicker we can leave again.'

'I hate this place.' Margaret sounded close to tears. She slid the shutter of the lantern wider open, allowing more light to escape into the room.

'Come on now,' Lorna encouraged. 'We want a list of the pupils.' The top of the desk was clear of everything except an inkwell, blotting pad and box of pens. The drawers were not locked.

'Here we are, lesson lists and a class list; that was easy.' Lorna handed the class list over to Margaret. 'Look for Sam Bellamy.'

Margaret's hand was shaking as she held the document under the light of the lantern. 'No, Miss. No Bellamies here.'

'Are you sure? Check again. Sir John must have had some cause for suspicion.'

'Quite sure, Miss.' Margaret scanned the page a second time.

Lorna sighed. 'What did that man mean by sending us here?' Grabbing the class list, she replaced it and opened the other three desk drawers. 'We'll check through these in case. You take the bottom drawer and I'll take the others.'

'There's nothing interesting in here, Miss,' Margaret reported. 'Stocks of pens, slates, a textbook or two and letters. Can we go now, Miss?'

'Read through the letters,' Lorna said. She took the top few and skimmed through, 'these are just copies of routine notes to parents.'

'Mine is the same,' Margaret glanced at the door. 'I thought I heard a noise.'

'Check the names for a Bellamy,' Lorna suggested.

'Wait...' Lorna scratched her head, knowing something was niggling at her memory. 'What did that maid say? She told me she was called

Mercy here. *Here*: that means that she is called another name elsewhere.'

'They do that,' Margaret said. 'When my ma put me into service when I was little they changed my name from Margaret to Nancy. I never answered to Nancy and what leatherings I got! So I run away.'

Lorna touched her arm. 'You are a stubborn little thing aren't you?'

'I'm Margaret Smith,' Margaret said. 'Nobody got the right to change my name.'

Lorna smiled. 'Well said, Margaret Smith.'

'Mercy's not a pupil or a parent,' Margaret said.

'No; she's a servant,' Lorna agreed.

'So she won't be in the same book then,' Margaret said.

'My goodness; you're right.' Lorna looked at her. 'Look for a staff file.' She rummaged through the drawers again.

'Here, Miss...' Margaret was looking at the bookcase. 'There's a book in here with no name.'

'We're not looking for that sort of book,' Lorna said.

'If I were hiding a book, I would put it here amongst all the rubbish...' Margaret turned the key and opened the glass door. She pulled out the book. 'It's all figures and things, Miss.'

Sighing, Lorna stepped over. 'I'm not surprised you get into so much trouble, Margaret; you never take a telling, do you? Let me see!'

Leather bound, the book was well kept, with lists of income and expenditure in neat copper-plate written columns. 'It's alphabetical,' Lorna said. 'Here we are, right at the back: wages. Mercy; two shillings a week and board. Ben: five shillings a week and board. No last names.' She closed the book with a snap.

'No Miss,' Margaret said. 'When I got took on at the farmhouse my Ma got money for me. See if there's anything like that.'

'You are the most stubborn young woman!' Lorna said but opened the book again. 'Here we are: *Sundries*. In the *paid to* column...' she followed the words with her forefinger. 'Paid to William Bellamy, wheelwright of Hollytree Farm Cottages, one guinea holding for his daughter: Susan Alice Mary Bellamy.' She looked up. 'The

241

Bellamy part is right, but she's called Susan; not Sam.'

'It's the initials miss: the first letters of Susan Alice and Mary. Sam Bellamy,' Margaret said. 'That's her!'

'So it is! Thank you, God,' Lorna said, and then, on an impulse, she kissed Margaret on the nose. 'And thank you, too, Margaret. Your stubbornness has been invaluable.'

'Here now, Miss!' Margaret recoiled, rubbing at her nose. 'Nobody ever done that to me before.'

'No?' Lorna smiled. 'A kiss on the nose is the best kind of kiss. Now we know who Sam Bellamy is we might make some progress. Thanks to you.'

'Are we going to ask her questions now, Miss? She'll be in her bedroom all alone.' Margaret seemed eager to press on.

'Not yet.' Lorna said. 'She's not going anywhere. Let's finish our search of this place first; other rooms might help.'

'Yes, Miss.' Margaret looked around the study and gave a dramatic shudder. 'I hate this place.'

'Come on Margaret; we won't be back in here.' Lorna led the way out of the room. The corridor was chilly.

'These are dormitories,' Margaret pointed to two doors on the next floor.

'I know,' Lorna said. It already seemed a long time since she had worked in this stifling environment.

'And that is Miss Appleton's bedroom.'

'We'll leave that room well alone,' Lorna said.

'We could set fire to it…'

'Come on!' Lorna did not want to test if Margaret was joking or not.

The thin beam of lamp light flicked before them, showing the steps that descended to the basement, where a stout wooden door barred their entrance. 'This won't take a moment,' Lorna bent to the lock.

'Were you a cracksman before you became a teacher?' Margaret asked.

Lorna smiled and shook her head. 'I grew up surrounded by soldiers,' she explained. 'Father had a soldier servant who was a bit of a character. When I was small, he showed me how to pick locks and other things.' Lorna closed the door quietly.

They entered another short corridor, with a door on either side.

The first door led into a sizeable stone-floored chamber with alcoves fitted with stone shelves, some stacked with wooden boxes. 'This was a wine cellar,' Lorna said. She opened the first box. 'Soap,' she said. The next was neatly folded linen, then candles. 'This is a storeroom,' Lorna said. 'We'll try the other door.'

The second door had a double lock.

'This one is harder to open,' Lorna said. 'Could you direct the light on the lock, please?' She knelt and inserted her pick. 'This one does not want to open.' Changing her pick, Lorna tried again. 'They must have something hidden in here.' There was a soft click. 'That's better: we're in.'

As the door swung open on greased hinges, Margaret directed the light inside. The beam shifted across a small room lined with shelves. Only two were heavy with folded sheets.

'Just another storeroom,' Margaret prepared to turn away. 'We're wasting our time here.'

'Why use such an elaborate lock on a near empty room?' Lorna wondered. She stepped inside. 'Let's have a look, Margaret.'

'What are we looking for?' Margaret stepped inside.

'I'm sure I don't know,' Lorna confessed.

'Miss: how about this?' Margaret lifted one of the folded sheets. 'It's a druids' cloak!'

'Nonsense...' Lorna began but stopped as Margaret revealed what she had discovered. 'That's unusual.'

'Druids!' Margaret said. The gown was ankle-length and white, with a deep hood. 'The witch is the murderer.'

Lorna nodded. 'I will not discount that theory, Margaret. Don't forget that there was also the woman in white that watched Findhorn.'

'And the women in white we saw on the path,' Margaret reminded. 'That was Miss Appleton and her Chosen Girls!'

Lorna unfolded the next garment: 'this one is the same,' she said. 'I don't know what we have here, Margaret, but I do know that I have never heard of a school that has this type of uniform.' She nodded. 'This must be what Sir John meant.'

'Druids.' Margaret said. 'Miss Appleton is the leader of the druids, and she murdered Mr Findhorn.' She nodded in satisfaction. 'Now you can tell the peelers, and they can hang the witch.'

'I don't know what it means, Margaret, but I intend to find out. We'll keep a close eye on our *alma mater* – our old school-and certainly, we'll inform the police what we have found.'

'Then they'll arrest the witch and hang her.' Margaret repeated.

Lorna sighed. 'That may be what happens,' she said, 'although I really can't see how a group of young girls could murder a big man like Findhorn.' She folded the white cloaks and placed them as they had been. 'Come on now; let's get away.'

'Yes, Miss,' Margaret said happily. 'I want to watch when Miss Appleton gets her neck stretched.' She put her head to one side, extended her tongue and made choking noises. 'It will serve the witch right.'

'We haven't finished yet,' Lorna reminded although all the evidence so far indicated that Margaret's theory could be correct.

Chapter Fourteen

'Hello Mercy,' Lorna walked casually up the path. Mercy was polishing the brass plate at the entrance to the school, rubbing furiously to bring up the shine.

'Hello Miss Buchanan,' Mercy hardly paused from her work. 'I was sorry when you left Miss. That was a wrong thing they did to you. I could not say that last time you called in case somebody was listening.'

'Thank you. I did break the rules, and I did neglect to inform Miss Appleton about a pupil breaking them.' Lorna shrugged. 'I could not expect anything else, really.'

Mercy looked up. 'Yes, Miss. I suppose so.'

'Was that not a terrible business about poor Mr Findhorn?' Lorna said.

There was a moment's hesitation before Mercy replied. 'Indeed it was Miss.' Mercy scrubbed so furiously at the brass plate that Lorna wondered if she would wear the letters away.

'They found him undressed,' Lorna said. 'And the police are searching for his clothes.'

'Is that so, Miss?' The assault on the brass continued.

'If they find the clothes, they think they will have the killer,' Lorna said.

Mercy's hands trembled. She did not reply.

'Now you and I both know that you handed Mr Findhorn's clothes into a pawn shop in Worcester.' Lorna spoke without any dramatic emphasis. 'How did you come by them?'

'I never…' Mercy turned away as if to run, only to find Margaret had climbed the outer wall and was standing behind her.

'You did, Mercy. Or rather Susan.' Lorna produced the page from the pawnbroker's ledger and pointed to the name Sam Bellamy. 'There you are.'

The tears formed quickly.

'Now, nobody is accusing you of murder,' Lorna said. 'Tell us what happened.'

'I was up the hills, and I found the clothes,' Mercy spoke through her tears. 'That was all. I never knew they were Mr Findhorn's or that he was killed or anything.'

Resisting the temptation to give Mercy a hug, Lorna kept her face and voice stern. 'Where on the hills did you find the clothes, Mercy?'

Sobbing now, Mercy pointed in the direction of the Herefordshire Beacon. 'On the old British Camp,' she said. 'They were stuffed into a hole in the ground.'

'Near the Alfreck Well?' Lorna asked.

Mercy shook her head violently. 'Nowhere near it at all. They were about a mile away on the other side of the hill. I never stole them, Miss. They were just abandoned there like the fairies had taken the owner away or he never wanted them anymore, or as if some man and a woman had ... You know ... And left his clothes behind.'

'Tell me exactly where you found them,' Lorna listened as Mercy described the location. 'Did you see anybody else on the hill?'

'Just some of the health seekers and the ghost,' Mercy said.

'The ghost?'

'Yes, Miss. There's a ghost; a white thing that walks the camp.'

'I see.' Lorna saw that Mercy was shaking; any story she told would be incoherent at best. 'I have heard about the ghost,' Lorna said. 'You saw some health seekers there too.'

'Yes, Miss.'

'What time was that, Susan?' Lorna asked.

'About ten at night, Miss.' Mercy was crying hard now.

'Is that usual at that hour?'

'I don't know, Miss. I'm not usually up there at that time.'

Lorna frowned. 'So why were you up there at that time? Did Miss Appleton send you?'

'No Miss. It's the Alfreck Well miss. If you go there, you can see the reflection of your future husband in the water.' Mercy looked away. 'I wanted to see if I would ever get married, Miss.'

Lorna felt a surge of sympathy for this little girl with the acne-scarred face and the life of toil. 'I see. I am sure you will, Susan. You're a hard-working, intelligent and respectable young lady. Someday a decent man will be proud to call you his wife.'

'Do you think so, Miss?' Mercy's eyes were liquid.

'Yes, Susan, I do.' Lorna said. 'Now, I have another question for you. Think hard please and tell me how many health seekers you saw.'

'Three miss. Three men.'

'Could you describe them to me?' Lorna saw the confusion on Mercy's face. 'What did they look like?'

'It was dark,' Mercy said, 'and I only saw them for a moment. One was tall; I know that. The others were quite bulky, stocky, you know? Like navvies or the like.'

'Three men and one ghost.' Lorna nodded. 'Thank you, Mercy.'

'Please don't tell Miss Appleton Miss,' Mercy pleaded. 'I'll lose my position, and then the police will send me away to be a demon. I heard the tales.'

Lorna eased her grim expression away. 'No, Mercy. I won't tell Miss Appleton, and I won't tell the police either. Nobody will send you to Van Diemen's Land or anywhere else. Now dry your tears; you've nothing to fear from me.' Finally, with all the information gathered, Lorna could follow her natural instincts. 'Come here.' She folded Mercy into a hug. 'It's all right, Susan. You'll be all right now. And you will find a good man when you are ready. I know you will.'

Lorna sighed. Some parts of this new job were as hard as anything she had ever done in her life. Now she had to meet Margaret and return to the hotel.

Chapter Fifteen

'Wait!' Lorna put a hand on Margaret's arm. 'Look at that.' There was a bar of light under the door, faint but distinct. 'Somebody's in our room.'

'It will be Mr Gibson,' Margaret said.

Lorna nodded. 'Maybe so.' She tested the door handle. 'It's locked.' She knelt and peered through the keyhole. 'No key in the lock either. Whoever is inside must have a false key to lock the door. On the count of three, we go in.'

'Yes, Miss.' Margaret sounded more angry than scared.

Lorna slid in her own key. It turned silently. 'Right!' she said and pushed the door open. It slammed back on its hinges as Lorna crashed through with Margaret a step behind her, shining the lantern.

Margaret's lantern-light flickered around the room for an instant, before fixing on a young boy who stood, momentarily transfixed like a rabbit caught in the glow of a coach's lanterns. The boy stared, goggle-eyed as the two women pounded into the room, and then threw his stubby candle at Margaret and dived for the open window.

'Not so fast, you!' Margaret lunged forward and grabbed at the boy's sleeve. She took hold of a handful of cloth. 'Got you, you little hedge bird!'

The boy twisted his head to look over his shoulder and for a second Lorna stared right into a pair of brown eyes beneath long, nearly girlish lashes. Then he ducked out of his shirt and slid to the window, leaving Margaret holding nothing but the rags of a dirty shirt.

'You little devil!' Lorna breathed as the boy vanished.

The candle the boy had dropped was rolling around the floor. Margaret lifted it up. 'Tricky little ding boy.'

Lorna stared out the window. The boy was climbing down the outside of the building, hand over hand, as he found gaps between the bricks.

'Here you! Stop!' Knowing that shouting was pointless, Lorna slid through the window and followed, feeling for handholds and footholds on the surface of the wall, kicking her skirts free as they encumbered her legs.

The boy looked up, his eyes wide as he realised that Lorna had followed him. He dropped to the ground, rolled, jumped up and ran. Lorna let go of her handhold, felt the momentary sensation of floating in the air and landed with a slight jar. She bounced back up, lifted her skirt above her ankles and chased after the boy.

'Stop, thief!' She shouted, hoping that some of the health-seekers may have chosen to rise even earlier than usual to walk the Malvern heights. The boy did not hesitate as he sprinted along the Worcester Road, only glancing behind him when he thought that Lorna had fallen behind.

After that first shout, Lorna saved her breath. She saw the boy hesitate as he reached the wall of a large house, and then he slid around the side of a boundary wall and disappeared.

Lorna increased her speed, turning the corner of the wall in time to see the boy run down a steep slope, his feet slapping on the ground and both arms pumping madly. Aware that Margaret had emerged from the front door of the hotel far behind, Lorna pointed down the hill, yelled 'Church Street' and followed the fugitive. The climb was steep and slippery with early morning dew, making if difficult for Lorna to keep her balance. She slipped, recovered and ran on, with the sound of her boots echoing around the street. A shutter creaked open in an upstairs window, and a white face topped by a large night-cap gaped at her.

'We'll have less noise, you drunken scoundrel. I'm trying to sleep here!'

Ignoring him, Lorna ran forward, to slide again, this time falling sideways and cracking her head against the stone wall to his right. She yelped, loudly.

'I say!' the man in the night-cap complained, 'enough of that awful noise. Great Malvern is a respectable town!'

Tempted to shout out that the respectable town was full of thieves, druids, and murderers, Lorna held her peace and ran on. The boy was now well in front and showed no sign of fatigue. He mounted a wall, glanced behind and saw Lorna still in pursuit.

'Halloa, woman!' The boy's voice was clear. 'You're old and fat and slow!' Balancing on top of the wall, he turned his back, hauled down his trousers and bent over to show his white backside. 'That's for you!' He slapped himself in undoubted triumph.

'You little scoundrel!' Lorna dived forward, but the boy pulled up his trousers, laughed and dropped on the opposite side of the wall.

'I see you!' Margaret had overtaken Lorna and vaulted the wall two-handed. 'You won't escape me you little bugger!'

Lorna scrambled over the stone wall to find she was in the graveyard of the Priory Church, with irregular rows of gravestones protruding through the ragged grass. The vast church dominated everything, windows glittering as the sun eased above the horizon.

No longer caring about propriety or respectability, Lorna shouted: 'Margaret!'

'Over here!' Margaret's voice floated toward her. 'The boy is behind one of these gravestones!'

'You stay put, Margaret and I will flush him out!' Lorna's voice was hollow in the semi-darkness. A blackbird called from a tree near the wall, the sound liquid, timeless, fitting for this place of memory and peace.

Lorna began to pace the rows of gravestones, peering behind each one and moving on to the next. 'You can't get away you know,' she called out, 'better for you to give yourself up and come peacefully.'

There was no response from the boy. 'If I have to hunt you down, I'll hand you to the police, and you'll get transported to Van Diemen's Land.'

The sun was rising, strengthening the light yet screening the lee of the wall and pushing long slanting shadows from the gravestones closest to the church. 'This is your last warning!' Lorna shouted. Margaret was standing at the opposite side of the graveyard, waiting to pounce the second the boy emerged.

'There he is!' Margaret shouted out.

The boy exploded from behind a half-recumbent stone, bare-chested and frantic as he rushed past Margaret. Lorna dived across the graveyard in pursuit. 'Right, you little monster!'

'Hoi!' The man's voice and the thrown rock that bounced from the gravestone an inch from her head made Lorna start. She flinched and looked to see who was shouting just as the boy scrambled past her.

'Here!' Margaret lunged out. Nimble as a ferret, the boy slipped under her arms and escaped. 'You little devil!'

They could only watch as the boy scrambled over the wall and disappeared.

'Another failure,' Lorna said. 'We're not doing well are we?' She brushed the dirt off her knees. 'Time for breakfast I think?'

'I can catch him,' Margaret offered.

'He'll be far away by now.' Lorna said. 'Come on: breakfast.'

Margaret scowled in the direction of the fleeing boy. 'If you say so, Miss, but I want to boot his arse until he can't sit for a week.'

'Quite,' Lorna hid her smile. 'Breakfast.'

They sat at the table in the hotel with the landlord bustling around and the cheerful clatter of crockery as a background.

'So what was the little devil after?' Margaret spoke through a mouthful of bacon, egg and devilled kidneys.

'One of two things,' Lorna said. 'Either he wanted to find out more about us, or he wanted to steal *this*,' she took the ancient silver coin from her pocket and dropped it on the table. 'There is nothing else worth stealing in our room.'

'It's only a scrap of silver,' Margaret examined it again. 'What value did Mr Temple put on it? Threepence was it?'

'Something like that,' Lorna enjoyed watching Margaret grow in confidence.

'He wanted information then,' Margaret said. 'The young one was finding out about us.' She grinned, 'you gave him quite a fright when you went after him down the wall: I've never seen any woman do that.'

Lorna smiled. 'I grew up in India, Margaret; we used to climb trees to chase monkeys.'

'Yes, Miss,' Margaret looked at her curiously. 'When you came into the classroom that first day you looked so lah-de-dah. I could not imagine you chasing monkeys then. Now I can!'

'What is more interesting than why that young boy was here is who sent him,' Lorna said. 'That man was not there by chance.'

'So the boy was working for somebody else,' Margaret said.

'Undoubtedly,' Lorna agreed. 'If we find the people who sent him, we can maybe sort something out in this mess.'

Margaret signalled for more bacon and kidneys. 'We have to find the boy first, and they all look alike; dirty, scruffy, smelly little tykes.'

'That is all true,' Lorna said, 'and you forgot thieving, illiterate, lying and cheeky. Yet that boy could be the key to this case: or merely another unfortunate little pawn.'

'We'll never catch him now,' Margaret said.

'We already know who he is,' Lorna watched as Margaret demolished another chop.

'How do we know that?' Margaret asked.

'He was the same little beggar boy who approached me the other day.' Lorna shook her head.

'Did you recognise his ar...? what you saw of him?' Margaret asked.

Lorna shrugged. 'Not through the part you nearly mentioned anyway.' They shared a secret smile.

'Dirty little tyke.' There was no malice in Margaret's words.

Lorna stood up. 'We have a lot to do now, Margaret. We have to trace this Navigator Wilce, find the beggar boy and watch the school for any untoward behaviour.'

'We should tell Sergeant what's-his-name to arrest the witch now,' Margaret said. 'Although I can't see any connection between Miss Appleton and that thieving little blaggard.'

'Nor can I,' Lorna was candid. 'There must be one, somewhere. What day is this? Thursday: we'll tell Sergeant Caswell about this morning's events and scour Worcester for this Wilce fellow. If he's known to the local police Caswell will help; if not it will be a case of searching through the lodging houses.' She paused, 'that's it, I think. Unless you have decided you no longer wish to help me.'

'I do want to help you!' Margaret nearly shouted.

Lorna smiled. 'As long as you're sure. I never thought this would be a simple case of navigators kicking a man to death, but nor did I expect women in white and druids and little bare-bottomed boys raking through my room.'

Margaret's smile was spoiled only by Lorna's view of the food she was still chewing. 'It's fun isn't it?'

Chapter Sixteen

'Margaret!' Lorna shook her awake, 'they're moving.' They lay in a slight hollow underneath a bush with the call of an owl echoing and the dew forming on their clothes.

'What?' Margaret opened bleary eyes, 'sorry, I must have fallen asleep.'

'The Chosen Girls,' Lorna reminded. 'They're leaving the school.'

'It's still dark,' Margaret huddled into her coat collar. 'I'm glad I was never one of the Chosen Girls. What do they mean by making the poor souls get up at this hour of the morning? That's just cruel hard.'

'Here,' Lorna handed over the small telescope she had purchased in a Worcester pawn shop. 'See for yourself.'

Margaret focussed the lens. 'This is fun, spying on the school like this.'

'Never mind that: can you see them?'

'I see them,' Margaret said. 'Miss Appleton and your old friend Miss Henshaw are on horseback, like shepherds with a flock of sheep.'

'A well-organised flock and each carrying a bundle of something,' Lorna said. 'We'll follow at a distance. I want to see where they are going and what they do when they get there.'

Miss Appleton and Jane Henshaw sat straight-backed and side-saddle on small cobs, with Miss Appleton in the front and Jane at the rear of the crocodile. Occasionally the headmistress barked something out, or Jane would poke at one of her charges with the long stick she carried.

'What are the horses carrying?' Margaret whispered. 'Look at the side packs.'

Lorna nodded. 'Something bulky. Keep quiet.'

Miss Appleton flashed the light from her lantern along the line of girls, then rode back, leaned out of her saddle and adjusted the school uniforms of a few of them. She snapped something, slapped her cob on the rump and led them out of the school grounds and downward toward the town.

Lorna allowed Miss Appleton three minutes before she followed, keeping quiet. 'Just keep your eyes on the teacher's lanterns,' she said, 'and when the light strengthens we will drop back a bit.' She judged the distance, slid out of cover and followed, with Margaret at her side. The crocodile moved quickly, with Miss Appleton leading and Jane prodding at any girls who lagged.

'They're going fast,' Margaret said, 'The witch is working these poor girls hard.'

'Easy to go fast when you're sitting on the back of a horse,' Lorna said.

'They're heading across the Wych to the Herefordshire Beacon,' Margaret said eventually. 'That's where these women found Mr Findhorn's body.'

'I know that!' Lorna's quick reaction proved the frayed state of her nerves.

The lantern light bounced; one instant showing a line of bonnet-adorned heads, the next an array of ankle length skirts, and then Jane shifted her stance, and the light flicked across the coarse grass and scrubby bushes as the crocodile filed onto the path. The pace slowed slightly. A fox barked, the sound eerie.

'She's taking them all the way to the top,' Margaret stumbled over a tussock of grass and swore.

'Mind your language,' Lorna said automatically, 'and keep moving; they're making ground on us.' Lorna lengthened her stride.

Margaret looked up from the uneven path. 'I can't see the lights.'

'Hurry up!' Lorna pushed up a ridge just as the lights became visible again, rising high and then dropping away. 'They are in among the fort's defensive ditches,' she glanced eastward. 'Dawn can't be far away now.'

'They've altered direction,' Margaret said, 'they're heading downhill.'

Lorna nodded, 'They're heading toward the Alfreck Well.'

'When my children grow up, I'm not sending them to school,' Margaret stumbled again and muttered a word that Lorna chose to ignore.

Lorna watched the shifting lanterns, and for an instant, she wondered at these other men who had stood where she was, many hundreds of years ago, and watched the lights of a Roman army surround the hill fort. Caractacus and his warriors must have felt the tide of history strong upon them as their old Celtic ways came into direct conflict with the most successful military machine in the world. Now she was an example of the most modern civilisation, a woman doing what many would consider to be man's work in the most progressive nation in this nineteenth century. Yet there was more than modernity here; something of the past remained. It was in the air, a whisper of something ancient surrounded her, soft sounds from forgotten foot soldiers, long gone memories; a feeling she had never encountered before and did not understand.

'You're never alone.' Amrita, her ayah, smiled through kind brown eyes. 'I am always here.'

'But Ayah,' Lorna looked around in the dark. 'I can't see you.'

'Even if you can't see me, I will be close by,' Amrita leaned closer. 'Hush now little poppet, and go to sleep.'

'The tigers will get me,' Lorna played for time and company.

'Neither the tigers or the cobras or the bad-mashes will get you when I am here,' Amrita said, 'and I am always with you.'

'Yes, Ayah,' Lorna said. She closed her eyes tight and sprung them open. 'I can't see you.'

'That does not matter. I can see you even when I am not in the room with you,' Amrita said softly.

Lorna smiled and snuggled into sleep.

It was the same feeling as she had as a very young child. She was not alone up here in these ancient hills. 'Stop!' She jerked back to the present and put an urgent hand on Margaret's arm.

The lights were static, glinting across the uneven contours of the hill, highlighting the greened branches of the mountain ash, reflecting weirdly from still water and rising pale to fade and die in a sky of pure ebony.

'They're at the well.'

'Can you see what's happening?' Margaret's attempted whisper might have reached Worcester had Lorna not clamped a hand over her mouth.

'Sshh! Margaret! Get down; down on the ground!'

Crawling, they inched closer, with Lorna following the line of dead ground so the coming dawn would not silhouette them against the skyline. She heard the cutting voice of Miss Appleton and the rustle of clothing, subdued whispers, and a giggle cut abruptly short by the sharp sound of a slap.

Dampness from the grass soaked through Lorna's clothes as she wriggled to the northwest of the well, hopeful that the darkness would conceal her better there. Settling behind one of the defensive ditches she eased her head up, taking care to move slowly and merge with the tussocks.

Miss Appleton had arranged the girls around the well and led them in a chant, the words of which Lorna could not understand. 'What are they saying?'

'It's not English,' Margaret replied at once. 'It might be Welsh: we get quite a few Welshies here.'

'Look!' Lorna peered through the pre-dawn dim. She was aware that something was happening but was unsure what until the girls stripped off their uniforms and donned the long white robes she had seen in the storeroom.

'What are they doing?' Margaret said. 'I told you they were witches and druids!'

'Hush!' Lorna pressed two fingers to Margaret's lips.

As they watched, one of the girls rose from the rest and walked forward. The chanting continued, soft, persistent, with the same phrases continually repeated, a litany of unintelligible words that Lorna did not understand. The girl poised at the edge of the well and, at a sign from Miss Appleton, discarded her white gown, so she stood, nakedly pale beside the dark water. She raised her arms toward the sky and then plunged in to stand thigh deep.

'What's happening?' Margaret asked.

'Shh and watch,' Lorna said.

Miss Appleton took three strides forward, reached out and pushed the naked girl right under the surface. The girl shrieked once as she was submerged. The chanting continued.

'They're drowning her,' Margaret half rose until Lorna grabbed her.

'No they're not! Watch!'

The chanting rose to a crescendo and stopped. The sun emerged from the horizon; watery, translucently pink it eased its light across the Worcestershire plain. Miss Appleton raised her hands as the sun's rays gold- tinted the tips of the grass while casting dark shadows into the depths of the defensive ditches.

As the first girl emerged, Miss Henshaw threw a blanket over her, and another took her place, stepping into the water as the others chanted. One by one, unhurried, methodical, all the girls stepped forward to immerse themselves in the well.

'Don't they realise that they are bathing in a well where a man was drowned?' Margaret asked.

Lorna did not reply for a moment. 'I think they know that very well,' she said softly. 'Remember that Mr Temple told us that the druids used to sacrifice a lusty man to give vigour to the water or some such? Findhorn had eight children; what more proof could he give of his virility.'

Margaret stared at her. 'You're thinking the same as I always thought,' she said. 'Miss Appleton murdered Mr Findhorn.'

'Heaven only knows what I think,' Lorna remembered that Miss Appleton had boasted that her Chosen Girls always found a husband and that a man needed children. 'We have a lot of work to do here yet, Margaret.'

'Girls!' Miss Appleton's voice was clear as the sun rose behind her, silhouetting her like a mythical priestess. 'You are my Chosen Girls. You have come to St Ann's College to prepare yourselves for life as wives. Men want women who will give them sons and heirs, and you must oblige. The ceremony you have performed is as old as the hills themselves and increases your chances of fertility, ensuring that you give your chosen men what they wish.'

The sun strengthened as Miss Appleton extended her arms in the shape of a cross. 'My girls!' Her voice boomed out, echoing across the scarred hillside. 'Here you are ensuring your destiny as wives; now we will ensure you fulfil your lives as women!'

The girls changed again, donning their school uniforms in a mad frenzy of activity while Miss Appleton and Jane encouraged them with harsh words and casual swings of her stick, and then

273

they formed up into their crocodile and followed her along the ridge that led toward Clutter's Cave.

'That's interesting,' Lorna said, 'I am curious to see what happens next.'

'They're moving fast,' Margaret complained, 'and we haven't had breakfast yet.'

'I doubt they have either,' Lorna reminded. 'Now keep down and keep away from the peak of the ridge. It's daylight now so they can see us as well as we can see them.'

The girls marched on with Miss Appleton in front and Jane Henshaw making up the rear. If a girl happened to flag or fell out of formation, Jane used her stick to prod her in the back or land a stinging blow.

'I hate both these witches,' Margaret decided.

The crocodile retained its formation, passing Clutter's Cave and around the next hill.

'Hangman's Hill,' Margaret said. 'I never seen a hanging there.'

'I *have* never seen,' Lorna murmured automatically.

Miss Appleton marched them down the reverse slope of the hill with the girls still straight-backed and quiet.

'Where is the witch taking us?' Margaret grumbled. 'Does she not know that I'm hungry?'

'Maybe you should run ahead and tell her,' Lorna suggested.

Margaret gave her a look of disgust. 'They've stopped,' she said.

Lorna lay on the ground and extended her telescope. 'They're clustered around something, but I can't see what. We'll have to get closer. I want to hear what Miss Appleton is saying.'

Moving from cover to cover, they inched closer until Lorna slid behind a wind-twisted thorn bush in the midst of a patch of rough grass. 'This will do,' she said quietly.

Miss Appleton was speaking again, quietly and earnestly. Lorna heard her tell the girls that they were every bit as important as men and to take their role as wife and mother very seriously, 'but never forget that you are also a woman. Take every opportunity to advance your cause; we want suffrage, we want entrance into univer-

sity, and you are at the forefront of our movement.'

'What is she talking about?' Margaret asked.

Lorna smiled. 'Miss Appleton is breeding a
whole generation of radicals,' she said. For the
first time, she could appreciate something that
the head teacher was doing.

'What's that?' Margaret pointed, 'what are
they looking at?'

Lorna focussed the telescope. 'It's like nothing I have seen before.' She said. 'It's a statue
of something, squat. It's ugly, misshapen,' she
handed over the telescope. 'See if you can do any
better.'

Margaret took the telescope. 'It's a statue of
some sort, but I can't make out any more than
that. It seems to be fixed here, like some Catholic
idol.'

'I doubt its Catholic,' Lorna said wryly. 'Listen!'

'We have this power,' Miss Appleton pointed
to the statue. 'It has always been known that we
have this power. Our Celtic ancestors celebrated
it, as we see here.' She stepped aside so her girls
could have a clear view of the statue.

'What is that thing?' Margaret muttered. 'I know what it looks like, but I can't be correct.'

'What do you think it looks like?'

'Something I would never show to my grandmother, that's what,' Margaret said.

Lorna took back the telescope. 'Oh dear God in heaven! I've seen a picture of that. It's a Sheela-na-gig!'

'It's disgusting!' Margaret gave her opinion. 'It's a woman pulling her ... her...' she stumbled over the words. 'Her thing,' she gestured vaguely to her groin. 'You know her *thing*! It's a woman pulling that open.'

'That's just what it is,' Lorna said. 'It's a woman parting her vulva.'

'I always said she was an old witch!' Margaret looked away. 'It's not right showing that.'

Lorna watched as the girls filed up to the grotesque statue and, one by one sat on it as Miss Appleton touched them on the head. 'I think it is a fertility symbol,' she said.

'I don't know what it is,' Margaret said. 'It's disgusting, that's what it is. Look; we're on the move again!'

'Back to the school,' Lorna took a deep breath. 'I think you may be correct, Margaret. Miss Appleton may be our woman.'

'I thought so,' Margaret nodded happily. 'She's a witch!'

'We'll go to Sergeant Caswell' Lorna said. 'And tell him what we have found.' Strangely, rather than triumph, she felt only immense sadness. There were too many pieces of this puzzle that did not come together.

'I'm hungry,' Margaret reminded.

'We'll have breakfast first,' Lorna said. 'And then go to the sergeant.'

'Breakfast is good.' Margaret agreed. 'Then we'll get the witch hanged.' She twisted her head in imitation of a woman being executed. 'I hope I get to watch.'

'Well Sergeant Caswell,' Lorna spoke quietly 'I have some scraps of information for you.'

Caswell nodded solemnly.

They sat in the police office in Worcester with two great mugs of tea on the table, and the door firmly closed at their back.

'I have made some progress as well,' Caswell said.

Lorna sipped her tea. 'Who will go first?'

'Oh, ladies first,' Caswell listened as Lorna explained her discoveries. He raised his eyebrows when Lorna related the tale of the young thief and frowned at the description of Miss Appleton's early morning excursion.

'Druids.' Caswell took notes. 'I will look into it. I know about the Sheela-na-gig. There are a couple of such things in the area. Little boys like to laugh at them. My information is less dramatic than yours. We picked up one of the three navigators who we believe *did* murder Mr Findhorn.'

'You still think it was the navigators?' Lorna did not hide her surprise.

Sergeant Caswell nodded. 'We do,' he said. 'As I said, we have one in custody.'

'Which one?' Lorna asked.

'A local man named Wilce,' Caswell said. 'We have him in the cells downstairs.'

'May I see him?' Lorna asked.

'Follow me.' Caswell put his tea on the table and rose at once. He gave a small smile. 'I hope you do not have delicate ears. These navigators can be a bit rough with their tongues.'

'I'm sure there's nothing I haven't heard before,' Lorna said.

The cells were small, cramped and clean with heavy iron-bound wooden doors each equipped with a spy-hole. The third door in the lime-washed corridor had the name 'Wilce' scrawled in chalk on a small board outside. Sliding aside the cover of the spy-hole, Caswell peered through. 'There he is; lying like a lamb.'

Lorna looked into the cell. The navigator lay on his back on a straw mattress, hands behind his head and narrow eyes returning Lorna's scrutiny. Apart from his probing eyes, he did not look much different from the farm labourers that were common throughout the agricultural areas of the country.

'May I speak to him?'

'I'll come with you,' Caswell said. 'He may be dangerous.'

'Thank you, Sergeant.'

'Constable!' Caswell nodded to a burly policeman who stood looking bored at the end of the corridor. The constable stepped portentously across and opened the door.

Wilce sat up on the bed as they entered. He was about forty, with well- developed arms and chest and a broad face. 'Is this more questions, Sergeant? Who's the lady?'

'I am Lorna Buchanan,' Lorna said, 'and I'm working for Lady Stanhope.'

'Oh yes?' Wilce surprised Lorna by standing up politely. 'And what does her Ladyship wish with me?'

'She wants to know if you killed Mr Findhorn.'

'Oh does she now?' Wilce gestured to the bed. 'You'd best sit there Lorna Buchanan because there's nowhere else in this room.' His grin was gap-toothed. 'I can't offer even offer you a cup of tea.'

'You watch your lip,' Caswell said. 'Miss Buchanan doesn't want any of your mouth.'

'Thank you, Sergeant, but I am sure it was kindly meant' Lorna said.

'I never did it,' Wilce said. 'I told the Sergeant that and I can't say more. I was nowhere near the Herefordshire Beacon that night. I was on the ran-dan in Worcester, and that's all there is to it.'

'Can you prove that?' Lorna asked.

'How can I prove it?'

'Who were you with?'

'There was me and my wages and a few glasses of rum,' Wilce said. 'There were other people there, but I don't know who. They were helping me spend my wages.'

'I bet they were,' Caswell said, 'and all the money you took from poor Mr Findhorn.'

'I never took anything from him because I never saw him.'

'Were you in a public in Worcester?' Lorna asked. 'Was it anywhere that you might be known?'

'I was in a lot of publics.' Wilce screwed up his face. 'I can't remember which ones.'

'I have men making inquiries,' Caswell said. 'We have covered all of this already.'

'I have something different to ask,' Lorna changed tactics. 'After Mr Findhorn fired you, or after Mr Findhorn was murdered, did you return to the navigator's camp?'

'Return to camp? Why would I do that?' Wilce said. 'I had no reason to.'

Lorna nodded, thinking of the items missing from Findhorn's hut. 'That can be proved. The other navigators or their wives would have seen you.'

Wilce nodded. 'They would that.'

'All right Mr Wilce; you are not helping your case here. Perhaps you can help me in another way. Could you tell me anything about Mr Find-horn the day, or days, before he was killed? Whether or not you killed him.'

Wilce shrugged. 'Oh aye; Findy was acting all queer. I don't know what was up with him. He was all excited. He was normally a surly sort of bugger...'

'Watch your language, Wilce,' Caswell said.

'Yes; sorry mistress.' Wilce nodded in Lorna's direction. 'As I said he was normally a surly sort of *fellow*, and that day he was all smiling. I thought he had been drinking or something until he let me go.'

'He was smiling? Do you know why?' Lorna asked.

'No miss. It was as if he's found a bottle of rum he forgot about or something. Queer it was.' Wilce shrugged again.

'What day was that?'

'The day he kicked us out. The 7th or 8th of March it would be.'

'Thank you,' Lorna said. 'You may have been helpful.' She paused on her way to the door. 'By the way Mr Wilce, what is the druids' sacred colour?'

'The what?' Wilce looked genuinely confused. 'What's the what's sacred colour?'

'What's the druids' sacred colour? Or the witches or fairies. What's their sacred colour?'

'Blessed if I know miss. I never met a fairy or a witch to ask them.' His grin was not offensive. 'Now can I get out of here?'

'You're suspected of murder,' Caswell said. 'You'll stay in there until I say otherwise or the judge decides to stretch your neck.'

Wilce shrugged. 'Free food and bed I suppose.'

'Thank you, for your help Mr Wilce.' Lorna said. 'I will leave you in peace now.' She hesitated. 'I don't believe you are guilty of Mr Findhorn's murder, Mr Wilce.'

'I do,' Sergeant Caswell said. 'And he'll swing for it.'

Wilce shrugged again. 'If I swing, then I swing, Sergeant, but either way I am an innocent man.'

Caswell ushered Lorna outside. The cell door shut with an ominous slam.

'I think he is innocent,' Lorna said.

'They all say they are innocent,' Caswell was smiling. 'I've yet to meet a criminal who admits to being a thief or a blackguard or a wife-beating scoundrel. If I was to believe them, I'd have a whole police office full of innocent little angels with blood on their knuckles.' He rapped on the door of the cell next to Wilce's. There was no chalked name on the board outside. 'Not all our prisoners are murderers. This young lad is only a little sneak thief. Have a look and see what we normally have to deal with.'

Lorna slid open the peephole. She frowned, instantly recognising the young boy who lay in misery on a hard bunk. 'I know this lad,' she said. 'May I have a word?'

'You know him?'

'We've met briefly,' Lorna said. 'I won't need an escort this time. What's his name?'

'He told us he was Tom Braeburn.'

Lorna nodded. 'That's as good a name as any. What's he charged with?'

'Petty theft,' Caswell said casually. 'If it's his first offence he'll get a few days in jail, or maybe only a few strokes of the birch. If he's a persistent offender, it could be much worse for him.'

'Let's hope it's his first offence then,' Lorna said.

Sergeant Caswell signalled to the watchful constable, who inserted a key into the lock and flung the door violently open. The boy inside cringed against the wall behind his bunk and drew his knees up to his chin. Big eyes stared from a filthy face.

'Hello Tom,' Lorna kept her voice cheerful. 'Do you remember me?' She sat on the end of the bed. The straw mattress was as thin as her finger and hard as the plank on which it lay. The cell reeked of urine from the chamber pot, and fear from the boy.

Tom shook his head. He recoiled as far as he could as if he was trying to burrow into the brick wall behind him.

'Oh, you must remember me!' Lorna smiled as if she enjoyed tormenting a boy who must have been suffering agonies of terror. 'You broke into my room, ran away when I returned, and then you hid from me in Malvern Priory churchyard!'

'No I never,' Tom's voice was little more than a whimper.

'Yes you did,' Lorna said. 'And you taunted me by showing off ... ' She delivered a sideways slap to his hip. 'That!'

Tom shook his head. Tears coursed white streaks through the grime on his face. 'No; it wasn't me.'

'Oh yes it was, Tom, my boy,' Lorna forced false joviality into her voice. 'And do you know what will happen now? No? Well, I'll tell you. Sergeant Caswell is holding you for petty theft as it is. He thinks that this is your first offence because you gave him a false name, didn't you?'

Tom started. 'How did you know that?'

'You just told me,' Lorna said cheerfully. She settled herself on the bed, hoping nothing was living within the straw. 'Right my little friend. The minute I tell Sergeant Caswell that you are a habitual thief and an area-thief to boot, he will increase the charges against you. Rather than a few days in jail, you will be facing a much more serious charge.'

Tom was sobbing now, wiping his be-slobbered nose with a ragged and filthy sleeve. 'No,' he said. 'No I won't.'

'It will be the birch first,' Lorna kept smiling. 'Perhaps twenty- five strokes, maybe more, and then what will they do with you? A boy who lives by breaking into houses and stealing? It will be transportation; seven years at least and probably more. Think of that, Tom; think of maybe ten years in Van Diemen's Land, on your own with all the grown men, all the murderers and thieves, the highwaymen and worse.' She pushed Tom's hands away from his face and stared into his terrified eyes, hating herself. 'Much worse.'

'No,' Tom shook his head and drummed his feet on the bed. 'No-o-o-o.'

Lorna let him sob for a long minute. 'Unless...' she said and stopped.

She waited for another minute, wondering if Tom would grasp at the slender thread of hope she held out. 'Unless.'

'Don't tell,' Tom said. 'Please don't tell.'

'Oh, but I will tell,' Lorna said, 'unless you help me.'

Only Tom's silence broke the thick silence in the cell. 'How?' He spoke from behind the shelter of his hands as if his interlocked fingers could shut out all the horrors of the world.

'Tell me why you broke into my hotel room first,' Lorna said.

'I never did,' Tom sobbed.

'I saw you plain as I see you now,' Lorna said, 'and so did Margaret, my friend. We both saw you then, and we will say that when you stand in court. Now, tell me why you broke in.'

'The man made me.' Tom's hands still muffled his voice.

'Which man?' Lorna gentled her voice slightly. 'You'll have to do better than that, Tom.'

'Just a man,' Tom said.

'What was he like?' Lorna heard the grate of the spy-hole opening and knew that Sergeant Caswell was watching her. 'Hurry Tom, or the sergeant will call me away, and I'll tell him all about you, breaking in and stealing from my room and then lowering your clothes and dis-playing your person to me. That will be another three years at least. Three more years in Van Diemen's Land with the tigers and snakes and murderers and other things … the great black spiders that come at night and the horrible men.'

'He'll get me if I tell,' Tom said.

'I'll get you if you don't' Lorna felt sick at this bullying. 'Tell me quickly.'

'He'll get me!' Tom's voice rose into a shriek that had Sergeant Caswell opening the door and barging in.

'Here! None of that!' He said. 'I'll have none of that bully-ragging of my prisoner. You leave that young lad alone, Miss Buchanan!'

Lorna felt a surge of affection for the sergeant. 'Oh, he's in no danger from me, Sergeant. Yet. If you could give me another five minutes alone with him, it may be to everybody's advantage.'

'If you say so, Miss Buchanan,' Sergeant Caswell sounded doubtful. 'But no bully-ragging, right? I don't hold to that sort of thing with the young-uns. I've got a son myself.'

Lorna touched his arm. 'It's all right Sergeant. It's all for the best, believe me.'

'All right then,' Caswell withdrew. 'I'm watching you!'

'There; just you and me, Tom, and you were about to tell me who this man is that scares you.'

'He'll get me if I tell,' Tom looked through a gap in his fingers.

'Not if I can help it,' Lorna said. 'Did he make you break into my room?'

Tom hesitated and then nodded.

'Did he make you break into any other room in the hotel? Or just mine.'

Another hesitation. 'Just yours.'

'All right,' Lorna said. 'Did the man tell you what to steal or what to look for?'

Tom closed his hands again.

'Come on; tell me. You're doing well so far. If you help me, I can help you. Did the man tell you what to steal?'

'Yes.' Tom's voice was very small.

'Good boy. What did this man tell you to steal?'

'Money.' Tom said.

That was not the answer that Lorna had expected. 'Money? I haven't got much of that. Are you sure? What exactly did he say?'

Tom's hands parted again, and one tear-bright eye peered out. 'Don't tell him I said.'

'I promise you that I won't tell him,' Lorna said.

'He said I was to look for a silver coin,' Tom said. 'And any other money I found I could keep.'

'A silver coin was it? What sort of silver coin.'

Tom shrugged. 'I dunno. He said I was to bring him a silver coin and all the rest I found was mine, even golden boys.'

Lorna nodded. A golden boy was the slang word for a golden sovereign. The mysterious man who had sent Tom was not interested in her meagre fortune then but only in silver coins. That could only indicate the single silver coin she had found in the hand of David Hughes, the dead navigator and which Mr Temple had assured her had virtually no intrinsic value.

'Thank you, Tom. Now only a few more questions. What was this man like?'

'If I say...'

'I know; he'll get you.' Lorna leaned closer and put an edge to her voice. 'What was he like, Tom?'

'Horrible,' Tom blurted out suddenly. 'He says he's my uncle, but he's not! He just stays in Malvern to rob people. He does the taking of the waters thing at the hotel and then talks to people and finds out who's got money.' Tom closed his mouth with a snap as he realised how much he had said.

'Three more questions,' Lorna pressed her advantage. 'Where does he take the waters, what's his name and what does he looks like?'

Tom shook his head. 'He's in the Sceptre but I dunno his name,' he said. 'I get to call him Uncle Charlie, but he's not my real uncle.'

'All right; that's a start.' Lorna said. 'What does he look like? Can you describe him to me? Is he tall? Taller than me?'

'A bit,' Tom said. 'Not much.'

'Old? Young? In between?'

'He was in between.' Tom's answers came slowly as if Lorna was dragging them from his brain with a pair of blunt tongs.

'Dark hair? Fair hair?'

'Dark hair.'

Word by word Lorna built up a picture of the man who had tried to rob her of her single ancient coin. He was a tall man with a big smile and a loud laugh, dark hair and a hard hand. By the time she finished, Tom was drained and limp, huddled on the bed with a tear-stained face and a faint voice.

'Was Uncle Charlie always alone?'

'No. He sometimes has his pals with him.'

'How many?'

'Two.'

'So there are three altogether.'

Tom counted on his fingers. 'Yes.'

'Three men; Thank you, Tom.' Lorna stood up.

'What was all that about?' Caswell asked when Lorna eventually emerged.

'I'm not sure yet,' Lorna said truthfully. 'When I find out I will let you know. I may be a step further forward, or I could be walking into a dead-end.' Lorna thought for a moment. 'Has young Tom seen Wilce?'

Caswell frowned. 'Not that I know of,' he said. 'The cells can't connect to each other. Why?'

'Can I borrow him for a minute? You can come too of course.'

'None of your ragging,' Sergeant Caswell said. 'Your young rascal's had enough for the day.'

'You'll be with me to make sure I'm as gentle as a dove.' Lorna promised.

With the sergeant a bemused spectator, Lorna took Tom to the door of Wilce's cell and opened the spy hole.

'Look through here,' Lorna said, 'and tell me who you see.'

Even on his tip-toes, Tom could not reach the spy-hole, so Caswell lifted him, quickly but gently. 'Well?'

'A man lying on his bed,' Tom said.

'Is that all?' Lorna said.

'Yes.' A small voice.

'Is that the man you called Uncle Charlie?'

'No!' Tom shook his head rapidly at a question he evidently considered to be stupid.

'Do you know him?' Lorna asked.

'No; who is he? I never saw him before in my life.'

'Thank you, Tom,' Lorna said. 'You can get back to your cell now. Come on,' she took his hand out of instinct, 'I'll take you.'

'How was the nipper?' Caswell asked when they returned to the office.

'Terrified and utterly filthy.' Lorna scratched at her leg. Something had undoubtedly bitten her in that cell; she needed a change of clothes and a long hot bath as quickly as possible. 'Could you oblige me with something Sergeant?'

Caswell raised his eyebrows. 'That would depend on what it is, Miss Buchanan.'

'Could the charge against Tom be dropped? He was most helpful to me, and I know he is terrified of a man he calls Uncle Charlie.'

'He is a thieving little tyke,' Caswell said.

'Of that, I have no doubt,' Lorna agreed. Fishing in her purse, she produced five shillings. 'If you get him bathed and cleaned up and give him this, he may keep out of trouble for a few days.'

'I can't make any promises,' Caswell said and sighed. 'I'll see what I can do.'

Lorna smiled. 'You're a good man, Sergeant. Oh,' she stopped as a sudden thought came to her. 'Did you or your constables search the navigator's huts after Mr Findhorn's death?'

'We did that, Miss Buchanan,' the sergeant said. 'And a rough time we had of it, too.'

'Did you find anything of Mr Findhorn's?'

'Not a blessed thing,' Caswell said.

'How about a round box, or any silver coins?' Lorna asked.

'The navvies don't hold money for long, Miss Buchanan. They spend as soon as they get paid, except for the few pennies their wives get a hold of.'

'Thank you, Sergeant.' Lorna had been concerned that the single silver coin she had found in David Hugh's hand could have come from Findhorn. Now she was convinced it had not. Hughes had picked it up in the tunnel itself.

Chapter Seventeen

'So Margaret, we may be a little further forward, or we could be chasing our tails.' Lorna sat back in her chair. Since the attempted burglary she ensured the door was kept locked and had Gibson fit an internal bolt. With the shutters folded back, late afternoon sunshine streamed through the eight glass window panes.

Margaret gave a little smile. 'You found out a lot.'

'Wilce said that Findhorn had some good news of some sort shortly before he was murdered.'

'Good news?'

'Apparently so,' Lorna sipped at her tea. 'Wilce said it was like he had found a bottle of rum. Drink seems to be the common currency of the navigators. Now, what would make Findhorn happy?'

'I have no idea,' Margaret said.

'We'll think about that,' Lorna said. 'Let's see what else we have. We know that Susan saw three men on the hill the day she found the clothes, and young Tom said the man who sent him here had two companions.' Lorna said. 'It may be a complete coincidence of course.'

'What does that word mean?' Margaret asked. 'Coincidence?'

'Oh – coincidence. It means that the three men in both cases may not be connected.'

'How about the ghost?' Margaret asked. 'You said that Susan saw the ghost as well. I think that's the druid.'

Lorna nodded. 'We now have two avenues to follow. We have your druid, or ghost or whatever it is, and we may have these three men: Uncle Charlie and his two friends.'

'Green cord, a man drowned naked, the witch and her Chosen Girls and a ghost seen nearby.' Margaret said. 'Miss Appleton is the murderer. I thought you were going to tell Sergeant what's-his-name to arrest her.'

'I was,' Lorna said truthfully, 'until I heard about Uncle Charlie. Miss Appleton is certainly not Uncle Charlie.'

'It's still Miss Appleton.' For the first time since Lorna had known her, Margaret sounded sulky.

'Why?' Lorna asked. 'Tell me exactly why you think that.'

'For the fertility well,' Margaret said. 'She wants to make sure her Chosen Girls make babies. Why would the three men kill Mr Findhorn?'

'Now that I do not know,' Lorna said. 'However, I think that this...' she produced the ancient silver coin, 'has something to do with it.'

'Mr Findhorn did not have that,' Margaret said.

'I know,' Lorna agreed. 'I have this, and Uncle Charlie and his friends wanted it. That is all I have to go on, and it's not much at all.'

'It's Miss Appleton and the druids,' Margaret insisted.

'You might still be right,' Lorna sighed. 'You might well be right; but in that case, where do

Uncle Charlie and his friends fit in? All right,' she said. 'We are going to go our separate ways.'

Margaret's face fell. 'No!' She stood up. 'I don't want to leave you!'

'You're not *leaving* me,' Lorna soothed her. 'I don't mean that. I mean that I am going to find out about Uncle Charlie and his friends, and you are going to read books.'

'Read books?' Margaret looked astonished as if Lorna had insulted her. 'I hate reading books.'

'Find out about druids, sacred wells and everything else you can,' Lorna said. 'Until we know more, we are struggling in the dark.'

'Where can I find books about that sort of thing?'

'Ask the prior,' Lorna said. 'He'll either have some books or will know where they are. I'll come with you.'

'Yes, Miss,' Margaret sounded happier. 'How are you going to find out about Uncle Charlie?'

'Oh very easy,' Lorna decided to shock Margaret some more. 'Young Tom told me that he takes the waters at the Sceptre.' She smiled. 'I am going to talk to some naked men.' She enjoyed

Margaret's open- mouthed astonishment. 'And I know a way that you can help if you are willing.'

Margaret flushed bright scarlet.

'Are you willing?'

'You know I am, Miss,' Margaret said.

'Well then.' Lorna's plan came fully formed into her head. 'We have some research to do first. Listen well.'

Margaret's mouth opened even wider as Lorna outlined her plans. 'You're a one, Miss, you really are.'

Lorna smiled. 'Let's get started then.'

Margaret's giggles echoed around the hotel room. 'You look very handsome, Miss.'

Lorna assumed a pose before the largest mirror the hotel had to offer. 'Thank you.' That was not quite right. She deepened her voice. 'Thank you,' she said gruffly.

'It's lucky that you're taller than lots of men,' Margaret said.

Lorna grunted in a most unladylike manner. 'My height has caused me all sorts of trouble throughout my life,' she said. 'This is the first time it has ever come in useful.'

Margaret's giggle reminded Lorna how young she was.

'What about your hair?' Margaret asked.

Sighing, Lorna ran a hand through her long auburn hair. 'I rather like my hair,' she said. 'I can either cut it short or pile it up and squeeze it under a hat.'

'Do the attendants at the Water Cure wear hats?' Margaret asked.

'The men in the Sceptre Hotel wear a sort of Scotch bonnet,' Lorna held one up and crammed it on top of her head. 'How does it look?'

'Crowded,' Margaret said. Reaching forward, she tucked Lorna's hair gently into place and adjusted the hat. 'Are you sure you want to go through with this?' Margaret stepped back. 'You're very brave.' She turned her head from side to side. 'That's much better now.'

Lorna could not restrain her smile. 'It will be interesting,' she said.

'You make a good man,' Margaret said. She looked Lorna up and down. 'Very handsome.' She repressed her laughter. 'What does it feel like to wear trousers?'

Lorna lifted her right leg and flexed it in the air. 'Quite nice', she said. 'It's very liberating really. I might get to like it.'

Margaret laughed again. 'They're a bit tight around ...' She pointed without speaking.

'They're tight around my hips,' Lorna smiled and ran her hands down her flanks, over her hips and down the outside of her thighs. 'Do those parts look too feminine?' She grinned with pure mischief. 'Maybe I should stuff something down there?'

'Oh Miss! You're terrible!' Red- faced Margaret said, stifling her laughter with her hand. 'No; you look very fetching,' she said. 'If you keep your hair hidden and maybe grow side whiskers and a moustache.'

'I can't do that.'

'I can draw a moustache on you if you like,' Margaret said. 'Sit down, Miss.'

'Now you know what you have to do to help?' Lorna asked.

'Yes, Miss ... Sit still, Miss! I nearly drew a moustache right up your nose!' Margaret narrowed her eyes in concentration as she continued her work.

'Your part in this is vital,' Lorna said.

'Yes, Miss,' Margaret said, drawing slowly. 'There; how's that?'

Lorna looked into the mirror to see her face adorned with a carefully drawn if thin, moustache. 'That's very lifelike.'

'Now your hair.' Margaret said. 'I'll do something with it.' She began to work on it until Lorna noticed the time.

'It will have to do,' she said. 'We have to leave.'

The reception clerk looked up as Lorna and Margaret passed, nodded acknowledgement and said nothing.

'He thinks I am a man and wonders how I got in,' Lorna said. 'That's the first test passed.' Her smile was more confident than she felt. 'There are far sterner ordeals ahead.'

'I hope young Tom wasn't drawing the longbow,' Margaret said. 'If he was, and your Uncle Charlie man is not there, I'll kick his bum so hard he won't know if it's Sunday or Christmas!'

'I checked, remember?' Lorna said gently. 'So there'll be no need for any bottom kicking.'

Margaret nodded doubtfully. 'If you say so, Miss. It would do the little devil good, though.'

'Of that, I have no doubt,' Lorna agreed. 'And you would enjoy it, too.'

Lorna had parted with a shilling to a donkey woman in exchange for information. The woman could not be entirely sure but believed that there was indeed a group of three men who met the description at the Sceptre Hotel in Wells Road, and one absolutely tallied with Tom's description of Uncle Charlie. With that knowledge tucked in her head, Lorna and Margaret had discussed their way forward. Now they walked the short distance to the side door of the Sceptre and waited for the next stage of their plan.

'Here he comes now,' Lorna felt her nerves beginning to tighten. Suddenly this did not seem like such a good idea. 'Are you sure, Margaret?'

'Stop asking me that,' Margaret whispered. She stepped forward as the young man approached.

'William!' Margaret put out her hand. 'I hoped you would be here!'

He was medium height with mobile eyes and a face disfigured with acne. 'Margaret; what are you doing here so early?'

'I've come to see you,' Margaret said.

'I have to go to work...' William said. 'It's my first day as a bath attendant.'

'I know,' Margaret said brightly.

'I'll take your place for today,' Lorna said gruffly. 'You two enjoy yourselves.' She slipped into the Sceptre before William could protest. A glance over her shoulder saw Margaret taking hold of William's arm as if they were old friends and guiding him toward the hills. It may not be in the most respectable taste, and it certainly would not be accepted in Malvern's polite company, but it cleared a space for her, and she knew Margaret could be trusted.

'Take care, Margaret,' Lorna breathed and then she had her own worries. She was sure that Margaret could look after her particular friend. She stepped inside the hotel and looked around.

'Are you William Griggs?' The supervisor was broad, tall and red-faced, with mutton-chop whiskers.

'Yes,' Lorna kept her face in the shadows as much as possible.

'I'm Mr Broadheath,' the man said. 'You call me Sir.'

'Yes, Sir,' Lorna resolved to give Mr Broad-heath as little trouble as possible.

Broadheath fished a silver watch from his waistcoat and glanced at the face. 'It's quarter from five,' he said and flamboyantly replaced the watch. 'At five you go to rooms six and seven. Wake up the gentlemen there, open the curtains, shutters and the windows; wide open remember, and ensure the gentlemen are out of bed. I will be there at quarter past the hour.'

'Yes, Sir,' Lorna said. That seemed easy enough. She hoped that she had chosen the correct hotel and the correct rooms. She also hoped that she had time to talk to the men without Mr Broadheath being present.

'There's the key,' Broadheath handed it over.

Rooms six and seven were on the first floor, side by side. Lorna hesitated for only a moment, took a deep breath and inserted the key, turned and walked in.

'Good morning gentlemen,' she walked quickly past the twin beds and opened the curtains and shutters as Broadheath had in-structed her. The room was stuffy, with both men still asleep in their narrow beds until she unfastened the window catch and pulled up the lower sash.

'I'll be back in a moment,' she said lightly.

That was the first time in her life that she had walked into a man's bedroom. Ten seconds later she entered the room next door.

'Good morning.' The room's occupant sat on the bed, perusing a newspaper. The curtains were already open so grey morning light augmented the yellow flicker of twin candles. 'You'll be the bath attendant.'

'Yes, Sir,' Lorna said.

The man stood up. He was tall, dark- haired and quite good looking. 'Thank goodness for some politeness.' His smile was friendly. 'The fellow who was here yesterday ordered me around as if I was his servant.'

'I won't do that, Sir,' Lorna busied herself fastening the shutters in place.

'I'm glad to hear it. Is it the same drill?'

'Yes, Sir,' Lorna felt even more nervous than she had expected. 'Mr Broadheath will be along in a minute, Sir.'

'There's no need to wait for him. Open the window; there's a good chap. I'll get the bed stripped.'

When Lorna turned back, the dark-haired man was stark naked and hauling the sheets from the bed.

The naked man looked around. 'There we are then, all set. 'What name shall I call you?'

'William, Sir,' Lorna had to force the words out. Talking about being alone in a room with naked men and the actuality of confronting them were two different things. She could not help the direction of her gaze.

'I am Charles Weaver,' the naked man held out his hand.

'Good heavens,' Lorna said at the frank admission of his first name. Despite herself, she added. 'You don't look in the least overweight, Sir.' She clamped her mouth shut.

'Come on man! Shake; I've no truck with this nonsense that servants and gentlemen can't converse.'

Hesitant, Lorna took his hand. It was firm and strong. 'Thank you, Sir.'

'Nonsense; grip man!'

Lorna squeezed tighter, suddenly glad that she had not had a conventional upbringing, so she was used to working with horses, guns, and tools. Her hands were stronger than most women. She altered the direction of her gaze upward to meet his bright blue eyes.

'That's the way man.'

Broadheath walked in. 'All ready? Here!' He threw a pair of blankets to Lorna. 'Put these over the mattress.'

That was easy enough, and she folded over a damply cold sheet next.

'On you go, Sir,' Broadheath said, and Weaver slid onto the wet sheet and lay face up, grinning at them.

Lorna averted her gaze as Broadheath wrapped the sheet tightly around Weaver's body, tucking it carefully under his chin. 'This is called packing' Broadheath said, putting both blankets on top. 'Go to that cupboard and get out the eiderdowns.'

Lorna hurried to obey and covered Weaver's cocooned body.

'Now this,' Broadheath produced a hot water pig and placed it at Weaver's feet. 'Now we leave you alone, Mr Weaver. As you will be aware, the coldness will encourage your blood to withdraw inwards to your vital organs. Within a few moments your body will create a layer of warmth between the cold and anything important, so you'll warm up soon.'

'Oh I'll jog along fine,' Weaver said. 'You fellows carry on with whatever you have to do.'

'We'll do that, Sir.' Broadheath said. 'Come along William; we have other gentlemen to attend. We'll return within the hour, Mr Weaver.'

The men in room six were still in bed when Broadheath and Lorna entered. 'Come along gentlemen,' Broadheath clapped his hands sharply. 'Up you get.' He lowered his voice. 'Take Mr Spalding; he's the one on the left.'

'What do I do?' Lorna asked.

'Copy me,' Broadheath walked to the bed on the right and without hesitation grabbed hold of the mattress and tipped it up. 'Up you get Mr Pickering!'

'Oh, Heavens!' Lorna saw Spalding staring at her through suddenly wide eyes.

'I'll get up!' Spalding said as Pickering sprawled face down on the floor with his flannel nightgown rucked high up his thighs and his hair a tousled explosion. He scrambled up, swearing loudly.

'Good man,' Broadheath said. 'Now we can get on with things.'

'Yes, Sir,' Lorna said. She hid her frustration; she had hoped for time alone with these invalids to question them. It seemed that Broadheath was intent on dogging her wherever she worked.

'Come along gentlemen, and we'll get you all tucked in!' Broadheath said. 'You know what to do, now!' He nodded to Lorna. 'You take care of Mr Spalding's bed, William, and I'll take Mr Pickering's.'

With both men safely packed on their respective beds, Broadheath nodded to Lorna. 'Now we get ourselves some breakfast' he said with a wink. 'Real food; none of that rabbit food that we feed to these poor invalids.'

'Rabbit food?' Lorna asked.

'Oh yes, the poor devils have to make do with miserable fare in the Sceptre. They pay a small fortune for the privilege of being soaked, sponged, douched and exercised.' Broadheath grinned. 'So all the more for us, William!'

Lorna stared at the thick mutton with gravy and peas that filled her plate.

'Go on William; eat up!' Broadheath bit into his mutton and continued to talk. 'You're not a local man are you?'

'No, Sir.' Lorna shook his head.

'What brought you to this job?' Broadheath's eyes were as dark as his hair. 'It's not everybody's choice, pampering fat old London aldermen, bilious barristers and such like who have spent half their life in gluttony and sloth.'

'It's a job,' Lorna said carefully. 'It's better than some.'

Broadheath swallowed noisily and took another bite. 'You'll start off polite and smiling,' he said. 'As I did, but after a few months you will grow to dislike the fat sows wallowing in their lard while expecting better men to run after them.'

Lorna nodded. 'That may happen,' she agreed.

'Where are you from, William?'

'London, Sir.' Lorna picked somewhere vast and impersonal.

'You'd be better staying there,' Broadheath said. 'I'm surprised you couldn't get a job in London town.'

Lorna cursed herself for that slip. 'I wanted to work in the country,' she said quickly. 'I like walking, and these hills are very inviting.'

'Oh?' Broadheath looked up, his eyes suspicious. 'Are you another of these health idiots? Or do you have another reason?'

'I just like to walk,' Lorna said. She heard her voice alter and deliberately deepened it. 'What other reason could I have?'

Broadheath was frowning. 'I don't know. There are all sorts of queer stories around here. I hope you don't believe any of them.' He gave a sour, humourless grin. 'Or not all of them.'

'I haven't heard any stories,' Lorna said. 'Except that there are ghosts or witches or something that prance about some of the wells.'

Broadheath's smile was more genuine as the suspicion died away. 'Oh, that old chestnut.' He shook his head. 'I've heard the tales as well. I've heard all sorts of rubbish about sacred wells and druids.' He laid his knife and fork down and swallowed. 'Some of it may be true.'

'Are you a local man?' Lorna wondered how long it would be before she could return to Mr Weaver. Charles Weaver... Uncle Charlie? Good Heavens, he was tall and dark ... And handsome. And might well be a murderer.

'I am from West Malvern,' Broadheath said. 'What did you hear about the witches and things?'

'Oh?' Lorna's mind was racing as she thought of Charles Weaver. 'Oh just that there are some druids or some such that use the old sacred well. Alfred, I think it was called.'

'Alfreck. What about them?' Broadheath asked.

Lorna shrugged, wishing Broadheath would leave her alone to think. 'There was something about the murder of poor Mr Findhorn.'

'I heard that,' Broadheath suddenly sounded quite excited. 'The druids or witches sacrificed him.'

'That's right,' Lorna said. 'That's what I heard.'

Broadheath shook his head. 'I am nearly scared to go up there, what with the navvies running wild with their randies and drinking and these druids murdering people.'

'You don't look the sort of man to be scared of anything,' Lorna tried sugary praise. 'You weren't up there when Mr Findhorn was murdered were you?'

'No!' Broadheath said sharply.

'That was fortunate,' Lorna said. 'I wondered if you had seen these druid people.'

Broadheath pushed his empty plate away. 'I'll tell you what I heard, William. I heard that a gaggle of women murdered Findhorn and that also scares me.' He stood up. 'Come on; it's time we got these fat invalids unwrapped and douched.' He gave a small smile. 'I'll do the first and leave you to the rest. This next part of the process is my favourite, William. I make them yell ... You'll soon see why!'

'Shall I take Mr Weaver?' Lorna asked. She did not care much for the idea of being alone with an unclad man, but if her disguise held, she should be safe enough.

'Can you manage him on your own?'

'He seems to know exactly what to do,' Lorna said. 'He can guide me.'

'You unwrap him and take him into the shower room for a cold douche.' Broadheath said.

'There are two types: descending douche or ascending.' He grinned. 'For the ascending, they sit down, and the water rushes up … and reaches all sorts of places.'

'Quite.' Lorna tried not to blush.

'Most choose the descending douche,' Broadheath said. 'I like it when they are new and don't know what to expect.'

'I can imagine it's a shock to the system,' Lorna said.

'The newcomers choose the shallow bath,' Broadheath said. 'Your Mr Weaver is an old hand.' He nodded. 'Off you go then, William.'

Suddenly wondering what she had let herself in for; Lorna left Broadheath and returned to Weaver's room.

'Welcome back,' Weaver greeted her with a smile. 'I'm sorry that I can't get up to greet you, but I'm a little tied up here.'

'You are indeed,' Lorna agreed. 'Not for long. I'll have you unwrapped in a minute and pop you into the shower: unless you wish the shallow bath?'

'Oh God no!' Weaver said. 'It's the descending douche for me! There's nothing quite so revitalising as gallons of freezing cold water dropping on one's body from a great height.'

For all her nervousness, Lorna did not have to force a smile. She rather liked this cheerful man, potential murderer or not. 'Have you been in Great Malvern long, Mr Weaver?' She began to peel back his covers.

'This is my second week here,' Weaver said. 'The second week of my third visit.'

'You must like it then,' Lorna nearly forgot to deepen her voice. She pulled off the final sheet, and Mr Weaver lay there in all his quite- impressive glory. 'Up you get, Sir, and we'll have you in the shower right away.'

Weaver took his time in rising, stretched and smiled again. He patted his stomach. 'You can see why I am here,' he said. 'Fat.'

'Hardly at all, Sir,' Lorna said. 'Did you hear about that terrible affair on the Herefordshire Beacon, Sir?'

'Johnny Findhorn's murder?' Weaver nodded. 'Yes, I know about it.'

Lorna tried to look away without being obvious. Interviewing a naked man was most distracting and much harder than she had thought. 'I hope you were not near the place, Sir.'

'Me?' Weaver shook his head. 'Oh no. I stay in the hotel in the dark hours. I have sufficient exercise during the day not to wish to walk all through the night as well.'

The shower room was a short walk, and when Lorna stared at the mechanism in dismay, Weaver smiled and showed her how it worked. 'Just pull that lever when I am inside and watch the fun.' He indicated a strange contraption of wooden slats above a sinister cave-like hole beside the shower. 'That is the ascending douche. I tried that once!' his laugh was open and hearty. 'Never again. I recommend it for murderers and the like but not for Christian gentlemen.'

Lorna tried to join in his laughter.

'I should not be laughing so soon after Johnny's death,' Weaver said, 'but I can't bring him back. Poor chap; he was a good friend of mine.'

'You knew him, Sir?' For the first time, Lorna could ignore Weaver's nakedness as she asked the question.

'Oh indeed. I employed the poor fellow.' Weaver shook his head as he stepped inside the shower cubicle. 'He was devoted to his family; quite devoted.' He glanced up at the tank of water with the nozzle that was suspended above his head, gripped the supporting rail firmly and smiled again. 'Ready when you are!'

Lorna took a deep breath and pulled the lever. There was a short pause, and then the nozzle unleashed a majestic deluge of cold water onto Weaver's naked body. He roared, gasping, and leapt out of the cubicle, flapping his arms and jumping around in a manner that Lorna found both distracting and entertaining in equal measures.

'Wow, that's cold.' He hopped on one leg. 'Oh sugar me all over!'

'Are you all right, Sir?' Lorna reached for one of the towels that she had draped over a metal rail.

'All right? Oh, that's the ticket! Oh, I'm going back inside young fellow. When it fills up, you just pull that lever! Oh, sugar!'

Weaver stepped back inside, blowing and slapping at himself. 'Oh, sugar that's cold! Sugar; sugar; sugar!'

'As long as you're all right, Sir.' Lorna was grinning at the antics of this naked man who was so open. *He may be a murderer*; she reminded herself. Oh, dear, God! She heard the water in the tank refilling itself, or perhaps some servant was busy with pails of water, she neither knew nor cared which.

'Oh, I'm all right, William.' Weaver blew again, dancing around disconcertingly. 'Yes, poor old Johnny Findhorn. He was always struggling for blunt you know, always doing without to benefit his family so when he came to me for a position I was only too pleased to oblige.'

'He came to you for a position, Sir?' Lorna heard the water above slow to a trickle and hoped she could find out a little more about Findhorn before she pulled the douche lever again.

'That's right,' Weaver gave a little shiver. 'I'm a shareholder in the Worcester and Herefordshire railway you see, so I can pull a few strings when needed.'

'Were you very friendly with him, Sir?'

'I've known him for years,' Weaver said. 'He was at Rugby with my pater so I had to give him a hand up when I could.' He glanced upward as the sound of water eased to a few final drips. 'He was like an uncle. Poor chap always had the worst of luck, and then he has that find and then...' He stopped. 'I wasn't meant to say that.'

'To say what?' Lorna asked. 'You weren't meant to tell me about Findhorn's find?' She felt the tension even as she forced herself to sound relaxed. She thought desperately, remembering the dust-free patch in Findhorn's hut. 'I did not know it was a secret.'

'You knew about it?'

Lorna nodded. 'I knew he found something.'

'Not enough to make him rich,' Weaver said. 'He was hoping to find more.' He looked upward. 'Ready, William!'

Lorna pulled the lever and the water hammered down on Weaver's unprotected head and body.

'Oh! Sugar, sugar, sugar!' Weaver rushed from the cubicle again, to dance as he had before, one leg in the air and the other shaking around. 'Sugar; sugar!'

Lorna watched, unable to repress her smile. 'That's enough of that, I think.' Taking a towel, it felt nearly natural to wrap it around Weaver and help him rub himself dry.

'Now that is over; you better have some breakfast. You will be going up the hills very shortly, Sir.'

'That's right; a bite to eat and then a tour of the wells, starting at St Ann's and working our way around as many as we can, drinking a glass of pure water at each. I'll be sloshing by the time I'm halfway around.' He took the towel. 'I can do that myself, thank you. I'm not an invalid.'

'Yes, of course, Sir.' Lorna stepped back.

'I'm *not* an invalid, you know,' Weaver said. 'You may have guessed that I am not entirely one of these podgy parties seeking to improve my health.'

'No, Sir,' Lorna said. 'You must have another reason to visit Malvern.'

Weaver nodded. 'The first time I was looking for the best place for the tunnel; the second time

I came for the camaraderie.' He grinned. 'There's quite a brotherly feeling in the Sceptre you see.'

'Yes, Sir,' Lorna remembered entering the Officer's Mess as a young child. Men together could be quite civilised. As a young woman, the atmosphere had been entirely different.

'You'd better avoid the mess in future,' her mother had taken her aside. 'You are causing quite a stir.'

'A stir? Why mother? Most of these men have known me all my life.'

'You're no longer a little girl,' her mother had said. 'You're quite grown up now. Some of the young men may get … The wrong idea.'

'Oh,' Lorna looked down at herself. There was not much to see up top, but she was quite aware of other changes. 'Yes, mother.'

Growing up among so many men had introduced her to many things, yet her parents had sheltered her from others.

Weaver rubbed at himself with the towel, wholly unconcerned at his state of undress. 'Naturally, the instant that Findhorn told me what he had found I made a few inquiries and dashed right over to see if I could find some myself.'

Unable to resist temptation any longer, Lorna asked. 'What did he find, Sir?'

'Did I not tell you?' Weaver sounded surprised. Dropping the towel on the floor, he began to dress.

Lorna kept her attention on his face and words. 'Not yet,' she said.

Weaver dropped his voice to a whisper as if somebody had crept into the water tank above and was listening to every word. 'Money,' he said. 'Findhorn found a jug full of silver coins.'

A jug: that would explain the circular space in the dust.

Weaver's grin made him look like a mischievous schoolboy. 'Pirate treasure!'

'Pirate treasure?' Lorna tried not to laugh. 'There are no pirates here; we are miles from the sea.'

'Well, maybe not pirate. At least not Captain Kidd or Blackbeard, but some kind of treasure anyway. These hills are filled with it.'

Lorna leaned against the wall. Treasure. Mr Findhorn had found treasure. Putting her hand inside her pocket, she fingered the silver coin she had retrieved from the dead navigator. *Keep calm.* 'I wish I could find some,' she said.

'You have to look,' Weaver said. 'I'm going to get the lie of the land and then walk the hills until I have to get back to business.' He was smiling again, excited at the prospect. 'I don't need the tin of course, but it's the fun of the thing. Imagine digging up buried treasure in the heart of old England!'

'What makes you think that there's more?' Lorna asked. 'Maybe Mr Findhorn found it all.'

'No no,' Weaver began to slip his coat on, with Lorna politely holding it for him. 'He only found a few dozen coins. There are more; why, back in '47 somebody found three hundred Roman coins in an earthenware jug, and only two years later, right on top of the Worcestershire Beacon they found the grave of a British king.'

'I did not know that,' Lorna said.

'Oh yes,' Weaver said. 'These hills are full of history and treasure.' He spoke seriously now. 'London and the Exchange are fine, but there's nothing more invigorating than the great douche followed by a walk up the hills looking for treasure. You meet all sort of chaps you know; splendid fellows. And chapesses too, if you see what I mean,' he gave an elaborate wink and a dig of his elbow. 'You know what I mean, old boy, lonely widows and the occasional looker if one is fortunate.'

'I see.' For some reason, Lorna felt a twist of anger at the thought of her naked Mr Weaver meeting a lonely widow. Suddenly she wished she could place him on the ascending douche and ensure the water was icy-cold and at full pressure. She nodded. Oh yes; *full* pressure and she would hold him down to ensure he got the full benefit of the coldest water in exactly the right place. That should sort his concupiscence for a while.

'One lives in hope,' Weaver had not noticed Lorna's sudden change in attitude. 'One can't be alone all one's life, however much fun one has and if I give a hint that I am searching for treasure... well, that adds a dash of romance, don't you know?'

'Indeed, Sir,' Lorna said. 'Are you going back inside for a third douche Sir? Or perhaps try the ascending douche again now you know what to expect?' She kept her voice innocent even as a succession of colourful images flitted through her mind.

'Perhaps next time. I'd better toddle along,' Weaver said, 'I have to get fit, don't you know. In case I meet a needy widow.' He winked, twirled his whiskers with an elegant forefinger, and stepped outside.

Lorna watched him leave. She was not one whit further forward with her quest for the murderer, but she may be a step closer to the robbery of Findhorn's hut. She shook her head; they might not even be connected.

'William...' Broadheath stepped in, 'where the devil have you been? And what's wrong with your moustache?'

'My moustache?' Lorna put a hand to her upper lip. It was damp where the water from the douche had splashed her.

'It's fading away!' Broadheath gave a great roar of laughter. 'You've pencilled it on, haven't you?' He gave Lorna a hearty slap on the back that nearly knocked her over. 'You can't grow one yet!'

'No, Sir, I can't,' Lorna admitted. 'I thought it would make me look older.'

'Well, now my lad!' Broadheath was obviously highly amused. 'We can't have that, can we?' He slapped her back again. 'We all have to grow up, Will. It'll come; don't you worry lad; it will come.'

'Yes, Sir,' Lorna said.

'Come on lad; wipe it away. We have things to do.'

Chapter Eighteen

Now Lorna had a great deal to think about. Treasure on the Malvern Hills? She shook her head as she walked away from the Pinnacle Hotel. If that was true, and Mr Findhorn had found something, it would explain why he was robbed and perhaps even why he was murdered, but not the method. Why would anybody go to the trouble of stripping him and tying him with green cord? Lorna shook her head as she made her way back to her own hotel.

There must be more to this. Lorna heard the frantic drumbeat of galloping hooves and looked up as Mad Jack clattered past with his mane of hair flowing behind him. She watched him for a second and returned to her thoughts.

Who would know about treasure being found? It can't have been widely reported, or Margaret would have heard about it.

Mr Temple would know. He was the local expert. Why had he not mentioned it before? Lorna shook her head: why *should* Temple mention it? She had not asked, and men like Temple would not give away their secrets in case somebody else got there first. Lorna resolved to go there as soon as she changed out of her male attire.

Margaret was waiting for her in the hotel room. She looked up right away. 'You look a bit rough, and you've lost your moustache.'

Lorna put a hand to her upper lip. 'How did you get on with William?'

'Very well,' Margaret smiled. 'Very well indeed.'

'I hope you have not done anything you'll regret later,' Lorna was suddenly concerned. 'You'll be ruined for life.'

'No! Of course not! I'm not that sort of girl.' Margaret looked genuinely angry.

Lorna nodded. 'Good girl. I thought not. I did not mean to insult you,' she said. 'Now I'll change out of these clothes, and we'll sit down, and I'll tell you all I've found out. Unless you wish to talk about William?'

Margaret shook her head violently. 'Not yet, Miss.'

'Lorna,' Lorna said quietly. 'Call me Lorna.'

'Yes, Miss. Lorna, Miss.'

They sat around the octagonal Spode Felspar tea-pot and two dainty china cups as Lorna related most of her experiences. She glossed over Charles Weaver, mentioning only the information he had provided.

Margaret listened intently. 'I never heard of any treasure,' she said. 'Not once. Roman coins and a dead king.' She shook her head. 'Well, I never did. She frowned. 'Miss,' she said.

'Lorna is better.'

'Yes, Miss; do you remember what that navigator said about Mr Findhorn? The one that was in the cell?'

'Mr Wilce.' Lorna reminded. 'He said that Findhorn looked happy; as if he had found a bottle of rum.'

'That's what I thought you had said, Miss. Now we know that it wasn't a bottle of rum he found. It was a treasure.'

Lorna nodded. 'It looks like it, Margaret. We don't know what kind of treasure but I would

333

hazard that it was either Roman or more of these.' She spun her silver coin in the air. 'Mr Weaver said he found a few dozen coins.'

Margaret caught the silver coin before it descended, and held it in her fist. She examined it again. 'A find worth a few pennies would not make much difference to a man with a big family,' Margaret said. 'He must have found an awful lot more than one coin. Mr Weaver said dozens. How many dozens?'

Lorna remembered the dust-free patch on Findhorn's desk. 'That must be it,' she said. 'That might well be it. Mr Findhorn found a jug of coins, and somebody murdered him for them.' She looked up, suddenly animated.

'Why?' Margaret said.

'What?' Lorna stopped in mid-stride. 'What do you mean?'

'Why murder him? Why not just steal the coins?' Margaret said. 'It's not as if he would have the treasure with him, is it? He would not walk around with his pockets stuffed full of gold and silver.'

Lorna sat down again. 'No; you're right. He would not.'

'Anyway, like I said Miss if the coins are only worth a few pennies, he'd have to dig up a whole lot before he was rich.' Margaret continued to dampen Lorna's enthusiasm. 'A few dozens at threepence each; say three dozen – that would be nine shillings, about three day's wages for a navigator.' She shook her head. 'It's not enough to murder for, Miss, unless Mr Temple got the value wrong.'

'Mr Temple was quite dismissive of the coin we showed him,' Lorna said. 'And he's the expert.'

'I didn't like him,' Margaret said. 'Why did he not tell us about the treasure? If anybody knew about it, he would.'

'That is a good point,' Lorna said. 'You're thinking well today, Margaret. Maybe he was worried that we might be after his antiquarian relics.'

'Maybe.' Margaret sounded doubtful.

Lorna sipped at her tea. 'I think we should have another word with Mr Temple. No,' she said. 'Perhaps not; not yet anyway. We'll find a numismatic somewhere and have him value our coin first. Get a second opinion.'

'A numis… what?' Margaret pushed the coin back to Lorna.

'A numismatic; that's an expert on coins,' Lorna said.

'I didn't know there were any,' Margaret said. 'What a queer sort of job to have. I've never met one in Malvern.'

'Oxford,' Lorna decided. 'We'll take the chariot to Oxford. That's the place to find one.'

'I never was so far away,' Margaret looked suddenly scared. 'I thought it was only the nobs that could go there.'

'You stick with me, Margaret,' Lorna patted her arm. 'You did well in Worcester; Oxford is only another town. Now; tell me all about William.' She smiled when Margaret coloured. 'I want all the details. Leave nothing unsaid.'

Chapter Nineteen

'Where did you find this, Miss Buchanan?' Professor Humphrey was around thirty years old and long- faced, with bushy side whiskers and bright eyes, nothing like the elderly professor that Lorna had expected. His room was bright and cheerful, with mirrors reflecting the light of half a dozen brass candlesticks and glass-fronted cases filled with scores of silver and gold coins.

'I found it on the Malvern Hills, Professor,' Lorna said.

'Near to the Roman finds?' Professor Humphrey turned his intense eyes on to her.

'It was in the new railway diggings,' Lorna said.

'Oh?' Humphrey looked surprised. 'Actually inside the diggings?'

'Yes, Professor.' Lorna said.

'That's very far down.' Professor Humphreys said. 'Was it under the ground there, or lying loose?' He examined the coin again. 'It still has dirt ingrained on the surface,' he said. 'It has certainly been under the ground for a long time.' He looked up again. 'Did you find it yourself?'

'No, Professor.' Lorna was slightly uncomfortable under the barrage of questions. She decided to turn the interview around. 'Could you put a value on it?'

Humphreys placed the coin on the table. 'Oh yes. As a historical artefact, it is quite invaluable of course. The ancient Britons were known to produce coins, but this is sharp and distinct. It's one of the best specimens I have ever seen.'

'Does it have any monetary value?' Lorna asked.

'Oh by George yes! Do you intend to sell it?' Humphrey asked. 'I would give you a fair price for it. A very fair price. Shall we say five sovereigns?'

'No, I don't wish to sell,' Lorna saw Margaret start at the value.

'That's a pity,' Humphrey said. 'A serious collector with deeper pockets than I possess would part with ten, maybe twenty guineas for a specimen such as this.' He rubbed a thumb across the face of the coin. 'I can write you a list of possible buyers if you wish.'

'How much?' Margaret had been awed into silence by the academic's presence. Now the mention of such a considerable sum of money, nearly six months wages for a labouring man, brought her out of her stupor.

'It could be as much as twenty guineas, Miss Smith.' The professor smiled at her. 'That would be enough to keep you in dresses and ribbons for quite some time.'

'Yes, Sir,' Margaret said.

'How much would such a serious collector give for many such coins?' Lorna asked.

'How many?' Humphrey asked quickly. 'Have you found more?'

'I haven't found any more.' Lorna said cautiously.

Humphrey's eyes were shrewd. 'But somebody has, I wager,' he said.

'Perhaps,' Lorna said. 'I am not sure.'

'I haven't heard of any such discoveries,' Humphrey said. 'If you do, I'd be obliged if you would tell me.'

'Would you be in a position to make such an offer?' Margaret asked quickly.

'Alas no,' Humphrey said. 'I lack the funds, I'm afraid. My interest is purely historical. Have you shown this coin,' he lifted it up, 'to Mr Richard Temple? He's the local antiquarian, you understand.'

'We did,' Lorna said.

Professor Humphrey raised his eyebrows. 'Just out of curiosity, what value did Temple put on it?'

'Mr Temple said it was not worth much,' Margaret said. 'He put it at threepence.'

'Now that does surprise me,' Humphrey said. 'He is usually very accurate about such things.'

'Thank you, Professor Humphreys,' Lorna said. 'You have been most helpful.'

'Twenty guineas!' Margaret repeated as soon as they stepped inside the chaise. 'If Mr Findhorn found three dozen at that price it would be...'

'Over seven hundred and twenty pounds,' Lorna said.

'A man could get murdered for that,' Margaret settled on the seat.

Lorna flicked the reins. 'He could,' she said. 'Where does that leave our druid theory?'

'Maybe the druids wanted the money for something?' Margaret said.

Lorna did not answer. Everything they discovered contradicted something else. Were all murders like this? She began to appreciate the difficult job that the police had.

The packet was waiting for Margaret at the hotel reception.

'Miss Smith?' The clerk smiled as she walked in.

'That is me,' Margaret glanced at Lorna as if asking for permission to admit to her own name.

'This was handed in for you, Ma'am.' The bald clerk handed over a small bouquet of daffodils, and a square box, together with a sealed note.

'Oh my goodness,' Margaret stepped back. 'They can't be for me?'

The clerk's smile was genuine. 'Yes, Ma'am. The young gentleman was most insistent that they were for you.' He lowered his voice. 'The young gentleman specifically stated that the packages were for Miss Smith's hands only,'

'Oh,' Margaret accepted the flowers and associated gifts gingerly as if afraid they would explode. 'Oh, my; thank you, Sir.' She glanced at Lorna as if expecting a rebuke.

'There is no need to thank me, Miss Smith.' The clerk said.

Nearly carrying her gifts at arm's length, Margaret walked to their room. 'I can't open these,' she said. She was trembling when she handed the note and box to Lorna.

'Yes you can, you silly,' Lorna felt a surge of affection for Margaret, who could be very mature and cynical one minute and so young and vulnerable the next. 'Go on; open them.' She took the flowers. 'I'll put these in water.'

Margaret's hands were shaking so violently that she had trouble breaking the wax seal of the note. Written in a laboured hand and on cheap paper, it was a simple message.

I hope we can meet again sometime. Your Friend William Griggs.

'It's from William,' Margaret held it out for Lorna's inspection.

'I rather thought it might be,' Lorna could not restrain her smile. 'What's in the box?'

Margaret was gasping for breath as she untied the ribbon and opened the lid of the box. 'It's jewellery,' she said. 'It's lovely!' She took out a handful of wood shavings and lifted a brooch in the shape of two intertwined hearts. 'Look.' She dashed away a tear. 'Nobody ever gave me nothing before.'

'Nobody ever gave me *anything* before,' Lorna corrected mechanically as she looked at the brooch. Made of cheap metal, it would have cost about two shillings, or three days wages for William; a lot of money for a working youth. The message was far more precious than the intrinsic value. 'It's beautiful' she said.

'Can I wear it, Miss?' Margaret asked.

'It's yours, Margaret,' Lorna said gently. 'You don't have to ask my permission to wear something of your own.'

'Oh,' Margaret said. 'Oh William.'

'I think you made an impression on that young man,' Lorna said.

'Oh Miss…' and Margaret began to cry.

Chapter Twenty

'So what do we have,' Lorna asked.

'A lot of confusion,' Margaret touched the brooch at her breast.

Lorna paced the room, stopping to look out of the window. 'I really don't know where to go from here,' she said. 'I didn't know that solving a murder would be so hard. I thought it would be a quick case of finding out who did not like Mr Findhorn and seeing where they were when he was killed. Anybody who had no alibi would be a suspect.'

'I still think it was the druids,' Margaret said.

'We'll get back to them later,' Lorna said. 'I have not forgotten Miss Appleton, the Chosen Girls, and their peculiar ceremonies. First, let's see what we have here.'

'We've got a man banged on the head, tied up with green cord and drowned naked in a sacred well,' Margaret insisted. 'And we have people wearing white druid robes. We have the same white robes in the school and the witch Miss Appleton as the headmistress. She killed him to get all her Chosen Girls fertile so she can find husbands for them.' She leaned back in her chair, smugly satisfied that she had solved the case.

'Did we not see Miss Appleton and her Chosen Girls that night?' Lorna asked.

'Yes we did, and they were in druid robes,' Margaret said in triumph.

'Which way were they walking?'

'Up the hill,' Margaret said.

'Up the hill to St Ann's well,' Lorna said. 'The opposite direction from the Alfreck Well. It would be a three- mile hike to get there, and three miles back, at night, unseen by anybody.' She allowed her words to sink in. 'And do you really think that Miss Appleton is a murderer? Or do you think that her Chosen Girls – girls from sheltered and respectable backgrounds – would strip and drown a man and walk calmly back to their lessons without saying a word?'

'How about the green cord then?'

'I don't know,' Lorna said. 'And then there's the treasure.'

Margaret stroked a finger over her brooch. 'I don't know, Miss.'

'I think we have reached an impasse. Nothing makes much sense.' Lorna sighed. 'I hate to say this Margaret, but perhaps it's time to visit Lady Stanhope and admit that I'm getting nowhere; thank her for her confidence and get back to London.'

Margaret shook her head violently. 'No! No Miss. That would not be good. You can't give up. Look how much you have discovered already!'

'What? What have I discovered?' Lorna's frustration burst out in an angry retort. 'I have – we have – found out a lot of things that don't help us in the slightest.'

'Sit down, miss.' Margaret said. 'You're only wearing yourself out walking up and down like that.'

Lorna continued to pace with her shoes silent on the carpet.

'You found out that there were three men seen at the murder site.' Margaret said. 'You discovered that that boy Tom was sent to rob us by a man called Uncle Charlie.' She waited for Lorna to respond and continued when she did not. 'Uncle Charlie had two friends, making three men again.'

'Three mysterious men,' Lorna said. 'And when I tried to interview the only three who fitted the description I found they were nothing like murderers. Indeed the man I spoke to,' Lorna smiled slightly at the memory, 'was a friend of Mr Findhorn's and had no reason to kill him.'

'Except for the treasure,' Margaret said.

'Mr Weaver is a wealthy man,' Lorna said. 'He holds shares in the railway company.'

'Everybody with any money has shares in a railway company,' Margaret said. 'And your Mr Weaver admitted he was here to search for treasure.'

'Yes indeed,' Lorna remembered Weaver's other reason for coming to Malvern. She had not mentioned his interest in lonely widows and conviviality.

'Treasure and druids,' Margaret said. 'Mr Findhorn found something, and then was killed by the druids.' She stood up suddenly. 'I bet that's it! She said. 'I bet he found something to do with druids and they saw him and murdered him for his fertility! Maybe it was druid treasure.'

'Don't forget that somebody robbed his hut and ripped pages from his journal,' Lorna said.

'I wonder why?'

'They must have given something away,' Lorna said. 'And then there is that mysterious woman in white who followed him.'

'She might be a druid too,' Margaret said.

Lorna nodded. 'She might be.' She could think of no other explanation.

'See?' Margaret said. 'You can't give up yet; you've found out so much.'

'I wonder why Dicky Temple told us that coin was worthless.' Lorna mused.

'Maybe he is not as good as people think,' Margaret said. 'Or he wanted to buy it cheap. He offered a florin didn't he?'

'We could ask him,' Lorna said.

'He would lie to us,' Margaret said.

'Come on!' Lorna slapped Margaret's arm as her mood suddenly changed. 'Get some warm clothes on and your heaviest boots.'

'What … why?'

'We're going up the hills!' Now Lorna had the idea she wanted to get moving as quickly as she could. 'Best take something to eat as well. We may be a while.'

'What are we doing?' Margaret was surprised at Lorna's change of mood.

'Three things,' Lorna said. 'We're digging for treasure; we are talking to everybody asking about women in white, and we are looking for three men together.' She smiled and kissed Margaret on the nose. 'Come along Margaret! I need you.'

'Oh…' Margaret's face was a picture. 'We're not giving up, then?'

'Never on either side of Christmas! Come along, Margaret; things to do!'

The Malvern Hills were busy as always, with donkey parties carrying the less able invalids from well to sweet well as the more fit dragged their often-complaining bodies over the undulating grasslands and up the steeper slopes with moans and great effort. A small group of entrepreneurs sold snacks from a small booth at the top of the Worcestershire Beacon, and a group of young bachelors indulged in a sing-song fifty yards away, tipping their hats and waving their walking-sticks to any woman under fifty who happened to be within sight.

'There are plenty of people here,' Margaret bit into the leg of a chicken. 'If they did not eat so much, to begin with, they would not need to torture themselves in such a manner.'

'Can you see three men together?' Lorna asked.

'No,' Margaret finished the chicken leg and dived into the case they had brought. She emerged with an apple and chewed vigorously.

'Nor can I.' Lorna took control of the food bag in case Margaret emptied it before the day was properly begun. 'Right; we'll start at Sugarloaf hill and work our way south to Worcestershire Beacon, Summer Hill, down to the Wyche, up to Perseverance Hill and end at the Holy Well.'

'That's a lot of walking.' Margaret spoke through a mouthful of apple.

'Tomorrow we will start at the Holy Well, work our way south to the Herefordshire Beacon and end at Hangman's hill.' Lorna pointed out the peaks to Margaret, who nodded.

'I know the hills better than you do,' she reminded. 'I don't need you to tell me.'

'Two places interest me most,' Lorna said. 'The Alfreck Well and Perseverance Hill.'

'I understand the Alfreck because that's where Mr Findhorn was found,' Margaret said, 'but why Perseverance? Nothing happened there.'

'I don't agree.' Lorna said. 'I think that a lot happened there. Now, look as if you are a health-seeker.'

'Yes, Miss. I'll have to put on a lot of weight then!' Her impudence was back.

'The way you're eating, Margaret, that won't be long.' Lorna murmured.

They walked on, waving gaily to people and stopped to ask a group of donkey women if they had seen anything out of the ordinary or suspicious.

'I have,' the older of the three donkey women said. 'I saw two women asking queer questions.'

'Two women?' Lorna asked. 'What were they like?'

'One was a stranger,' The donkey woman said, 'a tall, woman with an accent I never heard before. Sort of Welsh without being Welsh. A right nosey creature she was. And her friend was a local girl with a lost look on her face, a fancy brooch and apple juice all down her front.'

Margaret wiped her coat and touched the brooch she had fastened there. 'I don't look lost,' she said indignantly. 'That's not true!'

Cackling loudly, the donkey women ambled away, leaving Lorna and Margaret at the side of the hill.

'Come on Margaret,' Lorna said. 'We've a lot to do yet.'

It was pleasant to be up on the hills with the extensive views spreading around them and the wind caressing their faces. Lorna took a deep breath, comparing her surroundings to India.

'You'll like Home,' her father said. 'You've wanted to go there all your life.'

'Yes, Father,' Lorna stood beside the gangplank of the great three-masted ship. 'I know I will.' She looked back at the country in which she had spent most of her life. 'But this is Home too.'

Major Buchanan placed a single hand on her arm. 'I know that feeling,' he said softly. 'It is strange to possess such deep affection for a place that is so different from where one belongs.'

'I belong here, Father; India is my home.'

Major Buchanan shook his head. 'Not any more, Lorna. It's changed since the Mutiny. The trust has gone. You may come back, you will think of it often, but your home is there,' he pointed to the ship. 'Across the sea.'

'I hope so, Father,' Lorna looked back at India. 'I'm leaving you and Mother behind.'

'Your future is before you,' Major Buchanan gave her a small push up the gang-plank. 'Go and find it.'

'I can see why health-seekers come here from all across the country' Lorna said. 'The water cure may be torture, but this fresh air and scenery make up for it.'

'Miss: there are three men together,' Margaret said suddenly, pulling at Lorna's sleeve. 'Over there.'

'Don't point,' Lorna followed the direction of Margaret's finger. 'It's rude.' She concentrated on the three men and gave a little start. 'Good heavens; that's Mr Weaver and his companions. I misremember their names.'

'Mr Pickering and Mr Spalding,' Margaret said at once. 'Charles Weaver, was it not? Like Uncle Charlie that young Tom told you about.'

'That's right: Charles Weaver.' Lorna watched Weaver walking up the hill, casually swinging a stick and not looking in the slightest bit unfit.

'Your Mr Weaver looks nothing like a health seeker,' Margaret echoed Lorna's thoughts. 'He's well set up; quite a handsome fellow.'

'He's not *my* Mr Weaver,' Lorna said, far too quickly.

'Oh?' Margaret smiled and sensibly said no more. She touched her brooch.

Weaver and his companions walked briskly to the summit of Summer Hill, where they stopped and began to poke at the ground with their sticks.

'They're searching for treasure,' Margaret said.

'We'll leave them to it,' Lorna quickly turned her back. She was not sure if she was very keen to see Weaver again or desperately hoped to avoid him.

'Three men, Miss, searching for treasure.' Margaret continued. 'Should we not be watching them?'

'We can't go and ask them directly, can we?' Lorna could feel her face burning at the thought. 'Mr Weaver might recognise me.'

'Yes, Miss,' Margaret said. 'I think that should embarrass him more than you.' Even so, she followed Lorna's lead and walked away, although with more than one backwards glance.

It was mid-afternoon when they arrived at Perseverance Hill, with the sun sending lengthening shadows across the ground and a slight wind ruffling the grass. The sound of an explosion carried faintly to them as the navigators used gunpowder on some obstacle.

'There is nobody here except us,' Margaret said. 'All the other hills are busy.'

'I think people are scared of the navvies,' Lorna said. 'The tunnel is directly beneath us.' She smiled, 'if you put your ear to the ground you will hear them working.' Lying on her side, she showed Margaret what to do. 'See?'

Margaret joined her. 'So you can! I can hear the picks and shovels clattering away. Is that why we came here?'

'Not exactly,' Lorna stood up and brushed the soil and dirt from her clothes. 'I hope there are no grass stains on me. People might ask the most awkward questions.'

'Miss!' Margaret sounded scandalised, and then began to laugh. 'You're shocking; you really are! First, you pretend you are a man, then you bathe naked men, and now you are lying on your side to listen to navigators.' She shook her head, 'you really are scandalous you know.'

'That's what I am looking for!' Lorna did not respond to Margaret's entirely accurate state-ment. 'This must be it.' She pointed to a tall brick structure that protruded from the ground.

'It's like a chimney,' Margaret said.

'You are very close,' Lorna agreed. 'This is a ventilation shaft for the tunnel. It lets air down to the men beneath, and they pump up water when it gets flooded with all the rain in these hills.'

'Yes Miss,' Margaret looked bored. 'What has that to do with us?'

'When David Hughes died in the rockfall he had a coin in his hand. Our silver coin.'

'Yes, Miss. Professor Humphrey and Mr Temple both thought that was strange.'

'I would imagine that they did,' Lorna agreed, 'because the navvies are very deep underground burrowing through the hill. No Roman soldier or British warrior could ever have been so far underground to drop a coin and nobody burying treasure would dig hundreds of feet to leave it. It would be impossible with this very hard rock anyway.'

'Yes, Miss, so how did he get it?'

'Either he stole it from Mr Findhorn's find, and if he had the other navvies would have told us or, more likely, it dropped down when the navvies were digging this ventilation shaft,' Lorna said. 'I can't think of any other way it happened.'

'But it's solid brick,' Margaret pushed at the chimney-shaped shaft.

'It is now,' Lorna agreed, but it must have been an open hole before the bricks were added. The navvies must have dug through the rock somehow.'

Margaret nodded. 'Yes, Miss. Probably with gunpowder.'

'And who would decide where to sink the air shaft?' Lorna asked a rhetorical question. 'Why the contractor would, of course.'

'So Mr Findhorn might have found the treasure first,' Margaret said.

'Exactly,' Lorna agreed. 'That is what I think happened. Mr Findhorn seems to have found the treasure somewhere. He must have been here, so put two and two together, and we come up with a whole lot of silver coins.

'I am not sure why they wanted to kill him.' Margaret once again pointed to the glaring flaw in Lorna's theory. 'Why not steal the money and run?'

'I don't know,' Lorna admitted. 'I have not worked that out yet. That brings us back full circle to your druids and human sacrifice idea.'

'Miss Appleton,' Margaret said.

'It may be, although there are these three men to remember, and the sheer strength needed to overpower Mr Findhorn.' Lorna looked around. 'In the meantime, we have a job to do.'

'So if we dig around this area, we may also find something,' Margaret began to poke at the ground with her stick. 'This soil is very loose,' she said. 'It's like somebody has been digging here already and replaced the turf on top to hide it. See? My stick pokes through easily.'

'I see,' Lorna said. 'I think you are right.'

'It could have been the navvies when they were making the shaft of course,' Margaret said. 'Except that it's in the wrong place.'

'Halloa there!' The voice was cheery and familiar as Charles Weaver strode toward them with his two companions at his heels. 'What a grand afternoon!'

'It is indeed,' Lorna tried to look like a woman without a care in the world.

'Just out for a stroll?' Weaver asked.

'That's it; enjoying the views,' Lorna replied.

Weaver came closer with Spalding and Pickering at his back. He glanced at Margaret and away again to concentrate on Lorna. 'Charles Weaver,' he said, removing his hat and giving an elaborate bow.

'Lorna Buchanan,' Lorna said, 'and my companion is Margaret Smith.'

'Charmed to meet you both,' Weaver replaced his hat with a flourish 'These two fellows are Denis Pickering and Adam Spalding.'

Both men smiled and raised their hats, although they were obviously out of breath from the ascent of the hill.

'I am sure I know you,' Weaver said, leaning closer. 'Have we met before?'

'I am sure I would remember,' Lorna avoided the direct denial.

Weaver was frowning as he looked at her. 'You certainly look very familiar.'

'Perhaps we have passed in the street,' Lorna tried to move on. 'Are you gentlemen here for the health cures?'

'That and the company,' Weaver was surprisingly honest. 'One does meet the most charming company in Malvern.'

'It is quite a convivial environment,' Lorna had repeated Weaver's word before she realised it.

'Yes,' Weaver continued to study her. 'Oh I *am* sorry; you must think me most impolite staring in such a fashion.' He smiled and touched his stick to the brim of his hat, Lorna had a sudden recollection of him dancing naked with one foot and shouting 'Sugar'.

'Not at all, Mr Weaver,' Lorna said. 'These hills are made for such meetings.' She gave her most charming smile. 'Did you know that the name Malvern is from the old Celtic Moel Bryn?'

'No, Miss Buchanan. I did not.' He stepped back. 'Is there a meaning to the name?'

'Oh indeed, Mr Weaver,' Lorna said softly. 'It means bare hill.' She did not flinch from his gaze. 'There are a lot of bare things in this area.'

Weaver frowned again, evidently trying to place her. 'Good God,' he said, shaking his head. He leaned closer to Lorna. 'It can't be.'

Lorna smiled. 'I hope you enjoy your walk, Mr Weaver.'

When Weaver stepped back, his smile was a little uncertain. 'Forgive me,' he said. 'I must be mistaken about something. We must be on our way. Good-bye!' Lifting his stick, he marched off. Lorna watched him as he turned around on two occasions before squaring his shoulders and striding south in the direction of the Holy Well.

'That may have been very unpleasant,' Margaret said with a giggle. 'That poor man must be thinking all sorts of things! What do we do now? It's getting late.'

'We wait here,' Lorna said. 'And we dig.'

Margaret looked pleased. 'Really? Are we searching for treasure?'

'No,' Lorna said, 'we are *pretending* to search for treasure.'

'What if we find some?' Margaret sounded quite excited.

Lorna considered for a moment. 'Then I suppose we should hand it over to Lady Stanhope. After all, this is her land.'

'Oh; can't we keep it?' Margaret's excitement changed to disappointment.

Lorna smiled. 'If you find any, you can keep it if your conscience allows. If I find any, I will give it to Her Ladyship.'

'Margaret smiled. 'Let's get digging then. I wish we had brought a spade.'

'Like this one?' Lorna produced a small garden trowel from within her bag.

'Did you have this planned all the time?' Margaret asked.

'Yes,' Lorna said. 'If the air shafts were here, I planned to be seen digging. I hope somebody is watching us.' She stirred the already disturbed earth with the toe of her boot. 'Hopefully, the man who has already dug up here.'

'You are the cleverest of women,' Margaret said. Crouching down, she began a furious assault on the ground, throwing up dirt like a dog scratching for a bone.

'Dig nearer the ventilation shaft,' Lorna said. 'That's the most likely place you will find anything if there is anything to be found.' She looked around. With the evening drawing close the hills were quieter. The view west was astounding as the sun slid behind the blue mountains of Wales and shadowed the fields and farms of Herefordshire in heart-stoppingly melancholic beauty.

'Yes,' Lorna said quietly. 'This is the Home I dreamed of for so long.'

A part of donkey women and their customers wound their way down from the hills to the town below. A few lights began to penetrate the growing gloom, orange-yellow and friendly, highlighting the distance between the loneliness of the bare hills and the activity of the hill-foot towns.

'Only the memories remain,' Margaret's voice penetrated Lorna's thoughts.

'Which memories?' Lorna asked absently.

'The memories of the long- dead people who lived here.' Margaret was on her knees, still digging. 'They come out at night. This is their place then.'

Lorna tried to suppress the shiver and abrupt change of mood that ran through her. With the sun nearly down it was cold up here, although it was not the chill that raised the hairs on the back of her neck and made her start at the moan of the wind. The sun had all but gone now, with only a tiny sliver remaining and the land between darkening and quiet.

'Maybe this is not the best idea after all,' Lorna scanned the surrounding hills, part hoping to see somebody and part dreading who or what that somebody might be.

'What are you looking for, miss?' Margaret asked.

'A ghost,' Lorna said. 'Or a woman in white.'

'I can feel them.' Margaret was quite calm. 'They are all around us, watching, pressing close, wondering what we are up to on their land and at their time.'

'Have your people always lived in this area, Margaret?' Lorna asked.

'Yes, Miss, as far as I know. My mother and my grandmother are born and bred with Hereford-shire in their bones and blood, so my ma said. Dunno about my da though. He could be any wandering soldier boy with a roving eye and a saucy tongue.'

'If you are local, Margaret, then these people who lived here could be your ancestors. They could be looking out for you.'

'Maybe so, Miss, and maybe not. I dunno.' Margaret stood up. 'Not many of the locals come up here by night. It's not our time.'

'You're getting nervous,' Lorna did not like to admit that she was feeling the same way. There was something about the evening atmosphere of this place she did not understand. The bright cheerfulness of the day had vanished to be re-placed by something uncanny. She could nearly imagine this hillside when the Celtic peoples lived here, and the sound of children and lowing cattle filled the air.

There was also the far more recent memory of Mr Findhorn's death. It may have been at this time of night that Findhorn was alone up here in the gathering dark when somebody crept up behind him and bashed him over the head. Lorna relived that moment, visualising the sturdy railway contractor as he fell forward. There would have been a slight sound and then three men lifted him to the Alfreck Well. Or perhaps not three men; maybe it had been a group of women all clad in white. Perhaps it had been the spiritual descendants of the old druids who advised King Caractacus to make his stand here.

The last beam of the sun glinted on something. The flash was at the periphery of Lorna's vision yet caught her attention, breaking her chain of thought. Moving slowly, she turned in a full circle, taking in the darkening countryside as she had once done while hunting in India.

'Stay still Margaret,' she said quietly. 'We're being watched.'

'What? Where?' Margaret jumped up quickly.

Expecting Margaret to move, Lorna caught hold of her. 'I said stay *still*. I saw sunlight reflecting on something; I think it was glass.'

'Glass?' Margaret looked puzzled.

'The lens of a telescope I would guess,' Lorna said.

'Who would be looking through a telescope at this time of night?' Margaret asked. 'They won't see much!'

'Maybe whoever was digging here before us,' Lorna said. 'And they will see *us*. Now listen to me and do exactly as I say. Do you understand?' She spoke slowly and distinctly as if she was once more teaching a class.

'Yes, Miss,' Margaret said quietly.

'I want you to start digging again. After a few moments, stop and point to something under the ground. Look excited. Have you got that?'

'Yes Miss, but why?'

'I'll tell you later. Now off you go.' Lorna stood straight and looked around, searching for the elusive watcher. The sun had vanished behind the Welsh hills, and the Malverns were in shadow. She could not see anybody.

'Miss!' Margaret shouted so suddenly that Lorna started. 'Look!' She jabbed downward with her forefinger.

'What's that?' Fully aware how far a human voice could carry in the stillness of the night, Lorna spoke loudly. 'What have you found?' Keeping her back to the hidden watcher, she crouched down with Margaret at her side. They looked at the hole in the dirt.

'Right Margaret,' Lorna said quietly. 'If somebody's watching us, he won't see much in this light. Pretend to lift something and put it in the bag. I'll carry the bag.'

'Yes Miss.' Improvising with more sense than Lorna had given her credit for, Margaret lifted a fist-sized stone. 'Look Miss!'

Lorna clapped her hands in pretended delight. 'Put it in here,' she held open her bag. 'And let's get back to the hotel.'

'I thought we were looking for the ghost.' Margaret said.

'I think the ghost may be looking at us.' Lorna put her hand on Margaret's arm. 'Watch your feet and walk softly. I want to hear if we are being followed.'

'Yes, Miss.'

They picked their way over the rough grass and on to the track as true darkness closed in on

them. Twice Lorna stopped as if to check her surroundings and each time she heard a soft footfall
that ceased a moment later.

The footsteps were light and close together;
that meant a small man or even a woman: the
woman in white? Lorna gripped her stick. There
was a small wooded gulley ahead; that was a perfect place for an ambush, lonely, secluded and
dark.

'We're going to move faster in a minute,' Lorna
said.

'Are we being followed?' Margaret sounded
nervous.

'I believe so,' Lorna said. 'Hold your stick tight
and if we are attacked, don't swing it like a club.
Thrust like a sword.'

'Yes, Miss,' Margaret sounded surprised.
'You're a school teacher, Miss. You should not
know such things.'

'Aim for the face or the throat,' Lorna advised.
'If they are much taller than you, aim lower
down. You know where I mean.'

'No... Oh. Oh yes, Miss.' Margaret looked at
her and then away quickly.

'Right, deep breath and on you go.' For a moment Lorna contemplated sending Margaret on alone and turning the tables by slipping into the trees to wait for whoever was following. However, leaving a young woman to walk through the night unescorted did not seem sensible. It was better to stay together.

Margaret hurried, tripped over a straggling root and recovered with a gasp.

'Not too fast,' Lorna said. Taking hold of Margaret's arm, she held her close. 'Sshh now.' They were quiet for a moment, listening to the whistle of the breeze through the trees which muffled any possible noise of pursuit.

'All right. On we go.' Giving Margaret a slight push, Lorna followed. It was now full dark, and the path was faint between the trees. The bark of a fox only emphasised their position.

'Miss,' Margaret was gripping her walking stick so tightly that her knuckles gleamed white. 'I'm scared.'

'I'm still here, Margaret.' Reaching out, Lorna took hold of her left hand. 'We'll keep together.' She took a deep breath. 'I won't leave you.'

'Everybody leaves me Miss; my father left; my ma dumped me and...'

Lorna squeezed her hand, aware that she was being invited deep into Margaret's soul. 'I won't leave you. That's a promise.'

It took them another thirty nerve-stretching minutes before they reached Great Malvern and heard the friendly clop of hooves on the road.

'I'm glad to be back under street lights,' Margaret said.

'I'll be glad when we get back into our room.' Lorna glanced behind her. There were half a dozen people in the street, two courting couples, and two men walking alone. If somebody was indeed following her, she could not see an obvious suspect.

'Miss; what I said back there about the old people,' Margaret said. 'Don't tell anybody.'

'No, Margaret. Of course not.' For some reason, Lorna added, 'thank you.'

The hotel reception area was quiet, so Lorna caught the attention of the clerk without difficulty.

'Is the room opposite ours occupied?' She asked.

'Why no, Ma'am,' the clerk gave a little bow. 'That guest left only yesterday.'

'Thank you. That will be all.'

Margaret watched, puzzled. 'Why did you ask that Miss?' She scurried up the stairs, looking over her shoulder as another guest spoke to the clerk.

'We may move across there tonight.' Lorna pushed open the door to their room, entered and dropped into a chair. Margaret did the same.

'Why? And what was that all about, Miss? What's happening?'

Lorna forced a smile. 'I'm not entirely sure,' she said. 'Here is what I think. I think Findhorn found a jug or something similar full of coins when the navvies were digging the airshaft. One coin dropped, and David Hughes found it later.'

'Yes, Miss,' Margaret said. 'What happened to Mr Findhorn's treasure?'

'Mr Findhorn took them to his hut, and they were stolen from there. Now somebody must have seen him and hoped there were more coins so went digging at the same place. You saw the soft ground, remember?'

'I remember,' Margaret said.

'I thought that the digger, the treasure hunter, must have been back there to dig for more so if we were there, he would see us.' Lorna closed the door and turned the key firmly in the lock. 'I rather think it was him with the telescope.'

'I did not see anybody,' Margaret said.

'Nor did I,' Lorna admitted. 'I think I heard somebody from time to time.'

Margaret sighed and glanced at the door. 'What happens now?'

'We wait.' Lorna took the stone that Margaret had unearthed, 'and see if our friend comes for this.' She smiled. 'Last time he sent young Tom.'

'Do you think it was Uncle Charlie watching us?'

'I am not sure.' Lorna agreed. 'It may have been one of his friends. The footsteps I heard were light, but Uncle Charlie was involved in some way.'

'Charles Weaver.' Margaret said. 'He was one of the three men; he saw us digging on the hill and then he watched us come down.'

'Perhaps you are right.' Lorna hoped that Margaret was mistaken. 'Now I think we should leave this room for the empty one across the corridor and watch to see what happens.'

'They won't find anything.'

'Oh they will,' Lorna said. 'They'll find this.' She held up the stone. 'We have to make it look as attractive as possible for them.'

'We can put it in William's box,' Margaret offered.

'Are you sure? That held the first present that William ever gave you.'

'It was the first present that *anybody* ever gave me,' Margaret said. She handed it over. 'You're not getting the brooch, though.'

'Thank you, Margaret,' Lorna was aware of the depth of sacrifice Margaret was making. 'You're a brick.'

The stone fitted inside the box, and Lorna added a couple of half-pennies and a farthing to give some rattle, then tied the lid with stout cord. 'That should stop him opening the box inside the room,' she said. 'I want him to steal it and leave so I can follow him to wherever he lives.'

'We.' Margaret said.

'I beg your pardon?'

'You said *I* could follow him. I'm coming too.' Margaret set her chin stubbornly. 'I'm not leaving you alone either.'

'We'll discuss that later,' Lorna felt something swelling inside her. She knew how scared Margaret had been and here she was, offering companionship despite her fear. 'Now keep your clothes on and make the beds appear as if somebody's in them. If I remember you did that at St Ann's.' Lorna smiled.

Obviously unsure if Lorna was rebuking her or not, Margaret did not reply. Rearranging the pillows and sheets, they created the images that they were in bed, left William's box on the dressing table and lifted their outdoor coats, boots, and walking sticks.

'We'll need this,' Lorna lifted the candlestick. The light pooled across the table, momentarily settling on the gift box. 'Come on,' she led the way to the room opposite.

'Now we wait,' Lorna said. The room was not as luxurious as their own, with a single large bed, a dressing table and two chairs.

'This is exciting,' Margaret's voice trembled.

'Leave the door slightly open so we can watch,' Lorna said, 'and blow the candle out.'

The darkness seemed to emphasise every sound, so the creak of a floorboard echoed like the crash of a falling tree, and the distant barking of a dog caused Lorna to start.

'What if he doesn't come?' Margaret stifled a yawn.

'Then we'll have wasted our time, and we'll be exhausted tomorrow,' Lorna said. 'In which case, we had better try to sleep. We'll take it in turns; two hours each. You go first.'

'I'm not tired,' Margaret said.

'You were yawning a moment ago,' Lorna said. 'Off you go. Don't fall over anything on your way to bed.'

There were voices from below; somebody laughed; a woman scolded; a child woke, cried and hushed again. A carriage rumbled past with the horses' hooves clopping loudly then fading in the distance. Margaret's breathing became heavy and regular. Lorna smiled, settled back in her chair and fought the increasing weight of her eyelids. A shutter banged somewhere as the wind reached under unsecured fastenings. Lorna wished she had brought some knitting or sewing, realised that it was too dark to see either and endured the slow passage of the night.

'Fire! Fire!'

The woman's shout split the silence. Lorna widened her eyes. *What was that?*

'Fire! The hotel's on fire! Get up and get out for God's sake!'

Lorna recognised the second voice as belonging to the clerk at the desk. The acrid reek of smoke drifted to her, tickling her nose, so she rose.

'Margaret!'

'What?' Sleep slurred Margaret's voice.

Lorna shook her awake. 'Get up! The hotel's on fire. Quickly, now.'

Margaret turned on her side. 'Leave me; leave me, Ma; I never done nothing. Don't hit me again, Ma!' She curled into a foetal position with her hands over her head.

Lorna shook her again. 'It's me, Margaret; Lorna! Wake up chuckaboo.'

Margaret dropped her hands slowly. 'Miss?'

'Up you get!' Lorna shook her. 'Come on Margaret! The hotel's on fire.'

'Fire?'

'Yes, hurry,' Lorna dragged her from the bed. Mercifully Margaret had not taken off her clothes.

The hotel was alive with voices, and the scurry of frantic feet. Lorna pulled open the door and pushed Margaret into the corridor. 'Downstairs, quickly now.'

Light from candles and lanterns danced around, with a babble of voices. Smoke drifted; somebody was coughing loudly; a child was crying, a woman querulously complaining.

Candlelight confused Lorna's view of the stairs, so shadows merged with solidity, and the polished bannister gleamed like a highway pointing to the sanctuary of the street below. The harsh clatter of a bell made Lorna wince.

'Come on Margaret.' Lorna grasped her sleeve. 'Stay with me.'

A plump man in a long white nightgown blocked their passage, and then Gibson appeared, wringing his hands together.

'Oh, oh, please be quick; please be careful.'

The stairs disappeared beneath them, and they were in the hall amidst a milling mob of people, all asking questions or pushing at each other in their haste to escape. The front door was open wide, with the bald clerk now ringing a brass hand-bell and shouting:

'Fire! Fire; everyone out! Fire! Fire; everyone out!'

'Come on, Miss,' Margaret took the initiative. A little girl sprawled face first on the ground, howling. Margaret lifted her without hesitation, passed her to her equally vocal mother and pulled Lorna outside.

There was the sweet air of the street and a drift of rain, the wind mild and not unpleasant. Lorna looked around at women and men in their night clothes clustering around asking questions, pointing to the hotel, seeking friends and relations, some worried, some relieved, all curious.

'There are no flames,' Margaret pointed out.

Relieved to be safely outside, Lorna did not reply at first. She wanted to pull Margaret into a hug.

'Miss; there are no flames.' Margaret grabbed Lorna's arm. 'Where're the flames if there's a fire?'

Lorna looked up. Margaret was correct. Except for the meagre glow of candles and the directed light from lanterns, there was no flame.

'It may be at the back,' Lorna said. 'I certainly smelled smoke.'

'I didn't' Margaret said.

'Well, no harm done then.' Lorna said. 'We're safe and sound.'

'False alarm!' Mr Gibson appeared at the door of the hotel. 'I do apologise ladies and gentlemen; it is a false alarm. There is no fire in the hotel, and you are invited to return to your room. There is absolutely no danger.'

'What a waste of time that was,' Margaret grumbled sleepily. 'Getting us out in the cold for nothing.'

The crowd surged back inside, shivering, complaining or relieved to return, depending on their natures. One woman demanded a refund from Gibson while a man and a woman stepped wide apart as if to deny that they had escaped from the same room.

'Come on, Margaret,' Lorna said. 'Time to get back on watch.'

Heavy-legged, they clambered up the stairs to find the door to their room wide open and a candle burning in the candlestick.

'Miss,' Margaret said. 'The box has gone. The thief's taken the box.'

'Damn it all.' Despite growing up among military men, Lorna seldom swore. The fact that she did now only proved her frustration. All her planning and scheming had been for nothing, spoiled by an accidental declaration of fire at her hotel. 'He must have sneaked in during all the confusion.'

'What do we do now, Miss?' Margaret asked.

'We get some sleep,' Lorna said. 'It's two in the morning, and I don't know about you, but I am so tired I can hardly stand.'

'We can ask the clerk if he saw any strangers,' Margaret suggested.

'In that crowd?' Lorna gestured downstairs. 'He was too busy ringing his bell and getting people out safely.'

'There was no fire, Miss,' Margaret said. 'Do you know what I think happened? That Uncle Charlie gave a false alarm so he could come in and rob us.'

'That could be,' Lorna agreed. 'Except that it was a woman's voice I heard first.'

'The witch,' Margaret said. 'It would be the witch.'

Lorna covered a yawn. 'I'm too tired to think, Margaret. Get to sleep, and we'll worry about it in the morning.'

Chapter Twenty One

'You have been busy,' Lady Stanhope sat straight- backed in her chair, sipping from a cup of tea that a maid brought to her. She was so erect she looked like one of the marble statues that stood at various points around the pool of limpid water in her Italian garden.

'We've done our best,' Lorna said.

'You have discovered more than the police have,' Lady Stanhope said. 'However, there are still mysteries to unravel.'

'Yes, Your Ladyship.' Lorna agreed. 'I am not sure what Miss Appleton is up to with her Chosen Girls. She may only be preparing them for marriage as she says...'

'I don't like her methods,' Lady Stanhope said. 'I do agree that they are successful, but having them jump naked into a dirty pool of water and that other strange ceremony...' She rattled her cup in its saucer. 'We'll let that go just now. I know Mr Temple of course and I don't understand why he did not offer you a better price for your coin. Maybe he lacks the funds.'

'That is possible,' Lorna said.

Lady Stanhope held up her cup, and a maid appeared to whisk it away. 'Thank you, Mary.'

'I have met Mr Temple. We discussed the history of the British Fort, and I granted him permission to look for relics in my land, as long as he kept me informed of any significant discoveries.'

'Yes, My Lady.'

'Well, Lorna. Thank you, for letting me know what is happening.' It was a polite dismissal as Lady Stanhope stood up. 'Keep up the good work.'

'Thank you, Your Ladyship,' Lorna stood. 'I will try to find your murderer.'

'What are your immediate plans?' Lady Stanhope asked.

Lorna smiled. 'My young friend Margaret is meeting a young man just now...'

'Unchaperoned?' Lady Stanhope interrupted at once.

'Yes; they are both sensible.' Lorna said.

'I hope so,' Lady Stanhope said. 'You had better ensure they remain sensible. Human nature can take over when the fires of passion are kindled.' She stopped as if controlling herself.

'They have only two hours together,' Lorna said.

'That is plenty of time,' Lady Stanhope sounded calm again. 'I happen to know that young lady you see.'

'I did not realise that, Your Ladyship.' Lorna said.

'It was I who sponsored her for St Ann's College,' Lady Stanhope said. 'And that is quite sufficient information for you. Now off with you and look after her. And continue to search for that murderer!'

'Yes, Your Ladyship,' Lorna withdrew without another word. A male servant helped her into the chaise and directed her to the road to Great Malvern. Lady Stanhope was a woman with a finger in many pies.

* * *

'Miss!' Margaret tugged at Lorna's arm as they walked down Church Street. 'Look!' Her whisper was hoarse and urgent.

'What's that, Margaret?' Lorna asked distantly, still thinking of Lady Stanhope's agitation over Margaret.

'Over there!' Margaret pointed.

'Don't point, dear; it's rude.' Lorna said automatically, pulling Margaret's finger downward.

'That's Katherine Palmer and Alice Weatherby,' Margaret said. 'And just look what Alice is carrying.'

Lorna remembered Katherine as a well- behaved, shy girl and Alice Weatherby as quiet, very polite but with slightly shifty eyes. 'I see them.'

'That's my box!' Margaret said indignantly. 'Alice is carrying my box! I always said she was a thief!'

'They are also out of school bounds unescorted,' Lorna said. 'I would not have expected that from that pair. They must be on an errand for Miss Appleton.' She frowned as the import of Margaret's words hit her. 'Are you sure that it's your box?'

'Yes I'm sure that's my box!' Leaving Lorna's side, Margaret stormed across the road, nearly causing a gig to pull to an abrupt halt. 'Halloa Alice!'

'Margaret!' Lorna's attempt to call her back failed as Margaret approached Alice with her head high and her face set in a scowl.

'You stole that!' Margaret accused loudly.

'What? I never did!' Alice's face coloured as Katherine stared at her and two or three passers-by turned to see what was happening. One severe-faced woman tutted and swept her crinoline aside as if to avoid contamination from this young vulgarian.

'Oh Margaret; will you never learn?' Lorna muttered, lifted her skirt and ran across the road as quickly as dignity would allow. She arrived just as Margaret snatched back the box.

'I got that as a present!' Lorna was shouting now, attracting quite a crowd. A man ushered his lady away, with both throwing shocked glances at these boisterous young women exchanging words in their respectable street.

'Come now,' Lorna tried to calm them down. 'I'm sure there is a rational explanation.'

'You stole that from my room,' Margaret was not in the mood to be quietened or rational. 'You were always a thief, Alice Weatherby!'

'Enough now!' Lorna put a teacher's edge to her voice. She took hold of Alice in her left hand and Margaret in her right. 'Enough of this. You two: Katherine and Alice; what are you girls doing out of school bounds?'

'Miss Appleton sent us on an errand Miss,' Katherine answered at once.

'That's what I thought,' Lorna said. 'You have her permission then.'

'Yes, Miss,' Alice spoiled her meek reply by adding, 'of course we have.'

'All right,' Lorna took control. 'Katherine, you continue with your errand. Alice, you and Margaret come with me, and we'll get this cleared up.'

Marching them into a nearby teashop, Lorna sat them on opposite sides of a table. 'Right then, girls. I am sure this is just a misunderstanding.'

'She stole my box,' Margaret held the box tight to her chest.

'I found it!' Alice said. 'I did *not* steal it.'

Ordering tea, Lorna placed her hands flat on the table. 'Now Alice, I happen to know that this box belongs to Margaret. Where did you find it?'

Alice was quiet for a long time as her face flushed.

'Come on now. Where?' Lorna hardened her voice again. 'Was it in the street?'

'No,' Alice said. 'You know we're not allowed in the street.'

'Up the hills then,' Lorna suggested.

'No.' Alice dropped her eyes and shook her head.

'In the school grounds?' Lorna said.

Alice nodded. Moisture gleamed in her eyes.

Lorna glanced at Margaret.

'I told you!' Margaret said. 'The witch!'

'Where in the school grounds?' Lorna asked.

'In the ash heap,' Alice said quietly.

'Somebody threw my box on the ash heap?' Margaret said. 'Why?'

'Thank you, Alice.' Lorna glowered at Margaret. 'When did you find it?'

'Two days ago,' Alice said. 'I saw it when we came back from our walk and picked it up later.'

'That's that sorted then.' Lorna said. 'Now, I happen to know that this box belongs to Margaret's and she is going to keep it. Don't look so troubled, Alice; you are not in trouble. Dry your tears and go and finish your errand with Katherine.'

She watched as Alice walked away.

'It's the witch,' Margaret said. 'She stole my box. It has always been the witch.'

Lorna leaned back in her chair. 'We'll have to think about this,' she said. 'We searched the school and found nothing.'

'We found the druid robes,' Margaret reminded. 'And now we've found my box. The one William gave me.'

'That false fire at the hotel,' Lorna reminded herself. 'The first voice was a woman shouting. The clerk was the second voice. Come on, Margaret. Let's go and ask the clerk about the fire.'

'Yes, Miss.' Margaret held the box close to her and touched the brooch she wore over her heart. She said no more as Lorna addressed the clerk.

'No Ma'am.' The clerk shook his head. 'I never saw any fire. I was on duty at the desk. You know we keep open all night in case any of the guests require anything, or there are late arrivals.'

'I know that,' Lorna said.

'Well there I was on duty and a woman, a guest I did not know, comes running down the stairs shouting "fire, fire." So I says to her. "Is there a fire, Ma'am?" and she says. "There's a fire. You'd better get the hotel emptied, or there'll be a camality else."

'What did she say?' Lorna asked.

'She said, "there'll be a camality, else" Ma'am.' The clerk repeated. 'She meant a calamity, Ma'am.'

'I am sure she did,' Lorna said as a sudden memory set her heart racing. 'Are you sure that was her exact word?'

'Yes, Ma'am,' the clerk nodded his bald head. 'Quite sure. I remember thinking: that's a queer word to use, and then I thought of what she had said and of all the guests maybe burning to death, and I did not care about her words anymore.'

'Quite,' Lorna said. 'Tell me please, was she a tall lady with dark hair and a red shawl on her back?'

'Why no, Ma'am.' The clerk shook his head. 'She was a shapely little thing with the loveliest curly blonde hair.' He smiled. 'A man would go a long way for a woman with looks like that, Ma'am.'

Lorna forced a smile. 'Thank you. That is interesting. You have been most helpful.' Fishing a shilling from her pocket, she handed it over. 'If you can think of anything else, Sir, I would be most obliged if you told me.'

'Yes, Ma'am,' the clerk touched a finger to his forehead. 'There was one thing, Ma'am, that I thought most queer.'

'Oh? What was that, pray?'

'Well Ma'am, for a lady in such a panic, she did not rush outside as most would have. She ran back upstairs again. I thought maybe to get her things or rouse somebody.' A small smile lifted the corners of his mouth. 'I was a little envious of whoever she was rousing. He would be a fortunate man, I thought.'

'Oh?' Lorna stored that information away. 'Thank you. Did you notice when she went outside?'

The clerk crinkled his forehead with the effort of thought. 'Now you mention it Ma'am; I can't swear to having seen her leave at all. I was busy at the door what with the ringing of the bell and the shouting of "Fire! Fire!" though, Ma'am.'

'You said she was a guest you did not know,' Lorna said. 'Have you seen her since?'

The forehead crinkled even further. 'I can't say that I have, Ma'am. She might have been staying only one night, or have been a visitor to a guest.'

'Thank you.' Lorna handed over another shilling.

'There's no need for that, Ma'am.' The clerk did not even pretend to return the coin.

'You have been more than helpful,' Lorna walked away.

Dear God; that sounded like Jane Henshaw; young, bubbly Jane who had been so friendly when she arrived at the school. Jane had given the false fire alarm. Had Jane also stolen the box?

'What was all that about?' Margaret sounded confused. 'Do you know the woman who sounded the alarm?'

'I may do,' Lorna said. 'It was the thing she said: she called a calamity a *camality*. I have only heard one person make that mistake.'

'Who was that Miss?'

'Miss Jane Henshaw,' Lorna said. 'She said it when I met her on my first day at the school.'

'Oh goodness.' Margaret sat with her mouth open. 'Miss Henshaw. I always thought she was a bit too strict, but I never thought she was a thief.'

'Nor did I,' Lorna said. 'I wonder why?' The clerk's description fitted her perfectly, and Margaret's box had been found at the school where she worked. Lorna pondered breaking into the school again to see if Jane had Findhorn's stolen coins, but decided that was not practical with Jane sleeping in the same room.

'We should tell Lady Stanhope,' Lorna said.

'Would she believe us?' Margaret asked. 'She's a lady, and I'm only the unwanted daughter of a tenant and some soldier or something.'

'She might think more of you than you realise,' Lorna said.

The rap at the door was unexpected.

'Come in,' Lorna called.

'I am frightfully sorry to disturb you, ma'am,' the clerk gave a polite bow. 'There is a gentleman at the desk asking if he could have a minute of Miss Smith's time.'

'What sort of a gentleman?' Lorna was instantly suspicious.

'A young gentleman,' the clerk said. 'He asked that I give Miss Smith this as a token.' He handed over a single cut daffodil.

'Oh!' Margaret immediately coloured. She took the flower as if it was the most delicate jewel. 'That must be William!'

Lorna did not hide her smile. 'Do you wish me to chaperone you?' She teased. 'It might be best.'

'You will not!' Margaret's hot reply amused the clerk. 'I am perfectly capable of handling William alone.'

'As you wish,' Lorna said as Margaret paused in front of the mirror to adjust her hair and tug at her dress. 'He won't expect you to be in all your finery. Go as you are and he'll be all the more pleased that you did not keep him waiting.'

'But my hair...'

'Your hair is beautiful! Off you go...' Lorna gave her a little push. 'Go on!' She met Margaret's smile with another of her own, raised her eyebrows to the clerk and waited for Margaret to scurry down the stairs.

'She's nervous,' Lorna explained.

The clerk nodded. 'Yes, Ma'am. My daughter is much the same.' Bowing, he withdrew and closed the door.

Lorna checked the time and began writing notes on the case. The clerk's description of Jane Henshaw had given her pause for thought. She must be mistaken, surely. Not Jane! What could she possibly gain?

Sighing, Lorna wrote her notes, trying to make sense of all she had learned. After a while, she looked up at the clock. 'Where is she?' Margaret had been gone for half an hour. 'They must have gone for a walk.' After an hour Lorna rose and descended to the desk, slipped on the third step down, gasped as she twisted her ankle, tested it gingerly, and continued, limping.

The clerk looked up. 'Can I help you, Madam?'

'My young friend, Margaret Smith. Did she meet her young man?'

'Indeed she did.' The clerk said. 'He was waiting outside for her. I imagine they are happily walking out together, maybe visiting the wells.'

'I imagine so,' Lorna said although she had expected Margaret to come back much sooner. She returned to her room, wincing as her ankle began to throb. Sitting in one chair, she placed her sore ankle on another and hoped the rest would cure it.

After two hours had passed, she seriously began to worry. After three she pulled on her coat and limped downstairs. It was a different clerk on duty, a much younger man.

'I am going to look for Miss Smith,' she said. 'If she happens to return in my absence, pray inform her that I wish her to remain in our room until I am back. No, tell her that I *demand* that she remain in our room.'

'Yes, Madam.' The clerk did not look interested.

The street was busy with invalids returning from their tour of the wells, donkey women and their passengers and local people trying to earn a living. Lorna glanced quickly around for Margaret and limped heavily to the Sceptre Hotel where William worked. Luckily it was only a couple of hundred yards down the road.

'I am looking for Mr Broadheath,' she said to the clerk.

The clerk looked her up and down before replying. 'Mr Broadheath is not on duty today, Madam.' He said.

Lorna sighed. 'You have a young man here named William Griggs. A bath attendant...'

The clerk frowned. 'Yes, we have.'

'May I speak to him?' Lorna asked.

The clerk sighed as if Lorna's request caused him a great deal of trouble. 'Wait here, Madam,' he said and slipped away.

He returned within five minutes with a nervous looking William at his side.

'This is the lady,' the clerk said. 'Don't waste any time. The clients are waiting for you.'

'William,' Lorna did not waste time with niceties. 'I am looking for Margaret Smith.'

William flushed and looked confused. 'Are you, Madam?'

'You were with her a few hours ago.' Lorna said.

William shook his head. 'No, Madam. I have not seen her all day.'

'You came to the hotel with a flower,' Lorna had a terrible feeling of impending horror. 'A daffodil, a few hours ago.'

'No; no I didn't,' William shook his head quickly. 'I've been working here since early morning.'

There was no reason to doubt William's word. 'Thank you, William,' Lorna tried to keep her voice calm. She left the hotel with fear gnawing inside her. If that had not been William who called for Margaret, then who had it been?

There was only one terrible possibility that Lorna did not wish to contemplate. Had the same person who stole Margaret's box been watching them, so he or she also knew about William? But even if that was true, why had they taken Margaret away?

'Right,' she told herself. 'The only link I have is Jane Henshaw. I'm going to find you, Margaret, don't you worry.'

The gate to the school grounds was closed but not locked. Refusing to be surprised, Lorna pushed through and limped painfully up the familiar path. 'Where's Jane Henshaw,' she called the second she stepped in the front door.

Mercy lifted her head from scrubbing the floor. 'I don't know Miss,' she said.

'Mercy!' Miss Appleton appeared on the stairs. 'Leave us.'

'Yes, Miss,' Mercy scurried away in obvious gratitude.

'Miss Buchanan,' Miss Appleton stood at the first landing of the stairs. Dressed in black with white collars and cuffs, she looked much like a predatory spider waiting for an unwary fly. 'You are well aware that you are not welcome in this establishment. Please leave at once.'

'I will leave willingly as soon as I have fulfilled my purpose here,' Lorna stepped into the centre of the hall.

'You will leave now,' Miss Appleton stared down her imperious nose.

'I want to speak to Jane Henshaw,' Lorna met the stare with one of her own.

'She is not here,' Miss Appleton's reply was curt. 'I released her yesterday.'

Momentarily at a loss, Lorna could only continue her stare. 'Where is she?'

'I have not got the remotest idea and nor do I care. Goodbye, Miss Buchanan.'

'I wish to see her room,' Lorna refused to be brow-beaten.

'Goodbye Miss Buchanan.'

'I am sure Lady Stanhope would not wish to know that you refused my request.' Lorna took a step closer to the headmistress and balanced on her right leg, hoping she did not look too ridiculous... 'She is already perturbed at your antics with the Chosen Girls; your ridiculous ceremonies at the Alfreck Well and with the Sheela-na-gig. I would not presume to impose on Her Ladyship's good nature much further, Miss Appleton.'

Miss Appleton paled and stepped back as if Lorna had slapped her. 'You have five minutes,' she said. 'Then I shall call the porter and have you thrown out, Lady Stanhope or no Lady Stanhope. This is my school, and I shall run it to my rules.'

Without wasting time listening to Miss Appleton's final words, Lorna limped past and pulled herself up the stairs. Her ankle was throbbing badly and felt as if it was at least double the size it should be.

The door to Jane Henshaw's room was open. Lorna thrust in and stopped, unsure of what she was searching. It was evident that Jane had left in a hurry, with the bed not made and books and various papers scattered across the floor.

'You had better not take anything that is not yours,' Miss Appleton stood in the doorway, watching.

'I won't be long,' Lorna opened the top drawer. It was empty; as was the second. The third was jammed, and Lorna struggled to force it open. The fragment of green cord told its own story. 'Dear God in heaven,' Lorna breathed. She lifted the cord and ran it through her fingers; it was silk, identical to the cord that had been around Findhorn's wrists and ankles.

'Put that back,' Miss Appleton ordered.

'The police will wish to see this,' Lorna felt the increased hammer of her heart.

'In that case, they can come here for it.' Miss Appleton stepped inside the room. 'Put that back.'

Lorna deliberately folded the cord and placed it inside her cloak. 'This may be evidence in a murder inquiry,' she stepped forward, preparing to leave the room and her left foot scuffed something hard beneath the papers. Stooping, Lorna picked up the stone that Margaret had unearthed only a few days before. That was her final piece of proof: Jane Henshaw had stolen Margaret's box.

Oh God; I've done it. I've found the murderer. But where is Margaret?

'Here,' she tossed the stone to Miss Appleton. 'You can give the police this as well. A member of your staff stole it from Margaret Smith. I'll tell Sergeant Caswell the full story.'

'Oh…' Miss Appleton caught the stone and stared at Lorna with her mouth open. 'It's a stone.'

'Excuse me.' Trying to ignore the pain in her ankle, Lorna returned down the stairs.

'Oh Miss Buchanan,' Mercy jumped out of the way as Lorna limped to the front door. 'You're in a rush.'

'I am,' Lorna said. 'Now you're a smart girl, I remember. Have you heard anything of Margaret Smith or Miss Henshaw?'

'I haven't heard of Margaret Smith since I dunno when' the maid said. 'Miss Henshaw's left now.'

'Do you know where she may be?' Lorna was aware of Miss Appleton listening from the landing on the stairs.

'I can't say that I do, Madam.' Mercy screwed up her face. 'She may be with her sweetheart.'

'I didn't know she had a sweetheart,' Lorna said.

'Oh aye. That's why Miss Appleton got rid of her,' Mercy said. 'She was seeing the man after night.'

Lorna nodded. 'Thank you. Did you hear this man's name?'

'I heard it were Charles or Charlie. That's what the young ladies were saying.' Mercy's smile was a trifle wistful. 'They were saying that Miss Henshaw was out with that Charlie again.'

Charlie: Uncle Charlie. Lorna repeated the names as if chanting some pagan mantra. Charlie: Uncle Charlie. Jane and Uncle Charlie; Dear

404

God, she had known one of the culprits and had not realised it.

More importantly, where was Margaret and was she all right?

Where to now? Lorna limped away from the school. *Mad Jack had told her to check the school, and she had failed. Jane Henshaw was the culprit, not Miss Appleton. And now Margaret could be in danger. No; now Margaret was in danger. There was no 'could be' about it.*

The long shadows of evening were stretching across the ground as Lorna limped and hopped away, too anxious to be concerned about her dignity. *Where to? Where to? There was no profit in rushing around like a chicken without a head; she had to think quickly.*

Faint but growing brighter with the darkening sky, a full moon glinted above the hill-ridge. Lorna glanced at it.

'Full moon,' she said to herself. 'It was a full moon when Mr Findhorn was murdered. And now they have Margaret.' She did not know why somebody had murdered Mr Findhorn. She only knew that he had.

'The Alfreck Well,' Lorna said. 'They'll be at the well. It's the only logical place.'

It was a good two miles to get to the well, maybe further; she was tired, and her ankle throbbed abominably. 'I can't walk that far,' she said.

The chaise was sitting outside the stable block with Harold groomed and fed in his stall. Calling to the stable boy, Lorna urged him to hurry, using sweet words and an ever sweeter silver sixpence. Even so, it seemed to be an age before she was sitting behind the horse with the reins in her hand and the lanterns sending their dim light onto the road ahead.

'You be careful now, Ma'am,' the boy's words followed her out of the courtyard. 'It's full moon remember.'

With the wheels purring over the hard surface and the horse clopping cheerfully, Lorna knew it would only be a matter of minutes before she arrived at the foot of the Herefordshire Beacon. 'Come on now,' she cracked the reins on Harold's shiny rump. 'Sorry little horse but Margaret's life may be in danger.'

Until that moment Lorna had not considered what she would do when she reached the Alfreck Well. She was alone, with a weak ankle and had no real idea who might be there and what they might do. The sensible option would be to find a policeman if there was one in Great Malvern at this time of night. Lorna shook her head. She had no time to fetch the police; she was alone and would play it by ear. With the full moon rising, every minute might be precious.

'Come on!' Again Lorna smacked the reins on the horse's rump. Harold increased his speed slightly, accompanied by a sudden grinding from the offside wheel. Lorna glanced sideways. Both wheels were spinning, with the spokes as a yellow blur. She nodded, cracked the reins again and looked ahead, just as the offside wheel gave a distinct wobble.

'Oh God no; not now!' Lorna remembered Mr Farrell warning her about the wheel. She looked ahead; the moon highlighted the line of the hills, with the defensive ridges making the Herefordshire Beacon distinct, hard and somehow sinister. 'Hold out, chaise: take me just one mile further.'

There was a distinct crack from her right. Lorna watched in horrified disbelief as the off-side wheel spun slowly off its axle and rolled along the road at an angle to the chaise, which first slewed to the side and then toppled. Keeping her balance with great difficulty, Lorna hauled back at the reins. 'Whoa! Whoa; for God's sake Harold, whoa!'

The sound of the edge of the axle scraping along the ground set Lorna's teeth on edge as the chaise slid to an ungainly halt.

'Damn!' Lorna slapped her hands on the chaise in frustration. 'Damn! Damn!' she looked up at the hills. She was still over a mile from the Herefordshire Beacon, and she knew her ankle would not hold out for that distance. 'Damn and blast it to hell and gone!'

'Oh such unladylike language from a very engaging lady,' the voice was familiar. 'I use sugar myself. I say; we've met before haven't we?'

'You're Mr Weaver.' Lorna said. 'We met on Perseverance Hill.'

'That's correct! Charles Weaver at your service,' the smile was in place as the charm eased across to Lorna. 'And you are Miss Buchanan.'

Weaver looked at the chaise. 'You appear to be in a spot of bother.'

'Are you Uncle Charlie?' Lorna grabbed for her whip, ready to smash the stock across Weaver's head.

A shaft of moonlight gleamed on Weaver's face. 'Am I...? No, I am not anybody's uncle. What a queer question to ask.'

'Are you alone?' Lorna was not ready to trust Weaver yet. 'Where are your friends?'

'I'm quite alone; more importantly, are you all right?' Weaver dismounted from his horse and stepped across. 'Are you hurt? You seem distraught.'

Lorna stepped back. 'I'm not hurt.' She realised that Weaver had been riding in the opposite direction from Herefordshire Beacon and was alone; he did not have Margaret as a captive. 'I'm sorry Mr Weaver. I am a little harassed.'

'That's not surprising with only one wheel on your chariot.' Although Weaver's smile remained in place, his eyes were steady as he scrutinised her. 'Are you sure you are all right?'

'No,' Lorna lowered her whip and shook her head. She took a deep breath to steady her nerves and her voice. 'I am not.'

Weaver knelt beside the chaise. 'This is not too bad,' he said. 'The wheel is undamaged. I can slide it back on the axle without any difficulty if we have the retaining nut; did you hear it come off?'

'No, 'Lorna shook her head and blurted out. 'They've got Margaret! They might kill her; they might sacrifice her like they did Mr Findhorn.'

Weaver stood up. 'Who has Margaret? Start at the beginning.' He put strong hands on her arms. 'Come on now.'

'She vanished,' Lorna took a deep breath as her composure drained away. 'A man called on her and pretended to be her sweetheart …' she gabbled out her story as Weaver listened, nodding slowly, and then searched the road for the missing nut.

'I can't see it,' Weaver said. 'And you seem desperate to be on your way.' Here,'he whistled for his horse. 'Her name's Aphrodite; Aphro for short.' His smile was back. 'Go and do what you have to do. I'll get Aphro back tomorrow. She's not side-saddle I'm afraid…'

'Thank you,' Lorna was already hitching up her skirts and clambering on the back of Aphrodite. 'Thank you, Mr Weaver.' Once more blessing the fact that she was taller than most women, Lorna slid her feet into the stirrups, wondered briefly over her unladylike and unrespectable appearance, decided that other matters were more essential and kicked in her heels.

'Ride, Aphro,' she said, 'ride like a storm.'

'Oh sugar!' she heard Weaver's voice behind her. 'Sugar, sugar!' For a moment Lorna imagined him standing on one leg and shaking the other and then she forgot him in her anxiety to save Margaret.

Nearly an hour had passed since her chaise had lost its wheel and the moon was brighter, rising high in a star-punctured sky. With the straggled settlements of the Malverns bouncing past, Lorna pushed Aphrodite onward, feeling the perspiration dry on her face and the horse powerful underneath her.

She passed the Wych gap and pushed Aphrodite up the path leading to the Alfreck

Well. Trees on either side darkened the track, and Lorna recalled Margaret's nervousness when they were followed here only a few nights before. As the hill steepened, Aphrodite began to labour and blew hard in protest at this unexpected work.

'Come on girl.' Leaning forward in the saddle, Lorna fondled Aphrodite's ear, 'just a little further now, please.'

The track narrowed further, and the trees thinned. Lorna pulled to a halt beside a stand of silver birch trees. 'I'll leave you here Aphro,' she whispered as she climbed clumsily to the ground. 'Graze to your heart's content. Your master will be back for you sometime.'

Taking the riding crop from its holder as the only weapon she could find, Lorna stepped up the hill, wincing each time she put her weight on her injured ankle. 'That hurts,' she said softly and continued with the pain increasing with each step and the path coiling up forever into the moon-glossed night.

An owl called from the right, the sound drifting eerily; another replied from the left. There was no wind to stir the branches of the trees, nothing to whisper through the silver-green grass. Lorna heard the thump-drag-thump of her feet and the laboured rasp of her breathing; if she could hear that, then so could others. Stopping to rest her ankle and control her nerves, she seemed very far from the lights of the Malvern villages that hugged the foot of the hills.

There was a faint burr of voices from above. Two voices at least were male, with one lighter, female voice sharp among them.

'Is that Jane?' Lorna was not sure.

Riding the pain from her ankle, she limped on, gasping, halting, setting her teeth and moving again with the moon-glow illuminating the grassy ridges that had once defended this ancient British fort. Was Caractacus watching over her? Were there shadowy figures of Celtic warriors moving through the dark, ghosts of long-gone heroes as Margaret believed? Lorna stopped again, gasping, sticky with perspiration and aware she was becoming fanciful and light-headed with pain, fatigue, and worry.

'I'm coming for you Margaret,' she said. 'Hold on now.'

The lone mountain-ash tree thrust upward on the skyline; the budding branches stark against the moon. Two people stood at its side, with a third half crouched between them. Even at this distance, Lorna could see that the two standing were men, one tall and slender, the other broad and bulky. The third was Margaret.

'I see you.' Lorna gripped her riding crop tightly in her hand. She wished that she had brought some other weapon; a rifle would be good, a shotgun better and even a stout staff would be preferable to nothing at all. However, things were what they were, and she had no choice but to do her best with what she had, and what she could glean from her surroundings. Stooping, Lorna scooped a fist-sized stone from the ground, added another and ducked behind a straggling hawthorn bush. She looked upwards and felt anger chase away her fatigue as the broad man slapped Margaret across the head.

There was another bush on the lip of one of the defensive ditches about fifteen yards from the well, with the shadow of dead ground offering easy access. Holding her stones in the crook of her left arm, Lorna crept to the bush.

'Slow and easy, slow and easy,' Major Buchanan said. *'Take your time; a sudden move attracts them. Keep downwind, keep in the shadows and stay alert. If your prey has a mate, she might also be hunting you.*

The bush was half as tall as she was and armed with tangled thorns that caught on Lorna's cloak. She eased it free, crouched down and took a deep breath.

'Halloa!' She raised her voice, so it was high-pitched. 'Halloa.'

'Who's that?' The burly man turned around. 'Who's there?'

'It's me,' Lorna pitched her voice so he would have to strain to hear her. If in doubt, tell the truth. 'I've hurt my ankle; can you help me?'

'Stop playing silly beggars!' The voice was angry.

I know that voice, Lorna said to herself. What the dickens is he doing here? She peered. Yes; it was Ben the porter from St Ann's School, as grumpy-faced and bad-tempered as always.

'I need help; I can't walk,' Lorna said, faintly.

'Oh for God's sake!' Ben released hold of Margaret go and stalked forward, long-striding and round- shouldered. As Ben approached, Lorna lifted the first of her two stones. She would have to be fast and accurate for although she was tall for a woman, she did not have the strength of a man.

'Where are you Jane, for God's sake? Stand up, girl!'

Lorna waited until the porter came close and then rose quickly and threw the stone as hard as she *could.* Ben started as she appeared from behind the bush, but had no time to react before the stone crashed against his head. He swore loudly and staggered, giving Lorna the chance to lift her second stone and bring it down hard behind his ear. Ben fell, stunned, and landed face down in the middle of the hawthorn bush.

'I hope it prickles you!' Lorna glanced up. The second man had pushed Margaret to the ground and was striding toward her with a short, stout stick in his hand. Only then did Lorna see that it was Temple the antiquarian.

'I saw that! You're not Jane.'

'No, I'm not,' Lorna said and threw the stone she had used to knock down Ben.

More prepared that Ben had been, Temple saw the stone coming and ducked away, so it passed well above his head. 'Now I've got you!' He broke into a surprisingly energetic run.

Lorna heard herself breathing harsh and hard. She had not expected to miss with the stone. Now she had only her riding crop as a weapon against this active and angry man. Luckily Temple was no youngster, although fit as a man half his age with his daily wanderings over the hills. Lorna moved sideways around the bush and swung her crop, slashing Temple across the face as he closed. Temple yelled loudly and cringed, holding up his arms up to protect his face. Lorna swung, again and again, putting all her weight into each blow, hitting him on the side, the back and the arms, knowing she could not continue for long but determined to do her best. She had to incapacitate this man so she could rescue Margaret and escape before Jane and the third man, whoever he was, arrived.

With Temple cowering beneath the stinging lash, Lorna took a chance and gave him a mighty push. Already off-balance, Temple slipped and tumbled over the grass, to roll end-over-end down the steep hillside and disappear in the dark trough of the ditch.

'Margaret!' Lorna half hopped, and half ran to where Margaret lay beside the well. Still dressed in the clothes she had worn when she left the hotel room, Margaret was tied hand and foot and had a piece of cloth stuffed in her mouth as a gag. Her left eye was swollen and heavily bruised.

Unfastening the clumsy knots of the gag, Lorna eased it out of Margaret's mouth. 'Hold on; I'll have you free in a moment.'

Margaret looked up from wild eyes. 'Thank you, Miss! The clerk told me that William was outside the hotel and when I went out they hit me and dragged me into a coach.' She sputtered, tripping over the words. 'They're going to kill me, Miss, like they did Mr Findhorn.'

'Not now they're not,' Lorna said. 'One is face down in a thorn bush, and the other is halfway down the hill and still rolling. Even when he stops he'll be so dizzy he won't be able to do anything.'

'But Miss…'

'Sssh, now and let me get you free.' Rolling Margaret onto her side Lorna began working on her wrists. The knots were hard and tight, so she struggled with the tarred cord, gasping as she broke a nail down to the quick.

'Miss!'

'Keep still, Margaret!'

Intent upon unravelling the knots, Lorna did not hear the approaching footsteps. Something hard and cold pressed against her temple.

'I heard you were asking questions and causing trouble.' The voice was fruity and familiar. Lorna looked up into the red face of Broadheath. He ground the muzzle of his pistol deeper into her forehead. 'Get up.'

'Broadheath?' Lorna stared at him, feeling sicker than she had in her life.

'Up I said!' With his pistol boring into her head, Broadheath grabbed Lorna by the arm and jerked her to her feet.

Jane appeared beside Broadheath. She had a carpet-bag in her left hand, and her eyes were savage. 'I did warn you to mind your own business when you were still at St Ann's,' she said and landed a slap that jerked Lorna's head back and caused the muzzle of the pistol to scrape along the flesh. 'That's for what you did to my father.'

'Your father?' Lorna put a hand on her face. 'I've never met your father in my life?'

'You know him as Ben, the porter,' Jane explained.

'Ben's your father?' That explained the connection, if not the motive.

'Shut your mouth!' Broadheath pushed the gun-muzzle even harder into Lorna's temple. 'Or I'll blow your brains all over the hill.'

'Miss!' Margaret said. 'Please don't say any more…'

With Broadheath's eyes as uncontrolled as Jane's, Lorna clamped shut her mouth.

Ben and Temple both appeared; the former still holding his bloody head and the latter looking lean rather than thin, with mud over his clothes and, Lorna noted with grim satisfaction, a livid while welt from her whip across his face.

'What the devil will we do with this one?' Broadheath asked.

'Find out what we want to know first,' Jane looked at Lorna without real interest, 'and then…'

'We do for them both,' Ben smeared the blood over his face with an inquisitive hand.

'It's all we can do,' Jane said. 'They've seen us now anyway.' She leaned closer to Lorna. 'I didn't want this! If you had minded your own business none of this would have happened.'

'If you tell us honestly,' Ben said, 'we'll make it quick.'

'If I tell you *what* honestly?' Lorna asked.

'The Roman treasure,' Jane said. 'We know there's more. Findhorn found some and told us it was above the tunnel.'

'Why on earth would he tell you that?' Lorna asked.

'He said nothing at first,' Broadheath sounded quite pleased with himself, 'but when we said we'd do for his kids, he became uncommonly talkative. A right whiddler he was.'

'That would be after he went to Mr Temple,' Lorna began to piece the sequence of events together. 'But I am unsure how you got involved, Jane.'

Broadheath stepped back. 'You're not as clever as you thought, are you, Miss School-teacher! Jane and Dick were teachers at the same school, once.'

'I see,' Lorna said. 'Mr Temple wanted Findhorn's coins but did not know how to get them. He needed a woman's help!' She forced a laugh, hoping to make Broadheath lower his pistol.

'Enough of this,' Jane took control. 'We know you found something. I saw you were digging there.'

'So that was you with the telescope.' Lorna punctured Jane's triumphant smile.

'You found something,' Jane repeated. 'I saw you.'

'Is this all about money?' Lorna played for time, hoping that some health-seeker may arrive. 'You killed Mr Findhorn because of a handful of old coins?'

'More than a handful,' Temple said. 'When he brought them to me I could not believe it…'

'Never mind that,' Ben said. 'Ask what she found. How many there were.'

'Nothing,' Lorna said. 'I never found a single coin.'

'I saw you!' Jane nearly shouted. 'I saw you and Smith lifting something and celebrating. What was it?'

'A rock,' Lorna said. 'You stole it when you made that false fire alarm in the hotel.'

Jane's face darkened with anger. 'Kill them,' she said quietly. 'Finish them both.'

'We'll have to be quick,' Broadheath said. 'The same system is it?'

'Yes,' Jane said. 'We don't have to crack these two on the head. Strip them, tie them and drown them.' She spoke so casually that Lorna nearly doubted she was serious. 'Here,' Jane produced a coil of green cord from her bag. 'Use this. I'll be the ghost again to scare anybody that comes along.'

'On you go then, Jane; we'll take care of these two.' Broadheath lifted his pistol from Lorna's head.

It was only a slight move, less than an inch, but Lorna had been waiting. She knew that Broadheath could not keep the pistol pressed against her head forever. Ducking quickly under the muzzle, Lorna pushed at Broadheath with all her strength, thrusting him toward Jane. Taken by surprise, Broadheath staggered backwards; he threw out his arms for balance, and his flailing left hand caught Jane on the shoulder, so she sprawled forward.

'Run, Miss,' Margaret yelled. 'Save yourself!'

'I'll not leave you.' Lorna moved toward Margaret, only for Temple to wrap sinewy arms around her.

'You're going nowhere,' he said.

Lorna froze, allowing Temple to believe he had won, and then she lifted her knee, catching him evilly in the groin. His mouth opened in agonised shock and he clutched at himself, gasping. Lorna pushed him aside and bent desperately over Margaret.

'Oh God these knots!'

'Run Miss, please run!' Margaret screamed.

'That's far enough.' Ben grabbed her hair and pulled back hard.

Unable to restrain her yell, Lorna lashed out with a closed fist. Ben caught her arm with his left hand and gripped tight enough for her to wince.

'I've got her,' he said. 'Charlie; strip the clothes off her.'

'That I will enjoy,' Broadheath's smile was of pure malice.

'You're Uncle Charlie,' Lorna gasped, trying to free her hair with her left hand. 'It was you that sent that young boy into my hotel room!'

Broadheath grinned and twisted her hair. 'You're a bit slow in working that out, Miss Buchanan.'

'Come on, Charlie!' Ben urged. 'Strip her! We can't spend all night here!'

'Give me a hand, Temple. I'll hold her, and you take off her clothes.' Broadheath wrapped Lorna's hair around his fist and pulled her head as far back as he could. 'She won't get away from me!'

Lorna flinched as Temple unhooked her cloak and threw it aside. His slender and surprisingly powerful hands snaked obscenely across her upper body.

'Get away from me!' She struggled, tried to kick and missed.

'She's a game one!' Broadheath said. 'It's almost a pity to drown her. I could have fun breaking in this one. That's what you do with horses you know; you break them in and then train them up.' Using Lorna's hair as a lever, he pulled

425

her head from side to side. 'I'd like to do that to you; break you in and train you up as I want.'

'Stop talking so much and get her ready,' Jane had changed into a long, hooded white cloak. 'People might hear you.'

'At this time of night on a haunted hill?' Broadheath laughed. 'I don't think so! Go and do your ghost act and leave these two to us.'

Jane pulled the pointed hood tight over her head. 'I'll scare away anybody that comes,' she said. 'Get rid of these two. Father; make sure they don't waste time.'

'Get a move on!' Ben said.

'This next!' Temple grabbed at Lorna's dress. His eyes were wide, his breathing ragged. 'Hold her, Charlie!'

Broadheath twisted Lorna's arm behind her back. 'She won't move now, Temple.'

A cloud shifted across the moon, easing darkness across the hillside.

'Come on, Dicky!' Broadheath urged.

Lorna gasped and tried to pull away as Temple slid a questing hand across her body before he started to unbutton her dress. 'Get off me!'

'Oh not yet.' Temple said.

'Get off me!' Lorna tried to pull away. 'Get away from me!'

'You heard the lady, old chap; get off her!' The voice was cultured and completely unexpected.

'Who in God's name...' Broadheath looked around, peering into the dark.

'These are the chaps,' the same voice said. 'This is Margaret Smith; the young lady who saved your Edwin fellow when the tunnel collapsed. These unpleasant fellows are going to kill her.'

Lorna twisted around as a deep-throated roar sounded, and something like a torrent of bodies burst up and around the well. A dozen lanterns flared as the owners pushed back the shutters and Lorna had a vision of a horde of hard faces and harder bodies as a group of navigators and their wives charged forward. Lorna recognised Henry Clayton, Kate and Bridget in the crowd before they swept her aside.

Broadheath grappled for his pistol and fired a single shot before one sturdy navigator's wife crashed a billy-club onto his wrist and another smashed a bottle over his head. Temple gave a high pitched scream and turned to run. He managed a dozen steps before Clayton swung a pick-axe handle across the back of his knees. Temple fell, squealing. Clayton lifted him by the scruff of the neck and dragged him back to the well as easily as if he was an empty wheelbarrow.

'Good evening, Miss Buchanan,' Mr Weaver doffed his hat and bowed as formally as if they were meeting at a levee rather than on a windy hillside. 'I hope you do not object to my interference in this matter?'

'Not at all, Mr Weaver. Indeed I am rather grateful for your presence. It saved me the unnecessary experience of a cold bath at this time of night.'

Weaver grinned and bowed again. 'I do apologise for my somewhat tardy arrival. I am no use in a brawl and thought it best to collect some men of a more physical nature.'

Lorna curtseyed. 'Although I do accept your apology, Sir, I would be obliged if you come earlier the next time you rescue my companion and me from being murdered.'

'I will try to remember that,' Weaver said solemnly. 'I took the liberty of sending a fellow to contact the police. They should be here in a few hours if they have not been delayed by a case of furious driving or perhaps a drunken rascal shouting at his dog.'

'They *are* rather stretched with more important matters than murder and attempted murder.' Lorna knelt at Margaret's side. 'Do you happen to carry a knife, Mr Weaver? Poor Margaret has been tied up here for far too long.'

'Here!' Clayton dropped a knife the size of a bayonet at Lorna's side.

'Thank you,' Lorna sliced through the green cord around Margaret's wrists and ankles.

Margaret stood up slowly, rubbing at her wrists and ankles. 'Sorry, Miss. This was all my fault.'

'No, Margaret,' Lorna said. 'It was not.' Ignoring the navigators, their wives, and even Weaver, she pulled Margaret into a hug. 'I'm glad you're safe.'

'What shall we do with this one?' Kate and Bridget appeared with Jane struggling between them. Lorna was secretly pleased to see that Jane looked rather the worse for wear with her hair a mess and dirt across her cheekbone.

'Oh hold her until the police get here if you will,' Lorna said. 'You may wish to tie her up and throw her in the well if she resists.' She looked around. 'I have questions to put to her yet.'

Chapter Twenty Two

'We know they murdered Mr Findhorn,' Lorna looked around the police office with its high desk and uniformed constables in top hats and blue uniforms.

'We do,' Sergeant Caswell agreed. 'Now we need a confession, or at least proof to make sure that some clever lawyer does not wriggle them off the hook.'

'They were going to murder Margaret and me in the same manner,' Lorna reminded.

'I am well aware of that,' Caswell said. 'That alone does not conclusively prove that they did the same to Mr Findhorn.' He sipped at his mug of tea. 'I have a sure way of finding the truth. We'll put them together and allow them to accuse each other. Do you want to watch the next act in this sordid little drama, Miss Buchanan?'

Lorna nodded. 'I do,' she said.

'Then come along with me,' Sergeant Caswell said. 'You did extremely well in finding these unpleasant people. Now allow me to do my part.' He placed his cup on the table. 'This may not be pretty.'

'You're not going to beat them, or anything are you?' Lorna asked. 'I don't want to see that sort of thing.'

'God bless you, no,' Sergeant Caswell said. 'I don't hold with bullyragging at all.' Standing up, he signalled to a tall constable with impressive mutton-chop whiskers. 'Handcuff them, Dawson, and bring them all in. You better sit over in the corner Miss Buchanan. You don't want to be too near these four.'

Another constable brought a straight-backed chair, and Lorna sat down. She watched as the three men and Jane came in and sat at the table. None of them looked at her.

Caswell glowered across the table at his four prisoners. 'Well well,' he said with false joviality. 'Here's as pretty a bunch of murderers as ever I saw. Jane Henshaw, Charles Broadheath, Benjamin Henshaw and Richard William Temple, I charge you all with murder, attempted murder, assault, kidnapping, breaking and entering, theft and burglary.' He shook his head. 'Gallows bait the four of you, and especially you two, Temple and Jane Henshaw, both respectable people with fine upstanding names.'

'I did not kill anybody,' Jane said at once.

'We only have your word for that,' Caswell said. 'You were part of this gang of four that murdered poor Mr Findhorn in the most shocking manner. That's good enough for me and probably for the jury.'

Sitting in the far corner of the room, Lorna looked up as Margaret entered. 'You should not be here. It's not good for young people to see.'

Margaret hesitated. 'I want to know why Miss Henshaw did it,' she said.

'Why?' Jane turned with difficulty as the handcuffs around her wrists caught on the back of her chair. 'I did not kill Mr Findhorn!'

'You helped,' Caswell said quietly, lifting a hand to prevent Lorna from speaking. 'And you were all set to kill Miss Buchanan and Miss Smith as well.' He looked at Broadheath. 'Of course, you'll put all the blame on Broadheath and Temple and walk away scot-free. Did you hear that, Broadheath? You will end your life at the gallows while Jane Henshaw here will get a couple of years inside at the most.'

'It was her idea!' Broadheath said, as Sergeant Caswell took out his notebook and began to scribble furiously. 'When Findhorn found that jug...'

'It was an urn,' Temple said. 'Not a jug; a Roman urn! It was priceless, and you smashed it to get the coins, you buffoon!'

'Urn, jug; who the devil cares what it was called? As soon as Findhorn found that and began boasting about how much his wife was going to be pleased with his new wealth, young Miss Hopeful and her father here began to plan.' Broadheath shouted the others down. 'It was all their planning, Sergeant and I'm not going to swing if she walks free.'

Sergeant Caswell grunted. 'I don't believe you, Broadheath. Why would a respectable lady such as Miss Henshaw wish to kill anybody? I think the idea was yours and you dragged her along against her will. Mr Temple too; why he is involved, I cannot imagine.' When the sergeant looked up, Lorna saw the cunning in his eyes. She settled back down, as interested as Margaret was to see why Jane Henshaw wished to kill anybody.

'It was the money,' Broadheath said as Ben tried to keep him quiet. 'She hated working for that evil old monster Miss Appleton and wanted her own school.'

Lorna closed her eyes. She remembered Jane saying how much she wished to run her own school. She had no idea just how desperate that wish had been.

'And her father was treated like dirt by Miss Appleton you know. He and Jane got together and planned the whole thing. Kill Findhorn and dump him in the sacred well like a human sacrifice from the old days.'

'Why do that?' Caswell asked.

'To put the blame on Miss Appleton of course,' Broadheath said. 'Everybody knows that she takes her favourite class to the well in these white cloaks. Jane started the whole druid rumour and waited for people to blame Miss Appleton so she would lose her position and Jane could take charge of the school.'

'It's a very elaborate way of getting control,' Caswell said. 'You murdered a man for a few silver coins.'

'He refused to tell us where he found the urn,' Temple said. 'I am the antiquarian here, and I've been searching these hills all my life and this … this *railway* man finds an urn full of coins just by chance.' He tried to stand until the constable put a heavy hand on his shoulders and pushed him down again. 'It's not fair that he should have found them and I did not.'

'How did you meet these people?' Caswell seemed quite content to allow the four to convict themselves.

'I've known Miss Henshaw for years,' Temple said. 'She shares some of my interests in classical history. It was natural that she should turn to me, an expert when she heard about Findhorn's lucky find, and of course, he had come to me to get them valued.'

'And you agreed to the murder?' Caswell sounded surprised.

'These coins are mine by right,' Temple said. 'They should not belong to some lumbering oaf of a railway contractor who would or sell them to a pawn shop when I could give them a proper home.'

'I do see your point of view,' Caswell sounded quite sympathetic. 'After all, you are the local expert in such matters.' He shook his greying head. 'How many of the coins would you have got if you had been successful?'

'One- quarter,' Temple said. 'I will get a quarter of the find, or finds. I'll use them to build up the best Iron Age collection in this part of England. I'll be able to lecture; I'll be known…'

'You'll be hanged,' Caswell dropped all pretence of sympathy. He looked up to Lorna. 'I think that is all we need to know. Have you any questions to ask, Miss Buchanan?'

'Not even one,' Lorna said. 'Thank you, Sergeant Caswell. Come on Margaret. It is time we were out of here. Lady Stanhope will wish to hear all about it.' She turned at the door. 'No honour among these thieves, Sergeant!'

Caswell lifted a hand in reply. 'There never is, Miss Buchanan.'

Lorna had a last look backwards at Jane, turned her shoulder and left the police office.

'Well now, Miss Buchanan,' Lady Stanhope leaned against the stone balcony that overlooked the sunken pool. Steps descended to the limpid green waters, where flowers budded, waiting for the onset of spring. 'You managed to solve the murder, then.'

Lorna looked around. The pool was in a shaded corner of Stanhope House, from where Lady Stanhope managed her estate and another fifteen thousand acres of Herefordshire, Shropshire and Worcestershire. 'We were lucky,' she said. 'If Mr Weaver had not come to help we would have joined Mr Findhorn in the well.'

'Indeed,' Lady Stanhope said. 'If I heard correctly, Mr Weaver only came to help because you explained the situation to him after working out what had happened.' She lifted her glass of brandy. 'And I hear that you used some novel methods of investigation.'

'We did what we had to do,' Lorna said.

'It was all about money in the end,' Lady Stanhope sighed. 'For those of us who were fortunate enough to be born wealthy, money is not a concern. For those who were unfortunate to be born without, the pursuit of wealth dominates their lives and often warps their thinking.'

'Yes, Your Ladyship,' Lorna said.

'It may be true what the Bible says,' Lady Stanhope continued. 'The love of money could well be at the root of all evil.'

'Yes, Your Ladyship.' Lorna could say no more.

'There are still a couple of details about which I am unclear,' Lady Stanhope said. 'There is the lady in white who followed Mr Findhorn and the pages torn from Mr Findhorn's journal.'

'Oh the missing pages are simple enough,' Lorna said. 'Findhorn must have mentioned the treasure in them. Ben was the thief of course. He had worked as a navigator, so he knew his way around. He stole the urn and ripped out the pages.'

'And the lady in white was Jane Henshaw?'

Lorna shrugged. 'I'm sure it can't be anybody else. She played the ghost to scare people away or to make them think of Miss Appleton's Chosen Girls. What I don't understand is Mad Jack-Sir John's part in this. Why did he come to help and how did he know about the school connection?'

'Sir John...' Lady Stanhope smiled. 'There is nothing sinister, Miss Buchanan. He doesn't like the headmistress. That is all.' She stood up. 'Not everything was connected to the murder you know.'

Lorna stared into the pool. 'I see; when I was deep into the investigation, I was looking for clues and connections everywhere.'

'That was why I employed you,' Lady Stanhope stepped closer. 'I knew you would be thorough. Unfortunately, now that the case is solved, I am afraid that your investigating days are over. I will certainly call on you if I have any other distressing occurrences on my lands.'

'Thank you, Your Ladyship.'

Lady Stanhope nodded. 'Now, Miss Smith; I heard that you have been missing school these past weeks.'

'Yes, Your Ladyship,' Margaret said meekly.

'It would be better if you completed your education.' Lady Stanhope sounded grim. 'You started very late, so you have much to catch up on.'

Margaret stiffened. 'I'm not going back to St Ann's College,' she said.

'I would not expect you to as long as Miss Appleton is in charge. In which case, you will need a private tutor,' Lady Stanhope looked directly at Lorna. 'You are without employment at present; would you fulfil that role?'

'I have thoughts of going into business,' Lorna said.

'As what, pray?' Lady Stanhope's voice was suddenly sharp.

'As Britain's first female detective agency,' Lorna said smoothly. 'If that Scotsman Alan Pinkerton can found a National Detective Agency in the United States, then I can found one here.' She saw Lady Stanhope's mouth firm into a tight line; much worse was the expression of total dismay on Margaret's face.

'Of course,' Lorna continued. 'I will need an assistant, or it would hardly be an agency.' She looked at Margaret. 'I would like to recruit you if you are interested in the position? No pay, long hours, probably some danger and no guarantee of any work, even.'

Margaret's head was nodding so vigorously Lorna thought it might fall off.

'And,' Lorna continued, 'you would have to continue your education…'

Lady Stanhope's mouth softened into a smile. 'You will need some funds then.' She signalled to her servant, who immediately brought a small leather bag. 'Margaret Smith, I sponsored you from the workhouse to St Ann's so I am responsible for your present position.' She handed over the bag. 'This is my legacy to you; your mother was one of my tenants.'

'Your Ladyship!' Margaret opened the bag and poured out a stream of silver coins.

'There are twenty ancient British coins there,' Lady Stanhope said. 'Half what our murderers stole from Mr Findhorn. Keep them or spend them; that is your choice.'

'Oh!' Margaret stared at Lorna and said no more.

'There is one more thing,' Lady Stanhope said. 'Do you recollect that Ruth Finch immersed herself in the fertility well?'

'Of course,' Lorna said.

'She is with child,' Lady Stanhope said. 'She and her husband have been trying for ten years without success. It seems that the Alfreck Well's

442

powers are still strong.' She smiled. 'Mr Findhorn did not die in vain.'

'Told you so,' Margaret said, smugly.

'You, did,' Lorna agreed. It seemed that another chapter in her life was about to begin. The Four Counties Detective Agency. That sounded good.

Dear reader,

We hope you enjoyed reading *The Malvern Mystery*. Please take a moment to leave a review, even if it's a short one. Your opinion is important to us.

Discover more books by Helen Susan Swift at https://www.nextchapter.pub/authors/helen-susan-swift

Want to know when one of our books is free or discounted? Join the newsletter at http://eepurl.com/bqqB3H

Best regards,
Helen Susan Swift and the Next Chapter Team

Also by the Author

- Dark Voyage

- The Handfasters

- The Tweedie Passion

- Sarah's Story

- Women of Scotland

The Malvern Mystery
ISBN: 978-4-86752-844-0 (Large Print)

Published by
Next Chapter
1-60-20 Minami-Otsuka
170-0005 Toshima-Ku, Tokyo
+818035793528
10th August 2021